PENGUIN BOOKS

ARCHIMEDES AND THE SEAGLE

Born in Sydney, David Ireland has lived in many places and worked in a variety of occupations. He now lives in Sydney and writes full-time.

After some verse and playwriting, he turned to novels. Three of his novels have won the prestigious Miles Franklin Award: *The Unknown Industrial Prisoner* in 1971, *The Glass Canoe* in 1976 and *A Woman of the Future* in 1980. In 1985 *Archimedes and the Seagle*, his eighth novel, won the Gold Medal of the Australian Literature Society.

Also by David Ireland

Archimedes and the Seagle

A novel

David Ireland

Penguin Books

Penguin Books Australia Ltd,
487 Maroondah Highway, P.O. Box 257
Ringwood, Victoria, 3134, Australia
Penguin Books Ltd,
Harmondsworth, Middlesex, England
40 West 23rd Street, New York, N.Y. 10010. U.S.A.
Penguin Books Canada Ltd,
2801 John Street, Markham, Ontario, Canada L3R 1B4
Penguin Books (N.Z.) Ltd,
182–190 Wairau Road, Auckland 10, New Zealand

First published 1984 by the Viking Press
Published in Penguin, 1986
Copyright © David Ireland, 1984

All Rights Reserved. Without limiting the rights under copyright reserved
above, no part of this publication may be reproduced, stored in or introduced
into a retrieval system, or transmitted, in any form or by any means
(electronic, mechanical, photocopying, recording or otherwise) without
the prior written permission of both the copyright owner and the above
publisher of this book.

Offset from the Viking edition
Made and printed in Australia by The Dominion Press-Hedges and Bell

CIP

Ireland, David, 1927–
Archimedes and the Seagle.

ISBN 0 14 008090 2 (pbk.).
I. Title.

A823'.3

Preface

I wrote this book to show the world what dogs can do.

When I was three and grown-up and had taught myself to read I found another book, a marvellous book – the Book, I call it, with capital letters – the most precious possession I have. It's called the *Book of Knowledge* and has everything in it, and pictures, too. Well, almost everything. I read it every day, and think about it.

The Book is big and I had lots of trouble lugging it home, and once home, defending its presence in my abode. Every day was a battle. Julie was a great help; without her protection I couldn't have kept the Book hidden, nor could I have written my own book. Thanks, Julie.

Once I could read, it was a short step to writing, and from there to writing this book, which is short, compared to what I'd like to have done.

Since right now I've got more pressing and important things to do – I want to get started on my *Dog's Dictionary* as soon as I've finished this – I will not relate the extraordinary method I used to write it. The book itself must do, and I hope you like it.

1 / Dwellers in the Cracks

Before I go any further, a few words of apology are called for if this book is to escape even more severe censure than it certainly deserves.

Since I began to think, it seems to me to be more and more the case that an indefinite quantity of time can be spent exploring even a few moments of existence. For the more thoroughly you track down the contents of a moment, the more you find in it; and the more you think about it, the more you find that we live in moments, in little crevices in time. I however, deal in this book with a large tract of time – quite a few weeks, in fact. That means there are a great many moments of existence passed over, referred to briefly, elided or ignored; also that a few words are stretched out to cover complicated issues that deserve volumes. As well, there are some gaps in the narrative between the end of the children's August holidays and the start of the Christmas holidays; times when I did no writing of my own at all, being so absorbed in the Book.

That's enough of apology.

If only I could live long enough to write twenty books! Each, then, would be a chapter in the book of me. But not only that; and here we come to a serious part, which you may skip if you have no taste for serious things; each would deal in some way with the greatest and most complete tyranny ever clamped down over the life on this planet: the tyranny of humans over all else. Each would also tell of the ingenuity and resourcefulness of those of us who do not have the privilege of calling ourselves human, but who nevertheless manage to get along; exist; somehow survive in the few spaces between all those laws, territories, edifices and forbidden areas that humans have devised.

From being a proud part of the proud life on earth, we non-humans are reduced to the status of barely tolerated nothings; dwellers in the cracks, like insects; just like the human poor, who live in tiny, shabby, uncomfortable spaces the rich don't want.

Some of us they hunt for sport, some for food: all of us have only to get in their way, to annoy them, and they kill us without a second thought. They are the inhabitants of the earth: we are things.

To put it another way – dogs, cats, horses, cattle, whales, lions, tigers, pigs, leopards, seals, elephants, fish, birds and all the rest of us, are proletariat: humans are the world's citizens, the world's upper class, and not for one moment are we allowed to forget it.

Unless there are big changes, we can never be citizens of their world, bearing in mind that citizens are people who can partake of everything their civilization offers.

This has turned into a second preface, and that's quite enough. Let's get on to Chapter 2 and an important principle.

2 / Dogs Are People

Let me declare myself. I say dogs are people.

Humans are people too; cats are nearly people; birds are not people. The thing is, though, people can't fly: birds can. That's what's so infuriating about birds. Maybe that's why the official crests of so many nations – as I've seen in the Book – show eagles with wings spread, either nose-in-the-air or just plain murderous, with talons extended and ruthless beaks, (No national insignia show love-birds, budgerigars or doves.) as human homage to living beings that are fierce and can get off the ground unaided. Or even worship of such privileged beings. Yes, even that.

I deplore worship.

Still, everyone's got to live, and some people can live only by worship, or being thought to worship. I myself have to listen to all sorts of crackpot remarks from humans with little knowledge, and be thought to agree. They – the humans – think it's worship when I look up with my mouth wide open; or at least respect, since I don't answer back. Sometimes I can't help it and let out a short howl if they've said something unusually stupid, but at such times they say, 'Look at him! Wishes he could speak. If only he could talk!'

If only I could talk.

The plain fact is I *can't* talk to them. When I try to speak to them they call it 'barking' – dreadful word – and think I want something for myself. Well, perhaps not always. They know I warn them often, but often I warn them when they don't understand.

If I could talk, it would be easier for them to accept that I can think.

Because we don't answer when they speak to us they think we don't hear. Worse than that: they think we don't understand.

We ask questions, we criticise: but they don't notice. We suggest, we point out things, we alert them, we anticipate, we ignore things that deserve ignoring: they don't notice.

They know nothing of our dreams, our regrets, our memories; nothing of our broad apprehension of the sweep of animal life, bird life, insect life. (I leave out fish. I detest fish.) They are too proud to learn from our calm acceptance of life as it is. Always what we do seems to them to be in response to blind instinct, instead of being a thoughtful response to past experience, accumulated knowledge, and a reasoned evaluation of situations as they arise.

3 / Not Cathedral Street Woolloomooloo

I was bought by the Guest family for three hundred dollars when I was six months old. They came in their new car, the only new car they'd ever had, to Kellyville where our whole family lived as employees of Mr and Mrs Plowright and their children. They paid their money and I'm what they got. They had to like me or lump me. They decided to like me, and did themselves a good turn, because I'm a good employee: intelligent, amiable, reliable. How many humans can say the same?

On the whole I'm glad they bought me; it got me the Book, after all, though, in general, being a dog is no career to choose voluntarily. It's more a condition, an affliction.

To this day the smell of a new car reminds me of that day I was sold.

All my puphood I wondered what I'd do with my life, but after all the wonderful tales at home – with my father and mother and sister and brothers – of our hunting past, the practical reality was to take employment, do a reasonable job and avoid the death camps. Retrenchment, unless there was a neighbour who wanted a dog, meant off to the concentration camp, where they kept you for fourteen days, and on the fifteenth, if there was no buyer for you, it was needle and furnace. The Final Solution to the dog problem.

The people concerned about cruelty to animals made these rules, and I have to agree they're humane – if you allow for the human content of the word, which is over eighty percent. If the other humans that make up the public were left to themselves, they'd shoot us on sight the moment we got on their nerves.

The future seemed so big when I was a pup. When I came here to live, the future shrank to the size of a narrow block of land, a family of humans, and walks round my territory. I mind the house, look after the children, act as companion and friend. The pay's poor sometimes – when there's only scraps to eat – but they depend on me. (When humans are poor, their dogs feel poor, too.) These duties I mention are easy, but usually dull. Finding the Book was a marvellous thing for me.

When I first saw Woolloomooloo I thought: well, there's not much to be fond of here! But although the streets are narrower, the people, dogs and humans are just the same; the wind blows, the flowers blossom.

The sun also rises. And when it does, I get up and stretch my legs, go to where the backyard tap often drips, and take a drink from the pool there. Then I get busy reading a chapter from the Book.

The title of this chapter is Not Cathedral Street Woolloomooloo. If

I were to disclose which street I live in, I'd be tracked down and plagued by well-meaning people, sightseers, reporters and entrepreneurs trying to make news and money out of me, or even a circus dog – a freak.

Me – a freak!

But it's not Cathedral Street. All I'll say about it is that a row of houses along our street is rumoured to be up for demolition to make room for a freeway, and the Guests are in that row. Where we live now will eventually be a place for wheels only; just as white people once laid paths and put up fences, walls and houses on bushland freely roamed by tribal blacks two hundred years before, covering the footprints of feet now buried. They had to go: we'll have to go. Eventually, of course, the freeway will go, and something else will take its space, covering its footprints.

In the time I've been here in the city I've found that there's nothing basically special or naturally privileged about humans. Why do they go round as if there is, and put on such airs? They think they're so different from apes and monkeys, dogs and cats. Well, they're not; not to me, at any rate. So proud that they're not covered with hair; so convinced they're an exception to all the rules about animals. But they *are* covered with hair! I've seen it. Even on little Donna. What they're not covered with is *long* hairs. They confine their long hairs to the head, eyebrows, crotch and armpits. Older males add to this their chests, beards and longer eyebrow hairs. But what they *are* covered with is down: a fine, short, fluffy kind of hair. They've managed to make sure it doesn't grow beyond a millimetre or two, just to be one-up on all other animals.

They have such power over the rest of us, and that power is their ultimate privilege. Why do they have it, where did they get it? Is it because they can talk in words? Are the words themselves the secret? Does the possession of words make the whole lot of them cleverer? Or does it just make some of them superior? Is it because they can feel so solid amongst their human friends by virtue of their language and organization that they look down on us dog people, who are easily divided and split into units? To be picked off one by one, bought and sold.

Nevertheless, some of what they do to us is done to them, in turn. Mr Guest was bought by Associated Enterprises, who took over Gadget Distributors Limited, together with some employees, in one package. Not all the employees were bought; those who weren't bought had nowhere to go every morning.

So Mr Guest has Associated Enterprises for a boss, just as I have him for a boss. Wait a second. The whole family is my boss! Mr Guest, Mrs Guest, Jeff, Julie and Donna. Five bosses for one dog.

It's hard to get the Guests to stick to a routine they don't see the need for. I've tried to train them to let me see the television news on a regular basis, but they continue to think of television as a treat for me, and not something I could be interested in. They don't watch it every day, themselves. Perhaps they think news of the world is a treat for them. Or even that the world itself is a treat, and not to be had every day. I want to get as much of the world every day as I can. I want to fill myself with it.

They look at my face to see if I'm watching the screen. My trouble is, I'm responsive to them, and I can feel them turn their eyes on me, so I look at them. They think, then, that I'm not watching the picture.

4 / The Book of Knowledge

I was loping along Cowper Wharf Roadway, giving myself reading practice on street signs and the advertising on the Wharf Auto Port, thinking I was a pretty clever dog. I passed the two waterfront pubs, the Woolloomooloo Bay Hotel, and The Bells – Garden Grill and Bar – and turned left at the corner. I read the signs around the Woolloo-mooloo Auto Port:

Visit our new Shell shop
We must have something you need',

on the corner of Lincoln Crescent and Nicholson Street, crossed Nicholson and was halfway past the old deserted Plunkett Street school, alongside the concrete-post-and-wire fence, when there! – the Book lay near me on the edge of the gutter, resting against T2389, a timber electricity pole. I can still see in my mind's eye the 68 pressed into the hardwood and the green H sign nailed to the street side of the pole.

It was open, the cover was knocked about, and it lay face down. The words *Book of Knowledge* stared up at me in scratched gold letters. Some human had thrown it away, tossed it from a passing car.

According to the law of Finders Keepers it was mine. I would take it home, put it in my kennel and read it. Read it? I'd devour it!

But how to lift it? There was no time for regret that I had no fingers to grip; I had to get it home in my jaws. There would be damage to the Book: I had to make sure the damage was as slight as possible.

I studied the problem, trying to be calm when what I wanted to do was prance with excitement and joy; then I gripped the end of the spine with my front teeth, lifted, and when it was clear of the ground and the covers roughly parallel, I put it down flat. Next I manoeuvred it to the gutter edge so the whole spine was just over the edge. I stood in the roadway, gripped the middle of the spine with my jaws, and lifted the Book. One of my feet nearly slipped between the bars of the iron grating in the roadway just as a 311 bus whizzed past my rear end. The *Book of Knowledge* filled my mind and I didn't even jump. I stepped up on to the footpath.

I walked towards home. Eleven times I had to put it down and rest, each time leaning it against a post or a fence so I could pick it up easily. My jaws ached, my neck felt as if it would drop off my shoulders, but I got it there. When it was safely home in my kennel I lay down in the shade and panted a long time. My legs trembled. In my mind I still could see myself back where I started the journey: past the lights for the traffic set into the concrete of the kerb, past the two fine-leaved eucalypts and the struggling Cootamundra wattle. The signal box made digestive noises as I passed; it was a Philips box and its number was 211, with a number to call if it was out of order – 2113000. I was back there, trying to put out of my head all the usual things I noticed, in order to concentrate my strength solely on getting the Book home safe.

I was home, the Book was safe, but still I trembled. I pushed it further into my kennel so it couldn't be seen.

The moment Julie got home from school I showed her the Book. She knew right away that the rest of the family wouldn't understand, and would try to take it away from me.

7

My kennel is big. Julie went to the shed in the backyard where old things are kept a while before they're finally thrown away, and found an old school case that Jeff once used. She put the Book in it, and the case inside my kennel, and showed me how to lift the lid. I knew how to, of course; I forgave her for thinking I was helpless.

There was room in the case to open the Book out flat, which I did; and that's how I have it every day – I merely open the lid with my right hand, and there's the Book, open at the place I was last reading. I put some lick from my tongue on the pads of my right hand, in order to turn the pages. It's sometimes difficult to get just one page to turn, and at first I made plenty of mistakes – realizing I'd turned two pages when the continuation of a sentence made no sense or seemed strange.

I close the lid of the case when I'm finished reading, so the other family members notice nothing. Julie looks after the furnishing of my little house and gets fierce if the others butt in. She feels she understands me, and treats me as far as possible as an equal. In fact, she understands me a little in the sense that she tries always to be understanding, but she won't go anywhere near understanding *me*, until she can read *my* book, with *my* thoughts, written from *my* point of view.

I have Julie to thank for the linoleum in my kennel, and the mural round my walls. She tried to get Mr Guest to put a window in for me, to give me better light to read by than what the few gaps in the boards give, but he's kept putting it off. The whole family finds it hard to get him to do anything. He would call his strategy 'masterly inactivity' if he knew the phrase: Mrs Guest thinks he's just plain lazy.

When I've been out walking or on some excursion with the family, I begin to get anxious at being away from the Book. If I'm by myself I often break into a run to get home quicker in case the Book's gone.

Each time I get home panting and fearful, and find the Book safe in its case. I'm not ashamed to say I have tears in my mouth, tears of joy and relief. (I explain this in Chapter 47.)

Once, when all the Guests had taken me away with them to a house by the beach for a fortnight, I found, on jumping out of the car and racing round to my kennel, that I'd been invaded. Two thieves – a part-kelpie and a mixed collie – were at my kennel. I was so scared of something happening to the Book that I flew at them, biting and snarling, but mostly biting. I chased them out only as far as the front fence, since I wanted to go back and check that the Book was safe. They'd made a mess of my kennel, but they had no luck in opening the schoolcase the Book was in. I panted with fear and relief for a long time.

Mr Guest treated me with new respect after that.

'This dog's got a real killer instinct!' he marvelled proudly. 'I had no idea he was so fierce. I thought he was a lazy hound. Did you see how he chased 'em off? We've got a real watchdog as well as a pet. I think we ought to put him on extra rations.'

His good intentions came to nothing, though. Mrs Guest had firm ideas on what was enough for dogs. Only Julie realized why I had gone for those two thieves. She helped me tidy up my house, and was happy that the Book had come to no harm.

5 / Julie Christened Me

Julie saw me one day with the Book open at the early theorems of plane geometry and right then and there christened me Archimedes. I'd been content with Happy, or Happiness when she's particularly joyful, or just plain Hap, before; short for Harrison B. Guest. (You always take the name of your employer, for social purposes.) Harrison B. was given to me by my family's employers at Kellyville. I was Harrison B. Plowright then.

But why Archimedes? I was reading Euclid.

I looked up Archimedes in the Book. A good thing I did. Archimedes was a man who said he could move the world if he had a lever big enough and a fulcrum to work against. I'm just a dog, but I want to move the world, too, and this book is my lever.

Where's the fulcrum? The fulcrum I'm using is the Book.

Good old Julie. I'm happy with Archimedes. I must say, though, that even with a new name I still get Hap some of the time, even from Julie. And Happiness, or, more formally, Your Happiness.

In 212 BC Archimedes is supposed to have burned up an enemy fleet in the harbour at Syracuse by concentrating the light of the sun on the enemy ships. I wonder if ever I'll have the chance to do great deeds. I draw the line at destroying ships: I love looking at ships.

In the evening the neons lighting our street come on dimly at first, changing colour, shyly inserting themselves into the dark, until at full brightness they've defeated it, almost.

I wish I had a light in my kennel, so I could read at night.

When Julie comes outside to talk to me after her dinner, does she know or care, when she looks up at the stars and follows the Milky Way from one end to the other, that some of those stars are no longer there? She's only fourteen, but surely this knowledge should make some sort of difference to her.

I wonder what I mean, in saying that?

I think I expect that humans' ideas of themselves ought to change with every change in their knowledge; and that their behaviour ought to be different with every difference in their ideas of what the world is, where it fits into the universe, and where they stand by comparison.

6 / I Have to Keep the Book Hidden

The Guests are nice enough people, but they don't have it in them to understand someone who can concentrate on one thing for any length of time. They feel that's unhealthy. I've heard them pick on Jeff when he reads a book for more than an hour. But they have no need to worry about Jeff, he has no obsession with learning. The most frequent comment Mrs Guest makes to his schoolfriends who call in the morning to ask: Is Jeff here today? is 'He's not back from yesterday yet.' Well, no obsession with book-learning.

One Saturday in June when they were all at home, I'd been reading since sunrise. Really concentrating. I woke before dawn. The air was moist, as it was at the time of the last moonlit night, when I could feel the dew falling and imagined the moon was shedding tears; and I could smell the grateful thanks of the earth around me. (This morning the moist earth had something of the vague smell of mist, as if it hadn't enough strength to put out its special earth fragrance.)

The Guests were all up by eight and out in the winter sun by half past, leaving their radios on inside the house. Music is their most constant breakfast food.

For the next hour I could get no peace. All I wanted to do was sit and think about what I was reading; even to lie down and think. They wouldn't let me. It's not much to ask. It was a particularly difficult piece on the biology of the cell. I'd read it four times and still didn't understand it.

I'd had a virus a month before and while I was recuperating I read up about viruses in the Book. Viruses can have no progeny except by attacking a cell and tyrannizing it to produce more viruses.

I tried to picture in my head the virus attacking another cell, taking it over and forcing it to have its – the virus' – children. It's a violent thing, a sort of rape plus forced maternity.

I think I managed to picture it well enough, yet the ordinary eye can't see a virus.

(All living things fascinate me, even viruses. The life in living things pulls my mind towards them. Perhaps there are attractive forces other than gravity and electro-magnetism.)

I know from the Book that there are things all round me here in the Guests' backyard that are alive, yet I can't see them.

I wonder if there are live things that I don't know are alive – things I can see, which I think are dead. Well, not alive.

Trees don't move around much. (Yet I know there is nothing that does not move. There is nothing still in all the universe.) Trees are rooted in one spot and are at our mercy. Jack Jacaranda, for instance. Jack is my tree, my house is attached to him. He's alive, because he can grow. But clouds can grow, resentment can grow. Disorder can grow. Are they alive?

Jack has a circulation up from the roots to his leaves and back down again. Water has a circulation, newspapers too. Tides rise and fall, as if breathing; waves tear at the sea shore and eventually tumble great cliffs. Are they alive?

11

How about my rock in the backyard? She is made of sandstone, with moss and patterns and weather wear. Her name is Grok. She has a beautiful bumpy surface and feels good to be with.

Standing on Grok I see over the top of the grey timber fence to the grey ships of war at Garden Island. Is Grok alive? To me she is. Grok and I talk to each other.

Jack has stories of garden happenings reaching back many years, since he can see quite a few backyards from where he stands. He likes the fact that Grok has sloping sides that run water back down to his roots, for he gets very thirsty in hot weather and sweats a lot from his leaves. The ground under Grok stays moist – some of Jack's favourite roots rest and drink under Grok. They're very close, those two.

Jack, my tree (I say 'my' tree because he's my favourite tree and my friend) has a good honest plain Australian face. His voice is usually low and when the wind moves his arms about he sighs with pleasure. When I rub against him I can feel his warmth.

Jack tells me of spiders' weddings; the justice of cockroaches – who have a complex social system; the revenge of flies; epic stories of ants and spiders; the spitefulness of some garden gnomes; secrets about birds; all sorts of odd things about people. He never mentions dogs: perhaps he has some nasty things to say and thinks he'd hurt my feelings.

I never mark Jack off as my territory, he's a friend. All the fences are marked: that's enough. In the same way, I never mark the lemon tree, or the silver-leaved gum.

I've seen dead things. They seem to have no feelings, but do they? They rot. They eventually cease to exist. But that's impossible. I read in the Book that the bits they're made of, the electrons and suchlike (things we all believe in but no one has seen) live for ever. Well, practically ever – for millions of years. So they next go to make up other things. Perhaps many bits of us have reincarnation into many other things, so that the things we think are real are the truly temporary things and the tiny unseen electric charges are lords of creation.

Maybe on a larger timescale than ours, rocks like Grok wear away so fast that they look as if they're melting, or flowing like water. Maybe.

Perhaps nothing is alive; perhaps alive is the wrong word; perhaps what we call life is merely a particular form of temporary organization. In which case, what a strange universe we live in.

7 / No Answer

What chance has a single adult dog, in the isolation of employment, to do his proper community job of teaching the young how to live?

When young dogs are ripped out of their warm families, what are their chances of being able to grow into level-headed constructive adults, when their only teachers are a bunch of humans? I was lucky to stay with my family as long as I did.

The young dogs around Woolloomooloo have to pick up what information they can on street corners, so they get some good and some bad. But who's going to warn them of useless pride? – pride of money and possessions, pride of family, pride in connections and friends in high places? What dog of wisdom is going to burn into their thoughts the pathos of greed, the absurdity of selfishness, the short-sightedness of pomp, the idiocy of boasting, the horror and cowardice of cruelty, the madness of lies and deceit; the holiness of truth, the glory of candour and openness, the warmth of kindness and cheerfulness, the heroism of striving and effort, the sublime nature of courage, the humanity of persistence, the responsibility of talent, the benefits of law, the justice of mercy?

Who, indeed?

8 / The Seagull That Swore

This book I've written is partly about seagulls. I first got interested in
gulls when I was down in Hobart in the August school holidays with
the Guests. (The Book was in its case, safely under Julie's bed.)

I won't distress you with the frightful inconveniences I put up with
getting to Hobart in the plane, being sent on holiday in a crate
amongst the luggage in the belly of the plane, which would hit first if
we crashed, while the rest of the family sat above me in comfort, in
seats with windows. Still, I sang a few songs to while away the time –
'Dog on the Hill' and my favourite 'Green Grass For Ever' – to keep
my nerves from jumping; and tried to think of the Book.

I pretend I'm not afraid of air travel, but I wouldn't go in a plane if I
didn't have to. And in the pitch dark! If they were supposed to have
lights in there, they didn't work.

No, I won't distress you with all that.

When I first became a reader I read marvellous things in the Book. I
thought humans must be marvellous too.

They're not. I began by looking up to them, then changed to looking down on them. Now I look both up to them and down on them.
It's not an easy attitude to maintain.

There's a lot to criticise in humans. In dogs, too.

Much the same sorts of criticisms apply to seagulls, as to dogs and
humans. They could be so much better, they could know and do far
more; but they aren't and they don't.

As I said, I got interested in seagulls in Hobart. I'd just turned the
corner off Murray Street into Collins and was trotting calmly along
when I noticed a seagull ahead of me, among the pedestrians. Not
keeping pace, just ambling along as if it did this every day. I slowed to

a walk, and tried to engage this gull in conversation. The confounded bird didn't even look at me when I spoke! I drew level and looked more closely at him. He had the snowy white down, standard red legs and beak, grey on the wings, and appeared to be young. His light beady eyes were looking at me. He stopped and I made some remark about the weather. You know what he did? That cranky devil swore at me and walked on!

I thought birds were too scared to give cheek while they were on the ground. I made no comment, didn't even run at this individual to make him take off quickly, just trotted on down towards the paper shop where one of the Guests had gone for the Sydney papers.

The seagull caught up when I stopped, and walked past the shop, talking to himself. Then it hit me. That gull had spoken! And what amazed me even more – I understood! Not only could I read and write, I understood the speech of birds! I wish my parents were alive to see what I could do.

I waited for Jeff, the son of the Guest family, who's about eighteen, and when he came I set off with him with a good derisive flick of my tail. I hoped the seagull noticed, but I don't think he did. I have a beautiful tail; tails run in my family. I've never seen another dog family with such swishy, perky tails. My father used to say, 'Man created dog in his own image, in the image of man created he dog, male and female and all that jazz,' but he was being bitter and I could never understand – I was very young – how he accounted for tails, and by the time I was old enough to think about asking, he up and died.

My father died of heartworm. He was some time dying – it wasn't diagnosed early enough – and we young ones didn't know what was the matter when things were miserable in the family. I think they should have been more open with us about his illness, and then perhaps we could have said some of the things to him that we missed saying, things we thought of later.

He's buried in the bottom corner of the paddock at the Plowright's farm at Kellyville. Many generations of dogs are buried there. I won-der if grass grows greener in bone-fed ground.

We had a very happy family until then. Lots of dog people have no family; they're torn from the bosom of their mother as soon as they're born.

Before I even knew I was a young dog I'd been immeasurably influenced by my mother and her family tree, and by my father and his, way back when, in the distant past. I don't even have to know the thoughts of other dogs, to know my thoughts are in a tradition, in a line, with theirs. I've inherited a whole past. Where is it now? With me, in me. Where is it going? Nowhere, if I die in employment. Everything will die with me, since employment will not allow me to set up a family: I must be a single dog. Everything will die, unless I keep it alive in a roundabout way by means of my book.

We walked through the forest of slipped yachts in Sandy Bay and round to Wrest Point, and then back to where we were staying, and so the day ended.

I dreamed of that seagull pedestrian talking fifty to the dozen and thought of several smart things to say to him in case we met again – things I didn't think of quickly enough at the time.

9 / From Amoeba to Einstein

If I didn't have the Book, time would pass slowly when the children are at school and their father at work. Their mother is sometimes here, but often she's gone too: she has a job three days a week, sometimes four.

Both parents need to work, or they can't make ends meet. Mind you, it's very restful here in the day time, but rest isn't what I need. How wonderful to have all day for learning and reading! Most humans don't get that except for a brief childhood period at school. I suppose that means they haven't reached what you could really call civilization. Most people work and work and know next to nothing: they die ignorant. What if all of them had time to learn as much as they could hold?

What else have they got machines for?

When humans are around, I'm on stage, expected to put on a show whenever they feel like being entertained. Even as a pup I refused to do party tricks such as begging, though I'm tempted sometimes when

I see a certain look of pleasure in Donna's face as I do a few smart steps and make her look big in front of friends of her own age.

Just the same, it's a relief to get back to the Book, and tq have my own little room, with the mural all round me.

What if, as the Book says might happen, some other civilization from among the Stars contacts us in my lifetime?

I like saying What if. I'm sick of If only.

I was still pleased with What if? as I set out on my morning walk. Now I would see if Sydney seagulls were as bold as the pedestrian gulls of Hobart.

As I walked into the lane behind the house the smell of bone dust came to my nose, together with the smell of tomato plant leaves. Mr Sparrow, a neighbour, must have been tending his garden, and rubbed a leaf between his fingers.

If I could smell the crushed leaf at this distance, did that mean tiny bits of the leaf's constituents were able to travel through the air? I made a mental note to look it up in the Book.

The Book is my shield and my ladder: my shield from laziness and boredom, my ladder to the fascinating world of humans.

The Book is my escape to the ecstasy of intellectual exercise, from being a mere dog; even though I'm a dog with a shiny red coat, delicate featherings, and a high-domed head.

If only the knowledge in my head was equal to the knowledge in a single library.

Humans are lucky in having libraries; their existence means that everything in the collective memory – which is what libraries are – can be drawn on when needed.

Having the Book, and listening to the Guests, made me realize that most of their knowledge is not known by any of them! It's on paper. It took me days to get the full impact of this.

First, it means that a few can run human affairs, with the rest, the vast mass, knowing little, and being more or less passengers, and pretty useless.

Second, it means they're vulnerable. If anything happened to all that paper, all the books, all the libraries, filing cabinets, record systems ... they'd have to start many things again, at or near the beginning. Their whole civilization is a treasury of ideas, so rich that many futures are contained within it, but if lost ...

They must never lose it, yet they're in constant danger, since war is always close.

I've got an idea! In time of war why can't copies of all idea-treasures, suitably miniaturized, be sent into orbit until hostilities are over, then recovered; with the provision that if there's no one left able to recover them, they will make an unaided descent to earth, for whoever next is able to find, unlock and decipher them?

Other copies could be fired onto the moon for safe keeping.

Even a dog can get ideas, once he can read. Even a dog can appreciate the modest figure the earth cuts compared to the solar system, the galaxy, the universe; and even the clear plastic bag which contains our Universe – this clear plastic bag in the hand of a cosmic child, who may, on a whim, burst it suddenly.

The funny thing is, I don't feel small when I think of all that space, the size of stars and galaxies and the temperatures of globes of burning gas – I feel cocky that I, a dog on a small planet, can know about things so vast and far away, and all while I'm sitting here near my kennel in Woolloomooloo.

There's so much that's huge and wondrous. But the Book tells me that inside the small things, ordinary things – movement, words, sounds, thoughts, animals, insects, stones, trees, flashes of light – are huge and wondrous secrets; and that beyond the things we know are oceans of things we don't know. This fascinates me and draws me on. I like the idea that we will never know everything. In a way it's like the things I most like to read: they're things that have some meaning left no matter how many times you read them.

Why do I keep reading the Book, trying to read and imagine and *see* with my inner self all the things humans have had the opportunity of seeing? I'll confess it to you. I want to think further than the things I read, I want to travel a bit more along the road than the Guests have done. I want to discover something.

Perhaps I never will: I guess compared to Einstein I'm an amoeba. But I'll have tried, and maybe some day another dog will go further.

10 / The Drunken Seagull

I scrambled through my narrow gate that's let into the bottom of the back fence and walked out into the lane. The sun was strong, lights shone from grains in concrete, painted signs, shiny leaves of trees. None of my friends were around, so I went into Crown Street then Riley and up behind City Ford and took my special shortcut behind the Park Lane towers into little Phillip park, to the fragrance garden to sniff the pelargoniums, ran across Haig Avenue, up to St Mary's road, across the grass, up the steps, and I was home free on the grassed roof of the Domain car park. You have to watch out for dog catchers. There's a little black footpath on the street edge of the parking-station roof, set below the level of the grassed area; you can trot along there to the northern end without being seen by park employees up the hill. All you do when you get to the end is jump up to the grass, whip round the concrete wall where the trains go into and come out of the hill, then walk over behind the Art Gallery. Once you're near the Henry Moore statue of the woman it's easy to cross the bridge high over the expressway traffic past light pole 2326 and bolt across into the Botanic Gardens.

If I drew a dog's map of Sydney you'd see some interesting things . . .

I never leave my calling cards anywhere round on streets or paths, or the dog catchers would be waiting for me some day. If I'm by myself in the gardens, I go always under cover, behind a bush or into a little grove, wait till the coast is clear, then sprint to the next clump of bushes. A lot of my friends can't go for long runs like I do: they're too careless. Under the new dog laws they'd get their employers into all sorts of trouble, with fines and complaints.

Often I have to make sure one of my family takes me for my walk. The news comes on the grapevine – our underground news service – that the dog catchers are about, and I make it plain to my human family that their presence is required. A look of eagerness, a bit of snuffling into their hands with the wet of the nose, or even the tongue: that does it. If they're too lazy or dumb or obtuse, to come out – well, I must have my exercise, and one way or another, out I go. If I'm caught, my family will be contacted through my registration number. I have no money to pay fines.

It was good to be back among familiar haunts. It was a high sunny day, I decided I wouldn't go in the main gate, but stay on the ridge.

By the time I was travelling along outside the eastern iron fence of the Gardens I was feeling right at home, and feeling, too, that this was a day I was going to enjoy to the last drop of grass and sun and earth smell.

Along past Henry Lawson and his bronze dog, by the halfway gate, I came across my first seagull. I could smell sweet wine from a cricket pitch away. With a little detective work I found the wine too. It was an almost empty brown bottle of cheap sherry probably ditched by one of Sydney's many human derelicts through the bars of the outer perimeter fence. (At least they're not rounded up and if not claimed in fourteen days, given the needle and furnace treatment.) There it was on its side, still with a dribble of wine coming from its open mouth. The gull had found it, tasted, and it was good. An ironstone pebble under the mouth of the bottle had sticky liquid still on it, gathered to a puddle.

I tried to engage this disreputable bird in conversation, but it was hopeless. A few grunts, a strangled squawk and that was it. The gull lurched off down the slope of the grass and ended on the edge of a freshly dug garden, looking completely baffled. I think it was about to throw up.

A drunken seagull! I should have expected it of a Sydney gull, I suppose.

I moved on. When I looked back from under and between a Moreton Bay fig tree – if you know them you'll know how you can be both under and between – the feathered drunk was being attended by a gull that looked for all the world like a nun. Her chest was folded placidly, and though she was no taller than the miscreant, she contrived to look down, as she reasoned and reproved, and tried to help. Her legs were the colour of dried blood, she was old. On an impulse I sauntered back in their general direction, trying not to be noticeable, putting the nose down to the odd blade of grass, but keeping an eye on them.

I sat in the shade of a bush with yellow flowers, and observed in comfort. I was quite close. After a bit I found they were talking, having a conversation! I'd never heard gulls talk before, only swear, as in Hobart, or scream at each other. The Gardens around us were quiet, though the city was only a short distance away – I could hear the two gulls speaking in their otherwise inaudible voices. Dogs have very sharp hearing.

The drunk had once been a flying instructor, with a great reputation among waterbirds. He'd taught most of the accomplished flyers that were now in their prime. She was reminding him of his past exploits.

'You ought to get into the air more.'

'Beat it, sister,' answered the drunk. 'I don't need an ex-office girl helping me.' Light shone from a glob of spit, or dribble, coming from the point of his beak.

'I *was* a typist once,' she said in a dignified voice. 'Shorthand, too. But that's in the past. Like your flying career. I remember looking up to you when you showed your vertical landing technique to the kids. Very thrilling it was. Now all you do is scrounge on the ground. It's a pity. You could have been a fine example to the young on how to cope with fame and success; now what do they see? An old drunk that never gets airborne, just walks round picking up scraps. It's no wonder even the pinhead pigeons take no notice of us. They eat while we look: we threaten, they pay us no mind.'

She walked a few steps and took off heavily. The drunk didn't bother to watch. I saw her rise to cruising height and followed her flight as she glided down through the trees on to the sandstone parapet of Farm Cove. (We dog people have different names for all these things and places, but you put the signs up, so I'll use your names.) A party of gulls sat in the water of the Cove, doing routine maintenance, washing under their arms and so on; keeping cool. Do they sweat under the arms? And does their sweat smell?

I trotted from cover to cover, making for the Opera House and the Gardens. I took the high path, above the iron gates, up near the Governor's fence. There was a message for me on the low fence where the thick bamboo trunks push between the iron railing. It was two weeks old, a warning about dog catchers.

I like to stop there and listen to the bamboo talk. One of my first outings with Darling took us past that talking bamboo. We stopped to listen; in fact she pointed it out to me, and ever since, I can't go past without stopping to listen just as we did together that happy day. I skirted the Opera House, getting quickly to the boardwalk and trotting slowly behind an elderly human person as if he and I were together. In this way I keep under cover round Circular Quay and in the Rocks part of Sydney. Sometimes the human people understand that I'm using them as mobile bushes for cover, but mostly they don't. This old man's smell said he was miserable and poor and worried about everything in his life and never likely to be any different. He and I passed the place with the dreadful odour, where humans go to relieve themselves. They have different places for males and females, just as we do. The new laws about us dog people are aimed partly at our way of leaving it around, but it doesn't smell like theirs does, unless they feed us too much slops. For all their implied message that we're dirty and they're clean, the smells of their lavatories give it the lie.

The news placards at the Quay said gold was falling. Big deal. At least that meant war was less likely. The unhappy old man crossed Alfred Street and I was on my own.

Along near number 4 jetty a Labrador was sitting near a box of money, collecting for the blind and for guide-work generally. I passed the time of day with him, but he was weary, and didn't have much to say. The expression in his eyes was that of an old dog; something like my father's. My father was a very old dog when he came to die and there was sometimes a look of panic in his eyes. We noticed it, all the family. He couldn't have been afraid to die; all dogs believe not only that dying is quite easy, but that it's a dog's duty to show as little fear as possible. So why that look in my father's eyes? Was he afraid he'd get found out about something? If so, what? Was it because his eyes looked so big, with the lower lid having fallen a bit? He got more unpredictable as he approached his death, his eyes seemed to speak in a confused language, and made inconsistent signs. It still bothers me that I don't understand. Just as it still bothers me that in some places dog people allow themselves to be put on chains. Or farmed for food for humans.

West of the Quay I crossed the road and trotted through the park with the pepper trees, but I had to wait for a human person to cross George Street so I could go over unnoticed. The big mare in the old-style harness with the silver ornaments shining against the dark leather clopped along the street after I crossed, in the shafts of the blue Penfolds' dray carrying stationery about the city. Several tourists took photographs. I went along a bit, then ducked up a thin aperture between buildings, was heckled by an Alsatian on the way up the slope and came out at Harrington Street, where I have friends. However, no one was home, so I went back down Argyle Street to the western part of the Quay and had a short snooze hidden up in one of the raised garden beds where trees and shrubs have been most considerately placed. That aeroplane trip had taken more out of me than I realized.

I dreamed of myself when old: a lot of grey in my coat, and white whiskers. I'd really like to live for three hundred moons – that's the way we dog people count time – but I guess I'd be lucky to last two hundred. Once I counted up how many moons I'd already lived, meaning to keep count, but sometime later I forgot where I was up to. I'm hopeless with figures.

I woke still counting. I was near the overseas ship terminal, the one that's painted to be like an extension of the harbour. Sydney people want their harbour to extend as far as possible into the business area of their city, and who can blame them?

I made my way back, stopping whenever I heard seagull talk. This time the only seagulls I saw that were in any way out of the ordinary were firstly a gull that had gone into the priesthood to work among the poor, and an attractive gull that started out being praised for her looks, began to enjoy praise, and did whatever was necessary to keep the praise coming, and wasn't strong enough to avoid the other end of that slide: on the streets. I picked all this up from hanging about at the south-west corner of the Quay, where humans distribute crumbs to pigeons and gulls. As such, it was only hearsay, I know. I heard a gull mention the Tomb of the Unknown Seagull, and where it was, off the Opera House. I made a mental note to go and look.

I went home, happy that I'd seen some Sydney gulls, and determined to meet as many as I could during the next school holidays, which were coming up in December. Jeff, Julie and Donna would be able to come on walks with me.

In between those times I had lots of Book to read.

If I'm able to go on living and writing here with the Guests for the rest of my life, I'll have organized myself into a life of the most absorbing play. After all, the other work here, looking after the house, etc, is so easy you can do it sitting down.

11 / Love Grabbed Me

As I stretched out that night to go to sleep – first I stretch out, then I curl round, settle down, and hardly move all night – I reflected that I'd earned my keep while I was in Hobart. And a bit more. In addition to which, I'd learned something.

My first day back had been a full day. The only thing missing was Darling. How it would be if she were curled up beside me. And during the night, as we slept, we'd be touching . . . Ah! If only.

I suppose if I'd thought about it in that moment of meeting her those months ago – thought about the frustrations and separation and hardly ever getting to see her – I'd have drawn back. Well, for a second or two. I didn't draw back; I didn't give it a second thought. Love spoke to me, grabbed me and held me tight, and I'm glad of it.

I delight in smells. But there's one smell – a perfume – that lords it over all others, and that's the scent of Darling. When you get your nose close up to her, and preferably, buried in her hair, you inhale an essence that strikes right through you into that place where the greatest and most lasting impressions are made, kept, and folded away securely.

I wonder what Darling thinks about? I mean, does she think about things that happen around her? The news of the day? Could I teach her to read?

She has a beautiful voice that goes up and down like a melody, and only speaks after her eyes have thought for a while. When she speaks to me she talks in little bits at a time, and in her pauses I feel in myself a mixture of impatience, apprehension, longing for her voice and for the next words; and at the same time appreciation of the silver quality of the pause.

Last time I saw her at night I saw in her eyes the reflection of stars: pinpoints of light on the clear brown of her eyeballs. Her eyes are untroubled, candid, and happy.

No one taught me how to love her. It amazes me, when I think of it. I did it by doing. I watched her every chance I got, noticed everything about her, how she walked and stopped and spoke and ran and how beautiful it all was. And went on from there.

Poems are written about things that can't be entirely described. I can't describe how I feel about her, perhaps I ought to put it in a poem.

When I see her in the distance in Forbes Street, the day's full of joy and anticipation. She lives in one of the bright new houses down there on the flat. When I see her I go leaping and frisking towards her – it's not a stylish way of running, but it's how my feelings take me. When we laugh and talk and frisk about together, the world is bright with elation inside and sunshine everywhere.

She's just perfect. Her real name *is* Darling. Her human people sometimes call her Mrs Frobisher when she puts her nose in the air and looks down at them – she can look down her nose at you even from a sitting position – but between us we use her real name. It's much the same with me. My name is Harrison B. Guest, 'Happy' for short, as I said before, but my human family have it down as Spangler Red Brian Boru on their sheet of stiff pedigree paper. Other aliases I have, courtesy of human superiority are Blue (because I'm red), Dog, Mr Dogg, Towser, Buster, Red, Here Boy, Hey You and Hey Mong. Most of them are given to me by strangers and most of them I don't like and I don't come to any. I like Hap, for happy best. And Red. Red's a good nickname to have. I detest Mong; it's short for mongrel. I never use it, myself, about any dog person.

Darling is as bright as a button. She bubbles. She fizzes and lets off sudden noises. She prances and struts and makes a sudden turn-around, grabs at you, looks fierce sometimes, and laughs a lot. We were together, playing near the old concrete ramp round on the east of Lady Macquarie's Point and she slipped on the green slimy weed and let out a shriek as she tumbled into the water. She startled herself so much that she ran like the wind up the rise on to the grass and began shaking herself to get the water out of her long fair hair. She shook so quickly it was hard to follow her movements. I followed them, though. I couldn't take my eyes off her.

We go everywhere together, when we get time off from our respective jobs; which isn't much, lately. She does house duty and child-minding now, but way back before that the family came from the Shetland Isles. They were in the sheep business. She has a black patch on her back and on top of her head, with white everywhere else, and intelligent bright eyes. Her face is smooth, her coat smells beautiful, her undercoat is furry and white, and she has featherings on her arms, and nice legs. I feel bigger and stronger when I think of her.

I know – my father told me – that all things pass, but it's hard to believe my adoration for Darling won't be floating around in the soft blonde air of Sydney long after we've both left life. Floating like the echo of a song, perhaps, into all sorts of odd crevices and alleys and between the gaps in timber fences and the iron bars of park railings.

It was very pleasant, sprawled out, thinking of her.

12 / Human Smells

Going through leafy places, where shrubs are thick and spread over to reach the ground, and light is patchy with shade, I often come on the smells of derelict human people. They make little paths through the bushes, and hide at night and often all day with their bottles wrapped in brown paper. I smell loneliness, defeat. It's a rank smell; I don't like it.

I passed a man today, in his middle years, dressed in elegant clothes, the pink of health still on his shiny cheeks. His smell, though, told me he had lost his way, and was beginning to realize it. The smell of defeat wasn't yet on him, but it would come, along with the bitterness.

Once while the big apartment building was being constructed, up behind Riley Street, I smelled a criminal on the run hiding there at night. Jeff and I were out walking after dark, we walked up Haig

Avenue and took the path through Fragrance Garden. I caught the smell and stopped. Jeff knows that I often notice things humans don't, and obligingly stopped too. I could smell the ultimate in lifelong defiance and deepseated resentment on the evening air, resentment that embraced the whole world; I smelled a fear that was being strangled, but that still succeeded in living and rising from out of the defiance, and I smelled hatred and scorn. I suppose it was hatred and scorn of everyone who wasn't himself. That's the only way I can interpret it, but I don't understand people like that, whether human, dog or seagull.

Yes, it was hatred of everyone. He made no sound in the heavy, cluttered dark, but I could feel he was relaxed, probably sitting. He was anxious about something, too; it was an ordinary, trivial anxiety. Perhaps he was a smoking person and couldn't light up. We had to move along, then. I didn't have time to wait and smell out the fugitive's thoughts.

When school resumed last February after the Christmas holidays, Julie refused to go to the scripture class. At the same time she refused ever to go to church again. There wasn't much fuss at home, but she'd have taken her stand no matter how much fuss there was. I could smell her determination all over her, and the strength of her mind.

'They said animals have no souls. That means they can't go to heaven with us. Well, if Archimedes can't come, I don't want to go!'

And that was that.

13 / The Mystery of Now

As I was settling down last night to sleep I couldn't take my eyes off the stars overhead. I've heard Jeff and his friends, when they used to talk about school things, mention that the stars are burning and they're such a long way off that the distance itself is unimaginable and they could only talk about it with the aid of large numbers. They said that light takes millions of years to come here from some of those stars and that therefore what you see now is what was there all that time ago. And since then I've read it in the Book, with more detail.

What I'd like to know is: is it *now* everywhere? Is there such a thing as this moment, this latest moment, everywhere in the universe? I wish I knew whom to ask.

I wish I was *able* to ask.

The Book doesn't mention it. Or is it only for God that now is now, everywhere? Is God outside physics?

I stayed awake, thinking. I thought of the vast amount of time there has already been and how long it took for the first living organisms to spread and change and for some of them, somehow, to develop into things that were precursors of dogs and mankind. But how much longer it must have been for the first living organisms to arrive at living, assuming their ancestors had to start out as an assortment of molecules.

The numbers are so big when you think of time-spans like this, it makes your mind blur.

I was awake so long I had to get up and go for a short visit to Jack Jacaranda, my friendly tree, to rub against him, and to Grok, whose silence calms me.

Smells of Spring, when the wind's from the north, are almost too sweet for me. But if there's rain, the smell of wet earth balances the sweetness with its own subtle perfume.

Someone had left the tap on in the yard behind us, across the lane. I could hear a regular, slow drip into a pond below the tap, enough for me to catch the scent of fresh water. The Guests' tap was turned off, for once.

We have trees in our backyard. It's very small, and the trees are crowded together, but if there's one thing I like about trees it's the shady tunnels between the greenery. The air is cool in there. Sounds that are like poetry – leaves brushing, tree trunks rubbing, grass ends stirring – nothing in a hurry, just life, quiet life, all round.

When I go to sleep some nights in summer, or when I feel lonely, I sleep out there among the trees. The bosom of night comes down over me gently, and it's black. Before I drop off to sleep I think of Darling and hope she's not having nightmares. She gets them, but can't remember what they were, later, just knows she's had them. She's alone over at her place, too.

14 / The Night I Heard the Fire Start

One night in October a bit more than halfway between the coming of darkness and the morning, I heard a fire start. A short time later I heard a scream coming from a long way, and felt distant waves of human fear. I felt nervous, undecided, upset, all at the same time. I couldn't help it, I began to bark. Not a full-blooded bark that sounds savage, but a quick, nervy bark that was trying to say I knew I shouldn't bark at night except in emergencies, but something was wrong, and this was something I had to do.

I felt the Guests wake up, and stir, and start to blame me, then stop to get up and look outside. Just then, the first of the fire engines came howling down Park Street, along William Street. Mr Guest called out that he could see smoke from the fire, it was over the hill at Kings Cross, down past the Hyatt Kingsgate.

Jeff was up, and inside twenty minutes he counted twenty fire engines.

The Guests waited up more than two hours, and by that time, the first reports came over one of the local radio stations. Only one! It was enough to make a reasonable dog cynical about human communications.

I thought at first I was going to be in disgrace, but Mr Guest recalled that my bark came before the first fire engine's siren, and to this day my 'sixth sense' is a subject for pride in the family.

They don't know I *heard* the screams, and the fire! They can't entertain the idea that some of my faculties are keener than theirs. They'll admit it in conversation, but in practice: no. It had to be a sixth sense, something mysterious.

15 / Humans Are Mean

I've heard from dogs who were interned, then bought out of the death camps, that very few of the dogs whose turn it was to be taken for their needle on the fifteenth day (unsold) ever complained. Some did: most did not. They knew, and they went calmly, just like those kings and heroes mentioned in the Book, who made light of the rope, the fire, or the headsman's axe; or like the wives of Henry VIII. Even the public executions at Tyburn were enlivened by the witty remarks of male-factors, who often made a speech, or read a verse. Ned Kelly laconically said, 'Such is life'.

Even the two dogs at the Plowrights' that I saw taken at different times down the paddock, made no complaints and didn't ask for mercy. They went down – man, dog, rifle and spade – and after the rifle-shot, only man, rifle, and spade came back.

Here's my point. If one of us dogs has to die – like old greyface from across the street who had to be 'put down' because his employers thought he'd cost them too much in vet's bills if they kept him till the end – they see us go to die calmly. He did. We know there's no out. We put a brave face on it. But do humans credit us with courage, do they note that we don't even whimper? Do they see and applaud our fatalism, or our bravery as we approach doom with heads held high?

Never! They think we don't know – we're stupid because we don't make a fuss! Anyone would think the proper response was fear and flight; they forget their own history's record of heroic deaths, and think we should run or fight.

Humans are mean, to think we're not capable of the same heroism they can show.

16 / There Is No Mould You Can't Escape

My training taught me to trust no one but the family of my employer, to reject food offered by others, and only to accept familiarity from strangers if my human charges were on easy terms with them. My training taught me never to pick up scraps. My training taught me obedience, alertness, responsibility, and that humans come first.

But there is a part of me that my training did not touch. And that part, so strong in me, decrees that I always think about the words the humans, including my employers, use to me; about the things they do and say to each other; about the characteristics I pick up from their scent; about the ways their voices move when they deceive each other and try to deceive me; about the faces, the hands, the movements, the tentativeness, the eyes sliding sideways, the fidgeting, the odd display of courage which sticks out like a flower on a rubbish tip. And reserve my judgement and approval, no matter who tries to influence me.

That part of me, tucked away inside, is independent of their world. It's also independent of the dog world. It's independent of any training. It's the place where I am myself.

17 / The Dog That Can't Be Tamed

When they took me to the circus last April I walked along past the caged animals with Julie, and saw, in one of the lighter cages, as distinct from the heavy-duty cages that housed lions and leopards, a dog shaggy with hair, that looked angrily out over all who passed by.

'UNTAMEABLE DOG!' the sign shouted.

I managed to get Julie to go over with me so I could talk to the untameable person. We put our fronts against the cage and talked to her. 'Here, girl!' said Julie.

We barely had time to get away from the bars before the untameable person hurled herself against the part where we'd been, snapping and snarling. She set up a loud barking, and kept it up until we moved away. I tried to talk but I couldn't get a word in edgeways.

We went out of sight round a corner, and the barking stopped. I put my head a little back round the corner and there she was, watching. The barks began.

I had an idea. We went along behind the wall that hid us from her, and looked around. There she was, watching for us at the other end, where we'd been.

We stayed still, and soon the untameable one relaxed, sat down, then lay down on the floor of her cell. She showed all the signs of going to sleep.

When next we started along near her, she woke again, rushed at us, barked and snapped and looked fierce.

When we hid ourselves she subsided again. It seemed she had energy and motive to harass us only when we showed ourselves.

But she'd been tamed enough to get her into confinement: how could they say untameable when she spent her life in a cage?

I'd hoped, when they said this was a dog who could never be tamed, that I'd come across one who was still in touch with the common past of all dogs. No such thing.

Oh well.

Far from being untameable, I'm a very social creature. I love people around me. When I go out into the street and there's no one round, I feel funny.

18 / Tomb of the Unknown Seagull

Next day Donna was sick. She's four, a young pup of a person. Mrs Guest is proud of Donna. She's a pretty child. But Mrs Guest is even prouder of Donna's photographs, which make her beautiful.

She loves to water the plants in the garden and often tries to dig a garden for herself. She also loves to cuddle things. She constantly tries to catch me and lift me off the ground and always holds me tightly. I hate it. I hate being off the ground and I hate being held tightly. She holds me up as if *I* were a pup, too. I'm not!

I wonder if Donna, when she's seven and has been two years at school, will show the same dampening of her freedom with words and phrases as I noticed with the children of the Plowrights, back in Kelly-ville.

I had thought it was the effect of school discipline and the presence of adults who didn't love and cuddle them, but now I'm not so sure. What if it's the presence of the other kids?

Maybe it's just that there are so many things to learn that their confidence takes a dip.

I delayed my daily rounds until Donna had taken her medicine and was asleep. I also made a note to be home early. When I looked up the street and caught sight of the cathedral I thought of her and hoped she wouldn't be needing people to help her die. Then reproached myself for thinking of death. I nearly jogged back to tell her: 'You won't die! Of course you won't!'

I hope it's not serious.

I liked being on holiday, in a way, but it's better being home. It was full moon last night, and I went to the Opera House to pay my respects to the Unknown Seagull.

The tomb is a grey post sunk into the harbour floor, with a red light on top. At night the red of that light has a thick, bloodlike quality:

human people think it's a warning light to keep boats and ships and ferries off the Opera House perimeter. I was glad I'd heard it mentioned the day before.

I stood with my arms up on the fawn slabs of the low safety fence that supports the smooth round bronze rail, and gazed at the Tomb and meditated. It's fascinating looking at all the things I see around me, both here and in the Gardens, near the water and in the city. All the different things and people so busy being; just being. Perhaps everything in the universe knows what it has to do and does it, knows what it has to be, and becomes that. When I'd done meditating, I took my hands down and was glad to see a homecoming fishing boat surrounded by gulls. It was white, with a blue strip painted above the waterline. The fishermen were cleaning the decks and bits of fish were flung overboard into the boat's wake. From this distance the white birds looked like butterflies fluttering round a blossom tree.

In the sunny daytime surrounded by the flash of water and the grace of gulls it was a great joy to think of Darling. And how she loves the water and joyfully active things and coloured sails and calm ships. She and I are both happy, cheerful people. I used to have moods like other dogs, but one day I decided to be cheerful for ever. Or as long as for ever means to me. (All animals are ironic: dogs are more ironic than most, and know how short for ever can be).

Not far from the Opera House approaches there was a contingent of seagull protesters. They argue enough amongst themselves, they shout and yell and scream; I wondered what else they have to protest about. I followed the march and got close enough to hear the slogans. It was a march of gay gulls demanding that something be done about discriminating practices by heterosexual gulls. They marched round Alfred Street behind Circular Quay and nearly bowled over a tourist guide and a party of tourist gulls from the south coast who were ambling round to see the Opera House. Why do so many of them walk when they can fly?

I called round on Ben, an old friend of mine who lives with a caretaker up the hill in Phillip Street. I wanted to ask him about gulls. Old Ben was having trouble with his eyes and his feet were often sore. In his family that wasn't uncommon – the caretaker he minded had the same trouble. In addition to which, the caretaker was a prey to the worry lots of human people seem to have: he worried about not being able to make ends meet; money preyed on his mind. With some humans you can actually feel the rasp of their hunger for money, just by being near them. That's the best of being a dog and having given up things like clothes and pockets ages ago. We take with us only what we need right now, and trust to our smartness and initiative to live off the land.

Ben told me of the gull overseas news service, and how it was now possible for those gulls at the Quay to come in as tourists.

I woke early next morning thinking of little Donna, who was still sick. I knew she was sleeping easily; I could feel it: and when the Guests got up out of bed, it was true. But in the middle of the night, when something else woke me, I had thought of Darling and felt very warm and tender toward her. 'Love her, black night,' I said. And when the first glow of dawn woke me and shed the cold light of morning gradually everywhere around, it was delicious thinking of her.

I should never fret about Darling. I should take love easy, as fruit sets on the trees. Even if I don't get to see her, I know she exists and that fact is wonderful, by itself. The love I have for her is inside me, I carry it wherever I go.

19 / The Conspiracy to Change My Names

I like my names.

With someone like Jeff, though, a dog has to be always on guard. Things seem to be normal, day passes day, people go to work or school and come home; nothing out of the ordinary. That's when new ideas creep into the heads of restless people, specially if they're young. If they're seventeen as well, the new idea is all the more dangerous.

I know it was Jeff. I saw the way he looked at me, and I heard him float the idea in the Guests' kitchen to his mother. He wanted a dog with a name like a man: Rover. If he got his mother on side he'd have the vote, since Mr Guest will always sidestep decisions that have no bearing on his creature comfort.

I'm not a Rover; I'm not any other sort of dog: I'm a me, a Happy, an Archimedes.

When Julie came home from school I made a special sort of fuss, the sort she recognizes. We have a good understanding, so when I'm miserable, or when something out of the ordinary has come up, she knows.

We beat Jeff's conspiracy. Julie went in and asked her mother something I didn't hear, and Jeff came out later, angry. I knew Julie and I had won. I was Happy still, and best of all – Archimedes.

20 / The Setter

The setter is the world's most elegant dog, with long and subtle featherings on arms, legs and tail, and a finely sculpted head, with a high dome.

The setter is enthusiastic for work, and is remarkable in distinguishing between the scents of wildlife and the kinds it seeks as game.

Setters display canine intelligence at its best; a trained setter never makes a mistake.

Setters hold their heads high, noses in the air, and hold their point, motionless, at the game they hunt.

Setters have good looks, gentle manners, excellent temperament, wonderful sense of humour, and enjoy life to the full.

I'm glad I'm a setter. You can take it from me that if I hadn't been born a setter, I'd like to have become one.

People say my ears are too long. They're not: they're just the right size. When I was a pup, and growing fast, I noticed them a lot when I ran: they often got out of step with each other and one would flap up while the other was down. It used to make me feel a fool, and lop-sided. Even now I sometimes get a shadow of that old feeling pass across my mind when I'm loping along, and I stop, wondering if my ears are really flapping out of synchronization, and whether I look foolish.

Setters *do* look foolish, I know, a lot of the time. It's due to our eagerness and restless energy. We're used to it.

21 / A Ray of Sunshine

There's a neighbour up the street, who throws open the door at the front of his house and comes laughing onto his lawn. Every time I see him, I smile. I can't help it.

His name is Ray Cattleford. His friends call him Sunshine. His lawn is two rectangles of grass, each measuring about two metres by one metre. Perhaps he laughs at that. Even when he's been drinking a lot, he still finds plenty of things funny.

He keeps asking me to leave the Guests and go to live with him. He doesn't understand the conditions of a dog's employment.

He's very cheerful indeed, but I overheard Mr Guest once say to Mrs Guest that it was no use talking to Ray Cattleford if you didn't talk *about* him – he wouldn't be listening. Is that why he's so happy?

This joyful man has peculiar thoughts. I've allowed him to pat me and cup his hand over the dome of my head a number of times, and I felt his envy. He wants a handsome, cheerful, open-countenanced dog. Mixed with envy, though, is a sort of dog-in-the-manger attitude to the Guests and all who employ dogs. He feels they lack courage because they need to be guarded by long-toothed meat-eating animals.

Then, just as quickly as you turn a tap off, his cheerfulness swamps all other thoughts. It was the first time I felt the emptiness of it, placed like a mask over his real self, whatever *that* was. As if anything but happiness was immoral or to be hidden.

Perhaps his real self was the constant changing from one state to the other.

22 / I'm a Volatile Dog

I'm a volatile dog, I know that. It's not a great failing. But listen to this:

I had a cousin in the country who was a frenetic kind of setter; he ran everywhere, bolted his food, ran from person to person, from hand to hand. When he was near the river, he couldn't take his attention from the lights in the water; he got more and more excited as he tried to touch the water-dazzle, and since it always eluded him he got panicky with excitement. People had to walk away and leave him, he embarrassed them.

Sometimes he didn't follow, but continued his yelping and jumping up and down, even though no one was looking.

One day he bolted a big dinner, then looked round for someone to play with. His employers were all sitting round their own table, so he went under the house to lie down and sulk.

He didn't get up. Died where he lay. His name was Shrieker. Shrieker was held up to us young pups as a terrible warning never to bolt our food.

I remember, most of the time.

23 / Humans Have No Claws

Humans have no claws; and no teeth to speak of. Nature has given them no ornaments, only a thatched roof of hair and some bunches of fur where the limbs meet. I have my thick, shiny coat, my beautiful tail, featherings on arms and legs; others of the animal kingdom have similar adornments – if less spectacular than mine – but all have more than humans. Humans are naked, absolutely uncovered, unprotected; naked to the full extent, the ultimate meaning of the word.

Perhaps their art, their scientific efforts, their discoveries, explorations, their constant dashing about doing things; perhaps these come from their nakedness, as some sort of urge to cover themselves with the works of their hands. None of the rest of us are born naked; even fish have scales, and birds feathers. Humans provided for themselves only thin skin.

Humans often smell of fear. It reminds me of the water Mrs Guest throws out, when flowers have stayed too long in their vases, and have begun to rot. It reminds me also that they are animals, like us, subject to fear, disease and death.

Humans can't do something I can. Anytime I feel like it I can spring up and feel perfectly well-dressed. Humans can't. They have pants to put on – and pants within pants.

24 / When the Children Are Sick

When the children are sick I'm useful to them in ways I'd never have imagined when I was a pup.

Julie was sick for a week at the beginning of winter and I used to come in the house and go to her bedroom first thing and she used to pick things off my coat – bits of grass or leaves or the odd prickle from a spiny tree – and make up stories about where I'd been. She made me feel I was telling her a story; which I'd love to have done.

There's something pathetic about people who are so much bigger, when they get sick. It makes small people feel less small, to see them brought low, even if the small people have all the sympathy in the world.

I wonder if it's the same with female humans, when they see their men sick, or dying?

25 / What Women Want

I wonder why the Guest parents chose each other...to live with, I mean.

I suppose I'll never come up with a satisfactory answer to that one. The reason I ask is, I heard Mrs Guest talking at the front gate to a woman from a house three streets away, and that woman kept referring, every now and again, to a young man Mrs Guest used to go with before she met her husband. The way they both spoke of him, he was large, vigorous and very male. I asked myself why didn't Mrs Guest choose him? Mr Guest is quiet, ordinary, plain, and often has a bad back. The way they spoke of Don, it was clear Mrs Guest enjoyed him and he her. Then why not choose him? And he had a good job, where Mr Guest is often in doubt if he has one at all.

The City Gym has panels of photographs of body-builders, mostly male. Their muscles and veins stand out almost to the point of bursting.

I've been up there with Julie or Jeff, and I've heard passing girls and women talking about these males as if they were monstrosities; as if they found that weight of muscle gross, menacing, potentially uncontrollable. (Uncontrollable by a woman, perhaps.)

And I've seen that women, who seem to know about these things, maybe by instinct, don't exercise their bodies as much or as fanatically as men, yet they live longer.

If men's bodies and muscles are stronger, why don't they live longer than women? Is their back-up equipment weaker – their hearts and lungs, nerves and cells? Or is there something connected with their strength that cuts men's lives short? A balancing of an advantage against a disadvantage.

I'd like to reach back further into the past than Mrs Guest's choice, back to the time when humans' ancestors were making the choices that made them what they are today. Did the women of the past choose for mates the less hairy, less fierce, the more tamed, docile and steady males because they could manage them more easily, because they would be more obedient to the ground rules laid down by the women: more dependent on women, who rewarded them with constant temptation and constant availability and therefore were less of a nuisance to the women in the rearing of children?

If this were so, I thought to myself, thinking back to the parts of the Book that deal with ages past, what would be the effect on human society of women choosing the relatively gentle and harmless and less threatening? Why, it would tend to produce, instead of hairy, bullnecked creatures, the present smooth, hairless vulnerable mates that are called men – tenders of families, docile, obedient, able to adjust their few divergent and irrelevant desires to the peaceable bringing-up of children as manageable as themselves.

I was proud of this speculation, particularly as I thought it had a good chance of being somewhere near the mark. Then what happened? I found the very same thought later on in the Book!

It must be very difficult to have new thoughts. Writing has made me feel that ideas are floating around in the air, all over the world. You just reach up and grab them. Someone had grabbed this one first.

26 / The Dog with Pale Lips

Last night I dreamed of Leda and the Seagull, an ancient myth not yet invented.

I was a sculptor, and sculpted them engaged in a crucial act. I was a painter and painted flowing white wings covering Leda, and a prying red beak and aggressive red legs astride her. I was a poet and wrote impassioned lyrics from the point of view of every failed poet I could imagine; I was a historian and wrote a history of literature that had been altered throughout its course by the alteration to the Leda legend. I re-invented the Ugly Duckling, to erase the swan from folk memory and replace it with a seagull.

I woke feeling distinctly out of sorts. And no wonder.

It was one of those days when I feel slow. Not sick: just a bit off. I'd have liked Julie to come and read to me. She used to once when she was younger.

They don't talk to me enough. They don't realize that since my total life span is shorter than theirs, I have to pack a lot into each day. I can't take things as slowly as they do.

Always at the back of my mind is the dog with pale lips, who will come for me someday. I imagine his presence, for I've never seen him. I imagine his shadow, for he has none. He's not a dog for pleasure; he drives pleasure away.

Not for long, though, in my case. I'm not going to be intimidated by him; enough other things have intimidated me in my time. Well, one or two: that's enough.

If I have the picture of the dog with pale lips at the back of my mind, I wonder if others have the same dog at the back of their minds? Is it the same dog for others? Or does each person have his own dog with pale lips?

If each person carries his own special death with him, then there's a special thing about each person having a personal property in death.

I'll think about Darling. She has lips a soft shade of pink, and white teeth, and she comes complete with shadow. She has everything in good measure, and all lovely. When I think of her by day I want the day to have no end. There's nothing pale about her except her white throat and chest and stomach.

27 / Hey Readers!

Just listen to this. I read it in the Book just now and it really stirred me up:

> *'The behaviour of animals is derived from their perceptual present and their background conditioning.'* – Indeed! We have no memory, I suppose.
> *'There is no evidence that animals share this world (the human world) even in the smallest degree.'* – We're never happy or sad, heroic or cowardly, loyal or aggressive; just bundles of instinct, I suppose?
> *'In this fundamental respect humans are radically different in kind from animals.'* – Oh, you don't say!

I might accept a difference in function, but no more. How would they like it if I said 'the behaviour of humans is derived from their perceptual present plus their background conditioning?' What parts of *their* behaviour are not derived from their perception plus conditioning?

I've got over my first surprise that the Book isn't always right.

43

('Right' means 'up-to-date', since truth changes all the time, of course.)

It seems to me that a bird's nest, a spider's web, a bee's honeycomb, a squirrel's hoard, a beaver's dam, are, all of them, the product of thought.

How do humans *dare* to call animals' ways of solving problems instinct, and not apply the word instinct to *their* own behaviour and products?

> *'Animals make noises of expressive and signalling functions'* – And humans don't?
>
> *'Man describes and argues'* – And we don't?
>
> *'Language led to formulations, understanding, the concept of truth and falsity.'* – Yes, I'll go along with that, as far as it goes.
>
> *'Language is part of the development of reason.'* – Yes, part of it; it's the part of reasoning that is expressed in language.
>
> *'Man lived for ages in groups, roaming.'* – Like we did.
>
> *'Man was a social animal before a human.'* – Just like we are social animals, still, despite our confinement.

The Book omitted to say that Julie has her own language, different from Jeff's, from Mr Guest's; Mrs Guest has a language slightly different again, and Donna's is different from all of them. And each of their behaviours is their own.

They simply don't credit us with enough perception and mental life, and it's only through inattention and neglect. They refuse to study us! We have to study their behaviour, in order to fit in, in order to keep our noses clean, to survive.

Why don't they carefully watch what we do?

Why can't they see the extent to which so many animals' social organization is abstract; as are our patterns of communication? Maybe they don't recognize the abstract and ritual nature of a lot of their *own* actions.

> Look again at those examples I gave:
>
> A web is a spider's civilization,
>
> the nest is the civilization of ants, birds, wasps,
>
> the honeycomb is the civilization of bees, ·
>
> the dam is that of the beaver,
>
> the lair is that of the fox,
>
> the hoard of nuts in a tree is the civilization of the squirrel.

In the same way board and keep with a human family is the civilization of us dogs who left the wild.

Following the herds of foliage-eaters is the
civilization of meat-eaters, for example,
following herds of sheep and goats is the
civilization of the Bakhtiari, and
following herds of reindeer is the civilization
of the Lapps.

Just so, the protection, breeding, feeding, fattening, sale, slaughter, and eating of sheep, cows, pigs, birds, fish, together with the care and nurture, study, breeding and reaping of grasses, grains, trees, plants and so on is the foundation of the civilization of humans.

For how living things manage to live every day is a central feature of their lives and culture, and is reflected in their practical philosophies of life.

Humans are so taken up with the differences between them and other animals that they overlook the resemblances.

28 / A Water Chapter

I told you before of my delight in Spring, when I smell the earth itself rejoicing, and some nights even hear it talking.

One such night in November I went to sleep with those very thoughts in my head, and – perversely – dreamed of Australia as a poor land, a deserted country scarred by exhausted quarries, its metals and minerals long gone; a place peopled by humans who never had energy enough to make provision for holding the water that fell on it as rain, preferring to see it evaporate or find its way back to the sea. I dreamed that few had occupations that could be dignified with the name work; that all the dreamers had been repulsed and laughed at, who said rivers could be turned back to the dry inland, or that industrial plants could be set up on thousands of kilometres of coast to desalinate water.

45

Next morning the smell of dreams was still on Julie when she came out to say good morning. She smiled at me – just after she caught my eye, not just before, as she usually does. She'd got up early to work on a project for school, on the subject of water. She had it in her hand, and sat on the back step looking at it. I couldn't help myself, I went over to her, read what she'd written, and began to worry at her. If only I could talk.

For Heaven's sake, I could help her! Oh, how frustrating it was! I made all sorts of noises. I tried not to bark – barking alarms them – but I got my throat into all sorts of contortions, my tongue was in a tangle, anxiety made my face screw up this way and that.

'Desalination plants dotting the coastline; the retaining of monsoon rains; turning half a dozen rivers back into the dry; replenishing the great artesian basins' – these were the ideas I was dying to communicate to her. I was in a passion to tell her, to help her, to have her know I had an opinion.

The only sounds I made were strangled cries, grunts, half barks, moans, choking noises, undignified squeals. If only she knew what I thought. If only I could have formed one sentence, only one, and rolled it all out on my tongue, and said it; expressed myself, in one triumphant sentence! That sentence wasn't a sentence really, but contained all the suggestions I was capable of, in my desire to help humankind help itself on this unpredictable continent.

'Poor Hap. How you wish you could talk,' Julie said, and patted my head. She didn't know the half of it.

What was more painful, she didn't know *me*.

That afternoon, when she came home from school, I could smell tears. They smelled grey. Sure enough, Julie had a wet handkerchief tucked into the waistband of her dress. I gave her knee a nuzzle as she sat on the back step, and her right hand came up on to my head in recognition. I looked at her face. There were still some tears to come, and she couldn't speak; there was nothing I could do. Here was my best human friend, the one person who wanted me to keep the Book; who protected it, and me, and said nothing of my subversive educational activities to another soul; and I wasn't helping her in her sorrows.

I couldn't tell the origin of her sadness, neither on her, nor on her tear-wet handkerchief. But as I thought of this I knew what I could do. I began to nuzzle her knee, at the crook of the knee, then her feet, then between her knees, then stopped dead, and put my face up to look into her eyes. She burst into tears again, big floods of them, the handkerchief was wringing wet; they ran down her cheeks, into her mouth, off the sides of her chin. And gradually, she cried herself out. When I felt she was nearly finished I jumped up and down, nuzzled each of her hands, and her arms up to the elbows, and under her arms, where she tickles. I frisked and laughed and ran my long tongue over her hands, knees, then up onto her face. She began to laugh, and soon the tears were gone. We both pranced round the yard, laughing and making sudden little shouts and squeals. She was better.

There *was* something I could do, after all.

29 / On Really Bad Nights

On really bad nights in the winter when I'm hungry and the smell of meat is strong I'm allowed into the house. I have a special mat of sheepskin. They don't realize how I link up the smell of the skin with the occasional scraps of sheepmeat they allot me as part of my rations, and the fact of the mat, and their ignorance of my thoughts, cause me the odd smile.

I know, from conversations I've heard, that the picture on the front of the television box is a transmitted picture, from a centre where the action is dramatized and photographed and the pictures of it fed into the air waves. So I don't have to go through the business of making the discovery myself that the figures moving in the picture aren't real.

I know one old guy from Harmer Street, an airedale, who went around the back of the television set and peered in and found nothing but lumps and odd-shaped objects made of metal and glass, and wires, and traced the whole thing back to a cable fitting into the plug that sits on the face of the skirting board that goes around the outer border of the room. He knew, from seeing what happened with similar plugs in other parts of the house, that its button was in one of two positions, and when it had the red spot showing, that's when the action happened, whether it was a toaster, kettle, radio, or the television. He thought he was pretty shrewd. I didn't tell him I'd worked that out when I was a fraction of his age.

I'm cool with the television. Except when the little figures are going around killing people. At first I got a certain enjoyment from watching people shot with guns or broken up by heavy things rolling over them, but I got sick of it. And the time I got sickest of it was some moons ago when little Donna began to cry while she was watching a person with blood running down her chest. Donna shrieked, put her hand to the corresponding part of her, then settled into a helpless cry. By helpless I mean the cries seemed to come from well inside her and they shook her; they pushed and pulled and she had to follow. It was too much for me; I walked over to the cable and grabbed it with the back of my jaw where I have the strongest pull and the bluntest teeth and yanked it out. Everything stopped. Unfortunately for me, Donna cried worse than ever. They said a few hard words to me, but I didn't have to go out into the rain. They switched the TV to something else, muttering about censorship and human rights and who's boss in this house and all the time looking at me sideways. I had the sense to look ashamed, and they were satisfied.

The television upset *me* once, too. There was a dog story showing, and a film-starish dog person – female, and attractive – was prancing round in beautiful open spaces. I envied the expanse of grass, the rough rocks, shrubs, trees; especially the trees, because there were so many and they looked so shady and inviting. There was a stream bubbling over rocks. In the story the film-star dog has a frightful accident; she is rescued, but is dying. Her friends – in the story – gather around, and the whole thing is so sad that I have to look away. I try desperately to think of something else, but it doesn't work. I feel two large tears coming and I don't want the family to see. I mean, what confidence would they have in a security person out in the dark of night who cries at sad stories? I turn away and curl into a circle and put my head down.

'I thought you said he watched the TV and never took his eyes off it,' Mrs Guest said to Julie.

'He hates sentiment,' said Mr Guest sourly. He had wanted to watch sport but was out-voted.

30 / Donna

Little Donna gets half a dozen colds each winter. There's something the matter, and I don't know what it is. I have a feeling that if I knew what she ate I might have an idea about what's happening. It's a worry for her parents, as well as for me.

She loves me. She's always hugging me. When she does it in the street some of the passersby say: 'Look at that stupid kid. The parents ought to stop it. Never know what you can catch from animals.'

But only some. Trouble is, I'm always concerned in case Donna hears. There's time enough later for her to meet that sort of comment.

Last walk we had near the overhead railway, Julie gave twenty cents to a derelict who asked her for money for a cup of tea. As she went on, with Donna and me, she had tears in her eyes, thinking how dreadful it must be to be down and out.

As for the dero, he took the money and as we walked on he put the coin in his pocket and looked after us, then spat.

Donna was up early in the morning, and running about; trying to catch me, in her joy at being well, just as she tries to catch me when she is sick and sorry for herself, so the feel of me will be some comfort.

If I could speak, the things I'd say most often to Donna, would be things like this:

Sit still a minute and think.

Stop that – and think!

Don't look away: concentrate! Try to grasp the thought that's just slipping away, sliding out of your mind. If you don't catch this one, try catching the next.

31 / We Chose Silence

I feel a lot older than I was. Sometimes I wake worrying, just because human people are *so* big. Not as big as they seemed when I was a pup, but yet much bigger, because I know all the things they can do, and I know how fierce they can be. We dogs chose silence and a limited vocabulary. Man chose speech, and therefore insult, lies, orders, promises, excuses, gossip, demands, confessions, beliefs, lies, accusations, apologies, allegations, stammerings, scoffing, rumour, demagogues, flattery, manifestoes, guarantees, lies. But they can choose what they can do with speech. They're not forced to lie. Nevertheless, we made the wrong choice. Speech is better than enforced silence.

Mankind say they have a soul. That's what they tell themselves, but if they did have a soul, I don't think they'd care for its discarded case. Our people have souls, too; we don't care if its wrapping is left lying around after life has gone – in some street, or in a corner of the backyard in a favourite spot under the lemon tree. That's the test: if you care about your carcass, you're uncertain about your soul.

This morning the tide of water in the Harbour had been flowing to the sea; now it was coming back. Julie and I walked to the full extent of Mrs Macquarie's Road and on the way noticed a crazy gull, bullied by other gulls, prodded by pidgeons, scared by sparrows. I stopped to watch, and after a little pulling on my lead, Julie did, too. She laughed and I smiled at the antics of the idiot gull, and walked on, refreshed by the sight of glorious stupidity.

On the harbour side of the Opera House young seagulls were practising how to stand, without slipping, on the bronze handrail. Some could stay still for a bit, but in the end all of them slipped on the hand-smooth shiny metal. Their feet were hard and shiny too. I've always been a good balancer, so it was with great amusement that I watched them having a hard time keeping their footing. They like to perch there, within striking distance of the outdoor tables, waiting to swoop on food dropped or left for a few seconds unattended.

At the Quay it was lunchtime, and people from office towers hurried through the streets to get food. The sight made me think of the animals I'd seen when I'd been out in the suburbs near the western rail line – animals hurrying in captivity towards the abattoirs. I could smell their disorientation. Both hurrying: that's what caught my fancy.

At the Rocks Julie and I passed the Seagull Craft Shoppe, which had gulls serving behind the counter, and walking up the side lane past Phillip's Foote we saw – I saw; I presume she did too – seagulls cooking steaks in the barbecue. Unusual steaks: cat steaks, steaks cut in the likeness of humans, sparrow steaks; all hung upsidedown, pegged to a wire, waiting to be put on the hot-plate to sizzle. Seagull diners waited with knife and fork to have lunch. A building seagull stood at the door to the tavern and chatted to the publican about extensions to the timber tables and to the pergola on which climbed shady vines. Have you ever heard of such gulls?

32 / A Decent Life for the Guests

It's eight in the morning and there's that politician on talk-back radio again, talking of social cohesion. When that man talks, it's as if a tank of liquid has an open tap and his mouth is the spout. He's in opposition, so he has nothing to lose.

To my way of thinking social cohesion is money, employment, debts, traditions, churches, hospitals, access to water, food, amusements, electricity, fuel, marriage, taxes, police, schools, laws, roads, babies, holidays, advancement, opportunity, banks, garbage trucks, local government, records, public servants, freedoms, obligations, drains.

What he's saying is that we should all think the same and not argue

- especially against his point of view. He wants unity.

People like politicians can talk and the Guests don't seem to hear; the words flow over them like background music. Perhaps that's the function of such words.

Oh! I forgot the armed forces. They're part of social cohesion. Ours is not a world where you can afford to turn your back for long, unless you have a sentry.

As for unity, only in war are the people and the government as one; only in emergencies. The rest of the time the more voices, opinions, and conflicting aims expressed the better. The danger, ultimately to the state, is in opinions suppressed, aims not permitted to conflict, voices stilled.

The Guests are all in there, eating. I wonder if they hear that politician's talk about their duty to society.

The duty of the Guest family is not to serve their country, or be good economic units of Australian society: their duty is to themselves as a family, and next, to themselves as humans; to remain human and to revere the humanity of others. The duty of their country is to them: to help them live a decent life, to have an occupation that's not too dangerous or debilitating, and help them feed, clothe, and shelter themselves and their children.

Peace, order, good government – only with these things can the Guest family have that decent life.

The light is soft, this time of the morning. A faint mistiness can be seen in the sunlit air between my kennel and the hydrangeas, as if the warmth of the sun induces the ground to breathe out some of its moist breath.

33 / Strangers in the Blood

What if a new civilization was to begin here in the Guests' backyard, among one of the colonies of insects that may have inhabited the place for thousands of years?

Thousands of years? Certainly. The families and tribes of the meat ants, black ants, sugar ants, that have their living space in the back-yards of all the houses whose side and back fences join in these streets, could claim family connections or direct descent from ants who pop-ulated the ground before the original Australians ever came here from the north.

But if a new civilization arose, how would we know? It would be a precarious, hidden beginning, and while their community took hold they'd very likely keep their heads down and show themselves as little as possible.

And if a new type of person appeared among humans, they would feel their difference first, and keep *their* heads down, and would stay hidden until they were numerous enough to have their ways take over from the humans' ways.

A civilization will fight what is strange; a race will fight what is alien; the body will attack what is not its own. Little strangers invading the blood of a person will be attacked and destroyed because they *are* strangers, and don't belong.

Some of what is not its own, but like itself, the body will fight less vigorously.

When I think of these things, it seems to me almost that I am on the edge of understanding something about all life, but I cannot make the jump to a confident conclusion. What holds me back?

Something is pulling me down and I don't know what it is.

34 / A Dog's Eye View

Thursday I got talking to this dog on the next block. We dogs don't always have to speak in words: most of the time we see each other thinking; we know what's being thought, and we either agree, or disagree, or ask for further information. That's the reason you human people often think we're not talking at all, or even thinking. You often do the same thing, but you don't realize it. When two people meet in a doorway, you don't have to produce sentences of description of what's happened and what should happen and how you both are going to accomplish this: all you do is, one stands aside and the other passes; or one takes a step to the left and the other to the right. I see in human faces the thought that since we don't talk we don't think, and that's not good enough.

When we decide together on a common course of action, humans call it instinct or thought transfer. Always ready to downgrade us. What are they scared of?

I hope some day I can pass on my work to a younger dog, so that eventually books, and all the riches they contain, will be no luxury to dogs, no secret.

What makes a dog? Am I a dog because I look like a dog? Because I bark like a dog? Because humans say I am a dog? Or because *I* say I am a dog? Which is me and which is a dog? Am I a dog because I have such skill in sensing sickness in humans? – and hesitation, fear, guilt, dishonesty, meanness, uncleanness, murder, cowardice, approaching death?

I love the smell of fresh bread. Fresh bread smells like Spring to me.

When it rains, I smell the joy the earth feels; just as if its life-giving drops were raining inside me. I'm lucky I can feel so many things – all the more to fill my mind, all the more to think of.

Today, near the overhead railway, I smelled a baby in a pusher. It was a baby boy. I could smell the remote scent of a long life about him, and I bet his parents didn't even know. It was strange, knowing secrets.

There was an altogether different smell coming from Mr Guest today, when he came home. The smell was of cowardice. Something had happened at work, I would guess, and he hadn't spoken up when he should have. I sniffed him again, on the backs of his hands where everything comes out – he had been criticised by someone in authority and feared to answer back in case he lost his job. Poor man. Humans *do* limit their freedom, and just for an easy life of living on wages that come every week like a gift from heaven.

A woman passing in Cathedral Street had a perfume that reminded me of the wisteria in Hyde Park in Spring, which was a tumult of perfume. With a nose like mine it's a bit much, but I enjoyed the Guests' enjoyment of it and the pleasure of the other humans who sniffed it and took photographs.

When I had a short nap after reading my afternoon chapter of the Book, I dreamed Sydney was alive with the smell of the sea, which had risen and invaded the city, and already was lapping past Bridge Street. I watched it approach, knowing it would inexorably overflow my whole world and nothing could stop it.

When it came up to me, and lapped around me, I felt like a piece of the fizzing, foaming water that I've seen churned by ferry motors; soon to bubble, crackle and spit, and be no more an individual, but merge back into the sea.

God made a lot of his creatures with provision for four limbs. Some people use two of them as arms, some use two as wings, but dogs use them to run with. Angel, a dog I know, uses his four limbs to rush in where even fools would fear to tread.

Some dogs use their paws a lot to shake hands with humans. I don't mind it if they avoid pathos. To be pathetic is not to be a real dog. A real dog should be cheerful, or menacing; alert, admired; envied, even; but never pathetic or in need of sympathy.

All dogs are pure bred. All are bred from dogs. Only human people make a distinction between types of dog, and it's humans who are responsible for most of the breeding anomalies, the floppy ears, the short legs, the distorted jaws, the hips that get strained easily, the poor eyesight, the too-long torso, and so on. I'm surprised that humans' callous sense of humour hasn't yet bred a nude dog, in much the same way as they toy with the idea of dosing sheep with a drug to make all their hair fall out to save shearing. But I can't talk – I saw a sick cat last Christmas that lost its coat, and I laughed. Poor denuded cat! I hope you're clothed and in your right mind now.

That reminds me. Back where I came from there was a dog who lived in a tree. As a kid he always refused to scratch, to shorten his nails, and one day he found he could climb trees. His family hated him for it, since he could do something they couldn't.

How's that for an individual?

35 / It Rained Bones

Last night it rained bones in my dream. Some were dry with the dryness of roasting, some wet after boiling, some still springy with tendons which met muscle that hadn't all been eaten by the humans in their elevated heaven, before they were dropped en masse through the clouds. I pounced on them all.

There were thousands; they rained down on a vast paddock. I buried each one where it lay, working like a mad thing through the night. (I was aware it was night, even though it was a dream.) I smoothed over each grave-with-its-bone, until at last I was satisfied and sat down, looked around, and said to myself: 'Ah . . . All mine . . .' and woke up.

I was so ashamed of my selfishness that when I got up and began to walk round the yard, I slunk.

Dimly I heard Mrs Guest say, 'That dog has moods.'

I had to tell myself severely 'Pull yourself together. Hold your head up.' Which I did.

Mrs Guest had been watching me.

'Hey, everyone! The dog! I was watching him, and suddenly I saw him think!'

They all had a good look at me. I pretended not to notice, turning my head away and with one hand pushing at an ant. Mrs Guest was compelled just then by a sudden noise to look back at her pop-up toaster, only a month old, which made a strange noise and failed at that moment. I was forgotten, as she got upset then began to cry.

Poor Mrs Guest, her electric appliance wasn't made to live longer: it had to die because of the flimsy way it was made. Humans are funny: they talk about choice, but have precious little of it. I think Mrs Guest would have chosen a toaster that would last twenty years. Or would she? Some of them love change, at least in trivial things. Mrs Guest had been thinking of the past. The smell came to me of parties and dancing and music. And careless joy. Now it was overlaid by a sorrow for cash that she'd have to outlay to fix her toaster. She is the sort of human in whom the scents of joy and sorrow seem to have equal value.

She has a depressing tendency to sum up the future, gather it into a tidy pile, then soundly deplore it. In advance. What hope was there that she could ever enjoy it?

'Everything always goes wrong for me,' she cried. 'And it always will, as long as I live! I always knew it would, ever since I was a girl. I had such dreams of how life would be when I was grown up, and not one of the good things happened!'

Ten minutes later she was happy, I could smell happiness come from her. The sun was shining in her mind, she was twenty again; she stood on a bridge that floated across a narrow stream, and men passing underneath in boats admired her and called to her with urgent words, and when the boats carried them away they looked back, silent and full of regret.

She stood a long time, remembering and savouring.

36 / Packdog or Mandog?

I am torn between the two parts of my nature – the packdog part, and the mandog part. Sometimes the yearning to be away, to be running, surrounded by male and female dogs and the young growing up, in a strong pack, independent of humans, dependent only on each other and the pack, is so strong that I have to get right down at full stretch on the ground and put both hands up to my face to restrain myself. My legs want me to spring, to jump the fence, to head for bushland where the rest of the pack is waiting.

Later the other half of me asserts itself. I know it's an honourable thing to serve mankind, to watch and guard; and I know, too, that I owe to mankind all I have learned of things other dogs will never know: the history and insights and wonderful things in the Book.

I wish sometimes I was one thing or the other, but when I'm more myself I know I *am* two things; a packdog at the back of my mind, and a mandog seven days a week. I can never be free from what I am and what I've learned; and the best I can do is to know what I am, and use the best mixtures of the two parts of me, to be the best sort of dog I can be.

37 / No One Asks Anything of Me

When I was young I wanted to do heroic deeds. I dreamed of pulling a
heavy load, like a great dog my father told me of when we lived where
the great spaces were. I saw myself guarding a house of sleeping
humans, and giving the alarm when fire-flames rose in the night. I
swam a rain-swollen creek to save a child. I fought to save a family of
humans, against wild creatures.

The day I was bought and paid for, and had the car ride to the
Guest's house, I had a head full of excitement at the brave things I was
going to do, and at the same time a sort of sinking feeling that I might
not be equal to heroic deeds.

Well, I did pull young Donna in Jeff's billycart, but that's about it.
Oh yes! I gave the alarm for that fire over the hill in the apartment
building, before the fire-engines went howling to put it out. That's the
extent of my deeds, I'm afraid.

I wish someone would order me to do something brave, but round
here there don't seem to be many opportunities for bravery. No one
asks me to do anything.

38 / The River of Folded Water

The Book says I ought to be firm, precise and particular in what I put
down. Very well, then, I've put together a few lines about something
that affects me a great deal. That thing is light, which I find so won-

derful and mysterious.

I don't understand what light is: I have to be frank about this. The Book says that if you go right down to the smallest bit of light – the photon – then if you test this tiny character as if it's a particle, it'll come out as a particle, and if you test it as if it's a wave, sure enough it behaves like a wave. Maybe it's both. But if it's both, then maybe it's something else as well, and if we test it as if it's something else, then perhaps it'll turn out to be that, too. Maybe it's a lot of things we haven't thought of.

When I thought I'd try my hand at writing a poem about light I found that no matter what I wrote, something was missing. In the end, I kept the phrases I thought up, and put them down one after the other, and here they are, with a title:

The River of Folded Water

The dazzle of light on the water
The flutter of light in the leaves;
Fingers of light in poplars
Glitter of light on waves.

That's as far as I got. There *was* one line that strayed from my poem – it got clean away – and was just mooching around my kennel. It didn't fit. It said:

The puzzle of light on faces

but it didn't say, any more than the other lines said, what was happening to the light, or what was going to happen. It didn't go anywhere. The whole thing was a bunch of pictures.

Eventually I made a big effort to sit and look round and put down what I saw and felt.

The River of Folded Light

The sun lights up the air;
By day I see the sky.

The trees dress the hills,
Their leaves suck in gas, blow gas out;
Their roots are straws to draw
Liquid from under ground.

They sweat from many pores
To keep the cycle going,
To stay alive: (Once alive
Everything wants to stay alive.)

Grass covers the hill,
Gusts of mainly nitrogen
Make grass wave and bend,
Oxygen gusts too.
Fields of grass carry
ripples in their waving,
Blown in rhythm
by gases that grip the earth.

The air gets in my eyes,
I don't feel it. I run
On the floor of an ocean of air.
I drink the ocean of air.
I breathe on hub-caps,
They cloud over with fine drops.
I breathe gas in, blow out;
All my life I gasp,
even asleep at night,
for the prize of oxygen;
there's not a moment's let-up.

Birds and insects,
friends and enemies,
mothers, murderers,
hunter and prey
drink the same air.
They remain the same, they are
No more one happy family
With the same air, or without it.

Insects and prey,
Enemies and mothers,
friends and murderers
birds and hunters:
All continue, all goes on.

By night I see the stars;
the sun lights up the moon.

39 / I'm not a Revolutionary Dog

Twelve moons ago I had the idea it was my mission to talk all dogs into revolt. Chew your leads, and go free. But on the very day I thought of it, I followed the fortunes in the Book of a number of proletariats in revolt against the tyranny of government by upper classes, from Roman days to recent times. Their success rate was low. Low? It was nil.

I abandoned the idea. I want my life of effort to add up to something, even if it's small. I don't want power, I just want to know. You can't make slogans out of that – or battle cries. Next I want to spread what I know to other dogs. I want the humans, the upper class of this earth, not to be the only heirs to the future.

From what I've read of human history in the Book, it seems to me that every domination carries within it the motive and the means for its overthrow. The motive is obvious. The means is pointed to by the actual details of the working of that domination – the things spoiled, interrupted or forbidden by it, the people oppressed, starved of what is needed for a good life.

I'm not a revolutionary dog. I don't want people killed, either dogs or humans. I don't want life destroyed: I want life extended.

40 / The Fortunate Few

Hard times are here for some, and not for others. Some dogs I know are having things really tough and have lost their jobs; several were taken in their employers' cars a long way away and told, 'We have to let you go.' After which they were pushed out, and their employers drove off. Some made their way back home thinking a mistake had been made and all would be forgiven when they got back, but not so. They were hunted away.

They became what were called outlaw dogs, but they weren't really outlaws: all they were was unemployed, though they were treated as being outside the law. At the end of every street they expected to see the dogcatcher and in their mind's eye saw the concentration camp where bad dogs go, and cast-offs, from which the fortunate few might be redeemed for a fee, but in which the remainder, tens of thousands a year, perish under the needle and are incinerated. Just for losing their jobs.

In the hills near my family's home at Kellyville there was a dog ran wild; it would eat anything it came across. It was called the cannibal dog and they said it grew to the size of a Shetland pony, but I don't know about that.

On a walk with Julie up the hill near Fitzroy Park I met a baby, well-dressed, plump and healthy. She was just at the stage of walking a few steps, then toppling. She came up to me with all the confidence of human kind and I stood still. I could see she wanted to touch my face. I blinked my eyes slowly and gently so her parents would see I knew how to behave with their baby, and when her soft hand with tiny pudding fingers came near my eyes I turned my head away – not from fear for my eyes, but to show that my teeth were a long way from those whitely-pink fingers.

That same afternoon we met a tiny dog which stood shivering on a short lead outside a hotel near Hyde Park. When I say tiny, its legs – sorry, I mean his legs: he was so small I confused him with a wind-up toy dog – his legs were like fragile twigs and there was, in the way of flesh, hardly a breakfast on him. When humans came by, he skipped nervously away, his bulging eyes darting to their huge and dangerous feet. An old sign on the hotel advertised a restaurant upstairs, 'Cuisine minceur'.

Julie looked at me and saw me looking benignly at the chihuahua.

'Can't be cold, Archimedes,' she said of the little creature. 'Must be nerves. What do *you* say?'

But she looked away just when she should have looked at my eyes for my comment. Even Julie doesn't always believe in me.

41 / The Fortune-telling Cat

There's a cat up the road tells fortunes. A ginger cat that says the world of the dead is brightly coloured, not dull like this world. I first got to hear about her from a friend of mine, Moey. (He has a white moustache, though he's still young.) Moey once was known as a person who didn't care what happened, he pined for oblivion. Oblivion was all he wanted, he wanted it night and day. The ginger cat changed him. All he wants to do now is fight, he's forgotten oblivion and believes in the heaven of beauty and peace that the ginger cat says he's headed for.

He picked a fight today. He insisted his territory ran up to and included the timber electricity pole in front of the corner shop, knowing full well that was Nipper's run. I'd gone out to see what was going on and maybe have a short chat, but the fight was in full swing when I got there. No place for civilized people. I mooched off. There were more interesting things in the world than fights, especially over nonsense like territory.

Fortune-telling might be all right in its place, but I'll give it a miss, I think. Now that Moey's faith in oblivion has been replaced by belief in a cheerful beautiful world to come, with the unexpected result that he wants to fight all the time in this one – probably to counter the threat of endless peace – who knows what the ginger cat could do? I don't want to be changed.

We have our Moeys; we have oppression, immorality and crime, but we have no justice, because no one knows us well enough to judge. Man tried to teach us guilt and punishment with everything from rolled-up newspaper to poison baits, and the dogcatcher, the needle, and furnace is the final solution, but it was useless: there was no justice in it, only guesswork. We can do only dog things: we can't act outside dog nature.

As for the way we organize ourselves to get along together, it's much the same as humans do; as long as the weak and small show a decent respect for the big and strong, the strong don't need to lean on the weak too heavily. The smart dog knows his place, his size and weight, the length of his teeth, the speed of his limbs; and makes a similar appraisal of every dog he meets. He does his thing, doesn't tread on too many toes, and holds his head high.

42 / Idiots Abroad

Listening to them talk it sometimes seems the Guests are very ordinary people. Whatever they do, wherever they go, they are *under* others, never *over* them. They go humbly. They have no power to alter the decisions of those above them; for instance they didn't even discuss trying to get the airline to let me sit with them in the passenger part of the plane, they accepted that they had to obey the rules. They work *for* people, never for themselves.

Am I too hard on them? I think I am. But when I remember the efforts I'm making to educate myself, I think I'm too easy on them. They float, they drift, they never really try – they're passengers.

Life under humans – men and women, boys and girls – is a funny thing. We envy them some things: they've lost things we've kept. Yet it's not a balance. They are above me in the way their masters are above them. They speak: I jump. While they *feel* dogs are inferior, dogs *are*. We are obliged to show a suitable meekness, so that having seen this sign of their lordship, they don't have to keep on subduing us and proving their strength.

I've seen something of the same thing between Mr and Mrs Guest. If she seems to accept his superiority in certain things, then in return he accepts her authority in things where she marks out her territory, and he does what she says. For instance, in the house itself. Let her trespass on things where his man-pride is involved and you see a display of hostility and even force; and force itself is one of his territories: no one is allowed to oppose him there. But let him walk in places where she's the boss and she'll set about him with words, flaying him with phrases, which is a punishment he appears to hate most of all.

Dog politics consists in keeping things going along on an even keel; we can't afford to be zealots trying to get rid of human overlords. I guess we're like the conservatives in human politics: get into the saddle and stay there.

43 / I'd Heard It Mentioned

I'd heard it mentioned before, but I didn't believe it. It's one thing hearing it said by the Guests and quite another to read it in the Book. (Mr Guest, although he's nominally a member of Australian society, and has a vote, knows very little of what's in the Book.)

Do you know that humans in this country, and the next, and the next, and in all the countries, live in a constant state of debt? They don't have the money, yet they're out to buy the world. Everything's to be paid for later, and they find this a normal state of affairs. I call it stupidity and recklessness, but I feel more strongly about it than that. The system on which their world is based can never be sound if they leave their reckoning always to the future. In my opinion, the taker of credit is a thief of the future, and the giver of credit aids and abets the theft.

44 / You Aren't the Real Humans

I don't mind taking a risk, so I'll tell you humans of a tradition about you that has been kept alive in the dog world for thousands of years. According to my father, the tradition says that you are not the real humans. This is going to be a shock to you, but don't lose your temper. (Losing your temper is a sign of Inferior Man, as the tradition describes you.)

The real humans were bigger, healthier, and were capable hunters who knew co-operation. They were at one with the world around them. Inferior man learned the ways of agriculture and viewed the world as essentially hostile, a place of fear; this is the human whose outlook is to plunder, who is at war with the world.

You present bearers of the name humans wiped out the real humans. They weren't contaminated with your fear, but could keep to their habits of hunting only what they ate; they didn't learn acquisitiveness. Eventually you swamped them by sheer numbers, drove them out, drove their game away, and they disappeared from the earth. Vague legends persist of isolated pockets of real men in inaccessible places, but these stories smell of bad conscience and guilt, as if you want to assure yourselves that you didn't exterminate them, without trace, and didn't over-run the earth with your greed (which no other animal has), nor your desire to subdue the earth to your psychopathic need for conquest and dominance.

45 / My 'Dog's Dictionary'

There has never been a *Dog's Dictionary* before, and that's what I aim to write. My Dictionary will be a work that will supply mankind and dogkind with a base on which to stand in order that they may eventually know one another. It will be a way to sidestep the present inability of dogs to use their voices to make themselves heard.

In my mind's eye I see all the dogs who can read, teaching their young, and teaching those older dogs who want to; all over the world, a great movement, a great stirring of canine brain-power, a great raising-up of the grossly under-privileged to live better, fuller lives, the sorts of lives that humans – the upper class of this world – live now and have lived for all the known past. I want us, the lowly of the earth, to inherit the future, along with the humans, who are the rich.

Don't forget, 'dog' is a name given to us by them. We aren't dogs any more than a rose is a rose. Who bothered to take the time and trouble to ask it its name? No one. Humans just pushed in front of everybody and named the rose 'rose', and called us 'dog'. We have to dress in their words.

We are, of course, simply people.

Our system of names differs from that adopted by human people. The dog people create names far more appropriate to dogs' perceptions of character and traits, than humans can. For the purposes of this book I'll stick to human names, since it's only natural that human readers will understand them more easily. More easily! What am I saying? Humans can *only* understand human things. They're hopeless outside their familiar words. They couldn't possibly understand the depth of my achievement in crossing the boundaries between us.

Humans, of course, are people too; simply another variety of people. They go on four legs when young, closer to the ground, but later try to walk on two. They fall, and fall often, trying to stand taller than all others. We never fall.

How I'd like to be able to say: 'I must go now and get on with my Dictionary.'

46 / The First Day of the Christmas Holidays

It was Saturday, the first day of the school holidays, when I woke under the silver-leaved gum tree. Some ants not far from me had already been to the butcher's shop – their butcher's shop – and were carrying meat away. Their meat was a piece of worm that had dried to a red-brown colour, shiny and appetizing. I had to wait till they struggled past in case I rubbed them into the sand with my – compa-ratively – enormous weight.

I wonder what the bush looked like two hundred years ago, under-neath all the houses in Woolloomooloo? It was living space and hunt-ing ground for black people, but which black people? What a pity there aren't descendants of those same blacks still living around here. What a comment that would be on the magnanimity and farsighted-ness of the invaders!

Since the shops shut at noon, Julie and I had a morning walk across William Street and up the hill to Oxford Street. She had to buy meat for the weekend.

On the way up Riley Street a small pup was chasing its tail outside a house where, two steps up from the street, a small human with a bare white bottom was playing, trying to break down the wooden barrier that protected him from falling into the street. We smiled at both of them, but they were too busy.

Julie smelled of candour today.

I waited for her outside the butcher's shop. I'm not allowed in: they have laws against dogs. In the front of the window was the head of a pig with nearly closed eyes. His face had been shaved, he was very pale. The rest of him was chopped up and distributed in trays neatly arranged around his head. It made my mouth water, but at the same time I shivered, glad that the powerful humans didn't serve up dogs in shops. Glad it was Australia, not the East.

I wonder how they'd get our fur off. I suppose they wouldn't bother, just skin us like rabbits.

During the holidays there'll be so many things happening that it looks as if I'll have to make notes for my book and expand them later. There'll be no time each day to write everything down, if I'm going to keep up my reading of the Book, and get enough exercise as well.

47 / If They Can Fly, Why Do They Walk?

Saturday afternoon positively cried out for a long walk. I knew Julie's parents would want to rest on the first day of the children's school holidays – they were tired out at the very thought of it – so I went walking with Julie. (One good way of getting a walk is to lie around the place when they have work to do. By taking me out they have the double satisfaction of disturbing my rest and escaping their work. This method hardly ever needs to be used with Julie.) I got my lead down from the nail where they hang it, and she took it when I handed it to her. She fixed the clip into my new pigskin collar. (I know all the smells of other animals' hides, even if they're tanned and lubricated with leather-dressing oil.)

Just past the bridge in Art Gallery Road, past the beginning of the eastern iron fence to the Gardens there's a tree on the fence line that has two wide gaps on either side of it where the Park people had to cut the fence to fit the tree. I forgot momentarily and dived for the space between the bars.

'Hey,' said Julie. 'Dogs aren't allowed in there.' It's too nice for dogs, she thought. Even Julie doesn't understand that when she talks to me, I hear, and when she thinks, I'm listening to her. It's not right that we can't go round unaccompanied: we should be able to roam freely. Not to be able to is cruel – roaming is our nature. Dogs shouldn't have to deserve rights: rights should be free issue, simply because dogs are people. Julie doesn't walk quickly at all. I suppose humans must use an awful lot of energy in the effort of standing up. For us who walk on four limbs it's so easy. Why did they want to stand upright, all those thousands of years ago? First they must have *thought* they were different, then tried with all their strength to make it true, by standing up. They can see a lot further, I know that (what a pity they don't seem to see as much) – but at the cost of extra energy, less endurance, and it makes them far more conspicuous.

We walked along to Lady Macquarie's chair, watched the children fishing with their fathers, and all the time I was decorous, attentive; no barking, no comments, no wayward pulling, no calling cards on the bitumen – only a few brief messages.

I was enjoying myself so much that when we climbed back up to Mrs Macquarie's Road Julie turned right, past the bridge, for an extra treat, and we went into the Domain, one of my favourite expanses of grass because it has a gentle downhill at both sides. Sometimes the Park gardeners leave their taps slightly on. There's usually a pool under the one near the swings and the stone lion-ladies.

We love walking, Julie and I. She's a gentle walker. I shouldn't grumble when she goes slowly. It must be difficult, being human.

We watched the seagulls; we stood there quite a while, studying them. If there's one particular stupidity of gulls I thoroughly enjoy it's the habit of a few of them to bully as many other gulls as will take it. They run at another gull, and the other gull moves away. In most animals that's enough: the sign of avoiding a fight and wanting to live in peace satisfies most. Not these gulls. When the victim moves off, the aggressor comes after him. And again. The only thing that satisfies this type of gull is knowing he can intimidate everyone. When the others have reluctantly taken to the air and gone off fifty metres, he moves too, and scares them off from their new place. And not for food, just to say: clear off! It can't be territory, or not any *one* territory the bully wants to preserve: I think it's *all* territory! The others have no right to be *anywhere*!

There are some the bully can't intimidate, and he knows it. I've seen two or three bullies in a group, they never go for each other. Perhaps the ones they don't fight are relatives, or other Mafia members. Whatever it is, the sight of them squawking, running at others, dipping their necks down and up, scaring others off, then walking

71

around angry still but with a satisfied sort of anger, never fails to delight me. How can they be so clever in the air – wheeling, soaring, diving – and yet so stupid?

Seagulls are easy birds to admire in the air: so hard to like on the ground.

One other thing bothers me about them. If they can fly so thrillingly, so beautifully, and if there's no limit to how high they can fly, why do they hang around the shore and the parks, walking on the ground? Isn't there a gull somewhere that despises the ground for no other reason than that he can fly?

At the Opera House, around on the harbour side, there's a crowd of gulls that watch the tables for scraps. When scraps are light on, they practise balancing on the smooth bronze outer rail. Sometimes when a hydrofoil goes past, they leave the rail and swoop low over the waves, following the frothing wake, looking for anything the wake might churn up. When they find something, the rest settle in and take whatever they can get, or find nothing and come back to the rail. I wish I could do that! What a wonderful thing to be able to do, to get up in the air and go where you want.

Or when a full moon hangs low in the eastern sky, they fly off upstream, then turn and begin a sweep over the water flying towards the moon, waiting to catch the flash of fish in the reflection of moonlight. That's really clever; I'd say *that* strategy is the product of much thought, but the Book says it's instinct.

(Something troubles me about that. I'm not sure what it is. Maybe it's to do with the way the Book ascribes all sorts of canine strategies to instinct or some other handy word, rather than to thought. As if all dogs were the same, and there were no talented dogs, and certainly not a genius!)

I don't want to condemn the Book out of hand, but if it's wrong it's wrong, and I want to know it.

I wish I knew more. Perhaps if I ate less, I'd sleep less during the day, and have more time with the Book. But no – they'd think I was off my food, and therefore sick, and cart me off to the vet. Humans are very easy to alarm.

We walked home through the city. There's a pleasantly strange feeling about city streets when there are few people about and only light traffic.

Julie's the only one, apart from me, who looks at each face she passes. I look at everything. Nothing is uninteresting.

As a matter of fact, if anyone can tell me of something that's uninteresting, I'll be interested to see it.

I've been into a number of city buildings with the family, going through the foot-pressure doors with them or with unsuspecting human companions. I usually have a look round, get the atmosphere of the place, see how the humans look and feel when they're confined in large neutral places. A lot of the places I can go in by myself, but some of the pressures required for the doors to open are too great for my weight to operate. They don't like me coming in, generally; I feel their unease. I'm not a small dog, so they're wary of me. I'm not a noisy dog, or a dirty one, so they're usually content to wait and see if I make a fuss or a mess. When I don't, I can see them thinking how right they were to have been on their guard in case I did: they have no conception of taking us dog people individually and thinking that there are some dogs that are exceptional. If some are a nuisance, then all might be: that's their rule of thumb. It's not good enough.

It's funny, though, when I get into one of those airy, high-ceilinged places, all paint and light and shiny surfaces, and find I can't keep my footing on the polished floors. Once, coming in too fast to a bank with a polished stone floor I had a crowd of people in fits as I slipped and slid all over the place. The more I tried to keep my footing the more I slipped. My legs seemed to splay out in all directions. I ended with all four limbs pointing to the four points of the compass. I laughed with the onlookers and gave an approving bark to show I enjoyed the joke. It never works: it frightens them.

It's so frustrating that they never comprehend. It makes you feel somehow alone in a terrifying emptiness.

Some summer nights the Guests have a barbecue in their small backyard. It makes a late night but against that the smells that go out over the fences on all sides for hours make me something of a hero to my friends. It's a good feeling to belong to a family that has plenty of food, and a good feeling to have everyone around know it. Some of my friends have employers on social security, and it's hard to get their tails up.

When I've been depressed – you know, feeling life's so short and I'll die before I get to know even some of the things I want to know –

those barbecue nights have lifted me up, and the friends and visitors say when they see me grinning in the firelight, 'Doesn't that dog enjoy the company! Look at him laughing!'

And they're right: I *am* laughing.

The firelight pushes back the aggressive darkness – that always reminds me of the end of life – and makes something like a wild, shadow-dancing day; and a short night.

I'm not always laughing: I can cry, too. Last time I read a story in the Book about a dog, a very sad story of hardship, loss and cruelty, it had me in tears.

We get tears in our mouths, not our eyes; that's why you see us swallow sometimes. We're swallowing our tears. Then later, you'll see the renewed energy we get. You might think it comes from the emotional break the tears give, but no – it's from the tears themselves.

When we swallow the sadness down, then digest it, we get stronger and more lively.

During a short after-walk nap I dreamed of a pirate gull captured by law-and-order gulls and condemned to walk the plank with wings tied. He'd had a long and happy career taking food out of the mouths of other gulls.

He sank like a stone between the north-eastern corner of the Opera House and Man-o'-War steps. Only a bubble or two rose to the surface and went pop! – to show where he had breathed out his last breath of air, returning it to the general pool of air.

74

48 / Socks of Ice

When I was a kid at Kellyville there was a stream not far from the house where we went swimming. Once, when the children didn't go into the water in winter and I didn't register the fact, I splashed happily in, thinking they'd be in later.

I can still remember walking in that water, wearing socks of ice. I could hardly move, it was so cold. I got to the bank and shivered a long while, while the Guests laughed at me. 'Now can you see why we didn't go in?' they said to me in those voices that knew I didn't understand what they said.

I tested the water each time after that; I was never caught again.

I remembered my socks of ice this morning when I woke before dawn with my feet cold and my teeth chattering.

Do you know that before the sun rises, while the sky is dark, the coming dawn has its own smell?

49 / I Cried, and Nothing Happened

Oh, my parents! Those who owned *you*, sold *me*. I was your child, you were my father and mother. I was beneath you, you were my gods. You taught me, you fed me; taught me how to find food, and meat to eat. You taught me loyalty and to give my love and trust to my human employer, to accept setbacks and disappointments without a whimper. From the time I was born you told me to be brave on the day I came to be sold. Is that all a dog can hope for? Was your loyalty to me, to my best interests, less than the loyalty you expected me to have for the Guest family?

Now there is an empty space in me that I try to cover up, but it's impossible: everywhere I go, people can see this hole that cannot be hidden or covered up. I know it will never be filled; always I'll have this empty place; not even time can fill it. I feel so open. Everything I have in me threatens to fall out.

I hate it when self-pity strikes me. I hate the memory of that first ride in the Guest's new car, into employment with strangers, because I wept a few tears even while the children were patting me, for my home, my dead father and my brothers and sister, and my mother who watched me being sold.

I wept, and nothing happened. My mother didn't move, or say a word. I was separated from everything I knew and loved. I thought I would never see my family again, and I didn't.

This bitterness strikes me only rarely. I'm sorry if it makes you sad.

50 / My Beautiful Red Coat

My employers try to maintain the flowing lines of my coat by constant grooming. If there's a part that's matted and impossible to brush without hurting me, they cut away the clumps with a little pair of scissors that has rounded ends on both blades.

Mrs Guest knows how to do it best, but Julie is the most considerate. She's so careful to do nothing that will hurt me. My coat has never been badly matted; they've never had to take me to a professional groomer.

I like them for the way they feel good about the job they do in washing me and grooming my coat; when I'm all done and shining in the sun they gather round to admire me and exclaim about the lights they see in my washed and silky fur. They notice the sleek look in my eyes and attribute it to all the most unlikely things. Actually, it's a sort of contented joy that comes from seeing them happy. Humans find the world so complicated, and often get lost in the ramifications of everyday life. I like to see them happy; they're not happy often enough.

51 / A Secret Place

Each dog has his or her own song. There's a barking song for those inclined that way; a complaining song; a song of daring; a song of loneliness. Dogs get very lonely: I can't stress this enough. From being packdogs we've become mandogs; but our conditions of work in the ordinary family shut us off from the company of our kind. Dogs stick together, by nature; to have us isolated, one by one to a house, is a painful curtailment of our freedom to mix, and to roam free – and because of that, our opportunities to educate ourselves are limited.

Where was I? Oh yes, our songs. I have a song. I never sing in public – I hum it to myself in the privacy of my abode. Its a song of the past. In it there's my youth of play and grass and big open spaces and my brothers and sister; trees and long fences, sun and rain and happiness. I won't tell you any more than that – I have to have inside me somewhere I can be alone, a place where I can get my balance and constantly assure myself I'm me.

52 / Donna's Question

Today Donna asked her mother, 'Mummy, if I close my eyes does the world disappear?'

Mrs Guest said what a silly question, and put the cake mix under the beater.

Donna didn't seem to mind much, but asked her father when he came home.

'Of course not!' he barked, as if someone had accused him of something.

'I don't know,' Jeff said, when his turn came. 'How do you expect me to know? I don't know everything!' He sounded huffy.

Donna asked Julie as she was bringing my dinner out to me.

'Maybe it does,' Julie said. 'I don't think so, but it's impossible to check, with your eyes shut. But it's funny how quick the world you remember comes back the moment you open your eyes again.'

Donna thought about that. Then she said, 'Are we all dreaming? And we'll wake up some day and everything will be different?'

'Wow,' said Julie. 'What thoughts you get.' But she made no answer. I wish she'd stayed to go into the question, instead of trying to go easy on Donna. I think if Julie tries to be too merciful, she'll end by being unjust, or intolerant. (Perhaps they're cousins, these two things.)

53 / It's Black inside Me

Have you ever thought how inside your body it's pitch-black? And inside your head? All your arteries, your heart, your lungs, kidneys, liver, all the rest, are working away in the dark.

And when you're just looking around, no matter how your head seems to be filled with light, your view of what is out there is decoded in darkness. No light can enter that skull of bone covered with a thin skin of scalp that supports the growth of thatch that is hair.

And what about your blood, that has so many chemical functions, so many little beasties either floating along, or doing battle with other little intruders you've breathed in, or absorbed from your skin or stomach? It does its work, too, in the black dark inside you. Recognition of enemies, in those inland rivers, can't be by sight. It must be something else.

All this is in us, going on now, and we haven't an adequate picture of what it is or what it's like in there.

54 / Countries Where People Sit in Gaol

It was gloomy reading in the Book this afternoon. I read of countries where people sit in gaol and no crime has been done, though crime is recorded against them; where spies are many and some inform on others for pleasure and take no pay; where journalists, teachers, writers, artists, musicians, public officials, common people, all have the same opinions as the State; where there is no Parliament, no Opposition – except the people – where the Army is a back-up to the police. Where people may think what they like, but daren't say it, or even look as if they think it.

When I heard Mr Guest complaining to his wife about the outsiders coming into Woolloomooloo and buying up houses all around, I thought of those countries where the ordinary wishes and daily concerns of their people are so hedged with prohibitions and surrounded by menace, and I didn't feel Mr Guest had much to complain about. At least the social changes that he noticed arose from the differing abilities of different parts of the Australian population to make and save money, and not from an edict generated in a centralized, one-party State where the word democracy was used, but only as a lie.

Democracy.

When I first saw the word and knew what it meant, I loved it. Democracy: everyone can play, all they need is to want to.

In places where there's a crushing weight of authority pressing the people down, life must be much harder than places where the people don't feel that weight so heavily.

Democracy – an open society. An association of reasonably free individuals respecting each others' rights within a framework of mutual protection supplied by the State, achieving a growing measure of humane and enlightened life, through the making of responsible and rational decisions.

Democracy means the government can be removed, at regular intervals and without bloodshed, and the incoming government doesn't have to have the approval of the outgoing one.

Democracy, where the cry is often raised: Who's running the country? The answer is: no one person, no one group. Power is widely diffused.

In a democracy, the people ought to be careful that nothing they do or intend will reinforce the power of the State, for the State is not the people, no matter how piously the manifestoes read.

The difference between Australia's type of regime and the professed socialist regimes is that in Australia the lies drop from the mouths of governments, press, business, educationalists, and are left lying around. Those that want to pick them up, can just go and pick them up. In those other places the authorities don't drop the lies; they take a good hold on the lie and a firm grip on the citizen and ram the lie down the citizen's throat and watch to see it's swallowed.

55 / The Ten Things

When I criticise the Guests, it's not because they're typical Australians, just typical humans. I know I'm hard on them sometimes, but there are a lot of things to be hard on them for.

Just to leave you in no doubt about the matter, I'll set out the ten qualities I'd like to see in the people around me – dogs, humans, horses, cats: the lot.

Patience
Strength
Gentleness and helpfulness to others
Independence
An uncompromising attitude to one's own weaknesses
Slowness to anger
Concern for the future
Wide horizons and the long view
Implacable enmity towards greed and cruelty
A love for living things and for the planet itself.

Ten will do for a start. They're not commandments, as in Moses' collection of ten that he brought down from Mount Sinai – just qualities.

56 / The Spirit of Australia

Listen to it.

Can you hear it?

No?

Open a window.

Listen again . . . What comes into your mind?

You still can't hear it? . . .

Of course you can't. The spirit of a country isn't reached by sitting still, listening. It's out there, among the people whose lives dress up this land in so many colours; among those who know that every person is fallible and no one is all that much better than anyone else; who like to see everyone get a fair go at the good things; who don't like to see anyone, no matter how vile, trodden right down; in whose faces humour lurks and tolerance often shines; who will never take themselves so seriously as to believe in the destiny of nations or the divine right of anyone; who will give and take orders, if necessary, but would prefer not to; who are sovereigns of their souls, in an amused sort of way; who couldn't conceive of keeping, or being, slaves; who can, often, be trusted to work without a boss; who are capable of aspirations, but reluctant to talk about them; who will go to war to win, not simply to kill or to conquer; who value the good opinion of friends over the applause of strangers; who are proud of being people and therefore kind to beings less fortunate; who know in their bones that anyone wanting to lead others is corrupt already; who can see goodness in others, and half expected it; who can adopt isms, then drop them without regret; who can recognize their own guilt with a sort of surprised innocence; who know their own limits but wish wryly they weren't so easily reached; who fight well but prefer peace; who don't understand, but are rather proud of their uncomfortable country; who would sooner do a stranger a good turn than a bad one; who would rather enjoy being best in the world, as long as it was for something important, like sport; who are tolerant, but not to excess; courageous, but not stupid about it; patient, if patience is necessary or humane; uncomplaining, but not saintly; who often laugh at themselves, and with good reason; who are passionate, romantic, and would be more so if only they had more energy, if there were more hours in the day, and if there weren't so many more interesting things to do.

The Spirit of Australia is the people: not in the strange, sprawling land they squat on, though it has communicated to them some of its relaxed and ancient moods, as it did to those dark people who squatted here before the white people came.

The spirit of the land itself is secret for ever.

57 / The Other Spirit of Australia

Many Australians have a weariness that never leaves them. Too weary to think, too unused to thinking to think deeply; they're cut off, adrift. Australia is a raft and these Australians, on its surface, are lost. Perhaps they came here to be lost – by nature prisoners, their only happiness the happiness of confinement, of chains.

They don't belong here. They don't fit. The continent knows this, and changes them subtly. Something in the air (perhaps) gets to them; something that rises up out of the old rocks, the inert soil, the endless plains – a gas, a spirit, a thin soul – something enters them and turns their minds around, blurs their intentions, casts a haze over the withering future.

Is it a cloud of guilt? After all, the earliest immigrants weren't prisoners for nothing. Does their European guilt react with the aboriginal soil to produce the Australian haze, the crowded emptiness?

Yet even this emptiness is not what it seems; the emptiness of the continent is a strangeness, for although it's empty, there's no echo.

The silence is too dense to permit echo. The silence and apparent emptiness is full of something; something unseen.

I don't know what it is, yet even I, a European dog, feel the beauty of this land. In the next chapter is a sort of verse I wrote, to try to make it clearer to myself.

58 / Australia's Gift to the World

Australia is strange;
land of no time and all time;
outside time, containing it.
A place of desolate rocks,
delicate animals and humans.
Land of youth and brightness.

Land of sun, of light,
Land of perpetual day
where night is unthinkable
until it comes, and then
ignored, unrecognized.

Land of clear light –
harsh, unclouded, relentless;
strong, free of illusion,
And therefore mystifying.
Land the sun hates to leave –
where the sun lingers and waits
until suddenly called away.

Australia! If you want to,
you can be you! But you
don't know what you are;

you make no effort to find out,
letting events mould you.
You didn't quite make it
to the twentieth century, so
good luck for the twenty-first!

Australia! If you want to,
you can spread your good nature
and practicality, your casual
attitude in the face of pretence
and pomp, your idea
of fairness, all over the world.
The good Spirit of Australia
Is one gift you can give.

59 / Laughter in the Bedroom

I wish I could laugh, like the Guests. The family woke me this morning around dawn. It was the parents. The quiet of Sunday was gone before it started; their laughter and frolicking and general cries and muffled noises – muffled probably by bedsheets and pillows – brought me awake. Even neighbourhood dogs heard the commotion and started up from sleep and made alarmed, disgusted or irritated noises, depending on who the dog was.

Julie and Donna also woke. Jeff, who'd come home only an hour or two before, made no sound. Human people often take things to make them not see, and not feel. Jeff does: he drinks.

The joyful sounds died down, but knowing them, I knew their high spirits didn't cease. Keeping in mind all the human people I know, and that's quite a few, I know my family of humans are quite ordinary people, and sometimes seem unbearably stupid, but the two adults playing together in bed like happy children, sometimes have a rare love rise between them; and the kids know it, though they don't see it often or understand. (It was a surprise to me to find this out, each time it happened. I'd thought they were empty people, hopeless and lost in middle age.)

When I think of things like that, I remember my own boyhood. Everyone said I was the happiest pup in the street, and our street was well-populated. The backyard where I lived was as big as four backyards, and since then *became* four backyards – there were lots of vacant blocks then – and there was plenty of room for my whole family without going into the paddock where the horse was kept. My dad, my mother, three brothers and one sister, we all had lots of space, and at the bottom of the block there was a four-strand wire fence and on one whole side there was the beginning of the bush. It was outer Sydney bush; I guess you know that's ridges and slopes, well wooded on top of the ridges with low and stunted bushes and trees, and more thickly wooded on the slopes with taller trees, eucalyptus and turpentines, and softwoods bordering the creeks and making a covering mat from one side of each creek to the other, joining overhead.

It was a very happy place.

Now all the love my parents had for me is shrunk to two little graves on that same block, and the present families there of humans and dogs don't even know who's under their garden. Shrunk to an unknown piece of earth; forgotten.

No, it isn't! It isn't shrunk at all. It's with me. All the time that love is with me, in me; it *is* me! What a silly setter I am sometimes. And how can they be forgotten while I'm alive?

Once when they sent me away to the country – the family's children had gone to visit relatives at Wagga – they folded instructions in my collar, so people along the way would know my needs. I was humiliated at first, waiting in a box on a railway station, and I guess I made critical noises at the time. But I wasn't so downcast when I realized they only did it out of love and concern for me. That kept me going. They wanted me to be with the children, who got a lift back in their uncle's car and I was happy, sitting in the back with them, enjoying the view. Once they let me put my head out of the window and feel the air rushing past, and I grinned all the time. I know: they all told me.

I daresay dogs have come a long way since they first appeared on earth, running from the huge and terrible beasts our legends tell us of, and later, when we hunted in packs, tearing at those huge and terrible beasts in death.

I think humans learned from us. The moment they left their solitude and began to hunt in packs, that was the moment they started their rise. As for us, we've been fragmented for thousands of years – fallen from the position we once held.

There was another eruption of laughter and shrieking from the house. They were tickling each other and making a great racket. I couldn't help grinning at the sound. But I wish I could laugh out loud, like them.

Whatever the adults had been doing didn't tire them too much for a wonderful Sunday walk. The streets were quiet, like most streets on Sundays. A few people still in dressing gowns or pyjamas wandered back from the corner shop with the paper or milk or other comforts.

60 / On the Borderline of Begging

Princess is a party dog. She lives in Bourke Street. Our family was taking the long way round, via the Woolloomooloo wharves, heading up the green hill to the Art Gallery. We met Princess as we passed the house where she works. She believes in angels; she dreams of them and talks of them a lot.

Every time she knows people are watching her she does tricks. When she saw us she balanced herself on one side of the brick verandah and took off in an elegant jump to the other side, landing with all four feet together, looking round for applause. My people know how many bricks make five, and clapped. Next she stood on her legpaws with her armpaws in the air and clapped them. More clapping from the Guests. I pulled a bit on my lead involuntarily; it came out of Donna's grasp, and attention was unfortunately diverted from

Princess. If you ask me, Princess pines for a magic fairyland where she would be treated like a lady for the rest of her life, with appreciation and applause wherever she looks.

I'll never be a performer. I knew a terrier once that went on the stage. His act was to raise his leg against everything he saw and everyone he met, to make people laugh. I think it's disgraceful, demeaning. He ought to have more pride. Then he did a begging act. No pride at all. Begging is one thing I cannot stand.

Princess blamed me for the party moving off away from her little stage. She screamed out something highly offensive about me, and luckily my people didn't understand what she said. I'm afraid I snapped back at her before I could restrain myself and called her a disgrace to all dog people, and finished off with a threat of teeth. My teeth can be quite startling, seen suddenly and accompanied by a suitable snarl. She sprang back, and put her tail between her legs. She's too sensitive: you can't look at her sideways. She was in tears. I only meant her to pull her socks up and remember she's a dog, after all, not some cheap sideshow freak looking for the insult of pennies.

My people were looking the other way, and Julie got my lead and together we caught up. It hadn't distressed them at all. Perhaps they hadn't even noticed. If only I could talk like them, and they could see all I see. I felt bad about Princess later, remembering that dreadful time the children of her employers plaited her long fur, so that all over the underparts of her body little short plaits hung down. The humiliation affected her for a long time. Perhaps I *was* too hard on her.

In Forbes Street, just before Plunkett, Old Sorrowful lives. He's a retired basset; he has a younger dog to train for the job, so he takes things pretty easy, not like when he was younger. He was keen, then, almost officious, except that a natural incompetence seemed to rob his energetic demeanour of its effect. He was always going about, barking at nothing and saying 'I'll be damned.' Anything you said to him he'd come back: 'Well, I'll be damned.' He didn't mean it as swearing. I don't think he even knew.

I've known him for years, even before the new dog laws. They bring in new dogs laws all the time; they're very wary of us. Not that we have much political clout. But we have a negative effect, politically, that's dangerous for them to ignore.

We passed his front yard. He sat half in the sun, half out of it. His head was cool, the other end sunlit. There he was, practising Old

Sorrowful Eyes. You'd think he'd give up, now he's on the last stretch, his race nearly run. He was waiting for a pat and the sort of condescending sympathy human people give us because they don't know the extent of our knowledge. He got the pat, and even then, retired with a full belly, I could see the conniving going on in those eyes; working and plotting how to get a lazy meal out of impressionable humans. Well, they had nothing in their hands to give him, no matter how he put his nose up, no matter how imploring and well-mannered his closed mouth looked.

I watched him as we passed on; his mouth came open as he relaxed and looked up the street for the next prospect. I think that sort of thing's on the borderline of begging.

61 / I'd Rather Have It Both Ways

I'm an independent dog, having travelled the distance from packdog to mandog, and wanting to take a further step.

I'm distant from human concerns; detached.

When I feel the rasp of their hunger for money, I pity them.

I don't want to order others about, nor do I want to obey, but there's something deep in my nature that, I think, wants to obey a call to the service of something higher and more important than my self.

I want hands instead of paws, but I want to run fast, too.

If I had hands, I'd have less speed; if speed is what I want, then I must give up wanting hands.

I know compromise is the basis of civilization and consistency is impossible, but I'd rather have it both ways, and I can't.

62 / The Dog with Cold Teats

Joyful, a lady-like dog from Nicholson Street, has cold tits. She's had three families now and her employer sold her children and gave some away, and she was pleased they kept her. She's a very happy lady, but everyone who knows her will tell you about her cold tits. They're big and hang down, but that's natural since she's had twelve children and it must be a bit of a strain on any female. They say of her, 'Warm heart, cold tits'. But she doesn't mind what they say, or even that she tends to coolness in that area. She talks a lot and enjoys every day and I reckon that's the way to be.

63 / Lazy Bill

Lazy Bill is a different kettle of fish. He sleeps all day. What he thinks about in the short periods that he's conscious, I don't know, for he never says. Not to me, nor to anyone I know. He's a mystery. Once when I passed his yard and noticed him come briefly awake, I thought I saw a movement of his lower jaw as if he was preparing to speak. Expecting that a miracle was imminent I stopped, glad I happened by. I watched his face and waited. Nothing happened. Never mind, it might come, and it was worth waiting for. I waited. In the distance I heard the cheerful calls of two of my friends to each other several streets away. Then Bill's jaw moved down again. He's taking a deep breath ready to talk, I thought. But no such luck. The jaw dropped further, the eyes filmed, the lids shut from the edges inwards, the jaw closed with a faint snap. The eyes came a little open at the sound, then slowly closed, the head falling, falling, till at last it rested gently, then heavily, on his forearms. His chest gave a big soft heave with a grateful feel about it and he was off. He didn't move after that, apart from the gentlest of chest movements as his sleepy body required just a little more air every now and again to sustain what life he had.

No one ever saw him eat, either. I guess he was very little trouble to the family that employed him. Not a large claim to fame. Old Lazy Bill had plenty of chances to become a father, plenty of appointments, but he never ever made it in time.

64 / The Universal Critic

We passed the Art Gallery just as a surly seagull was coming down the steps, muttering. We were quite close and I looked at her with a question-face.

'But is it art?' she muttered, 'I don't call *that* art,' and crossed the road, deep in thought.

'What is art?' I thought, and felt like Pilate asking what's truth.

Julie and I went for a little run on the Domain grass. I was careful not to tire her.

Going down Macquarie Street I was glad to find that the Guest family, who don't get to see the city often enough, really appreciated the new statues that line both sides of the street, from Queen's Square to the Opera House. For the sake of people who haven't seen them, they're statues of ordinary people: not long-dead statesmen or colonial officials, but the sort of people in the city every day. There's a barrister, with gown flying and one hand up to keep his wig on; a ferry deckhand; a librarian; a shopkeeper looking knowingly but anxious, cheerful but wary, all at once; a clerk eating a sandwich in the park; a telephonist; a street-sweeper; a policeman on horseback; a tourist; a shop assistant; a parking policeman with notebook; a busker; a notable derelict; a foreign sailor ashore; the plastic-bag lady who feeds the pigeons; a grazier down from the country; a tired mum with kids; a retrenched man of fifty reading the paper in the park – that sort of thing. Twenty-four in all. We passed down the hill, left into Bridge Street, across tiny green and shaded Macquarie Place, with the anchor, the cannon, and the monument to distance in this country of distances, and down Arbitration Street past the Paragon Hotel to the Quay. My people were enjoying it: every now and then I looked up to see their faces. The parents that loved each other so much looked at everything we passed. I felt very approving towards them, they showed promise.

At the Quay they stopped at one of the shops – there ought to be twice as many shops there! – and got drinks for Donna and Julie, looked at the two chain links symbolizing the convict past, and the statues from Tasmania of the four seasons and the bush pools, and across the street, under the railway, to the water.

Small ferries bumped up and down invitingly, kids fished from the railings; men too. Buskers played music at about a dozen spots along the concourse between the railway wall and the iron railing over the water – the railing ornamented with sea-horses – and the ferry wharf entrances. It's a beautiful place. I love seeing lots of people; and so many different sorts of people.

As you stand near the water's edge at the iron railing and look back up at the overhead railway wall, the new mural looks straight at you. It's near a hundred metres long, stretching the length of the railway wall above the concourse.

All of Sydney is there in bright colours; the harbour, the parks, the people, streets, shops, fountains; the sports, the things people do – theatre and music and painting and everything! – and the whole thing gives you the sparkling, cheeky, dancing feel of Sydney. It's the most famous mural in the world, partly because its always being added to, always changing in one thing or another. There's a permanent scaffolding there, on wheels, so it can be moved along as it's needed.

People coming from overseas to the nearby passenger-ship wharf see it the moment they round the Opera House and slowly berth in Sydney Cove. People on their way to work in the morning by ferry see it and it makes them smile. It's lit up at night and people on the water and coming over the Harbour Bridge see it and shake their heads – amazed that a city can be so beautiful.

I think the thing about it I most enjoy is their enjoyment.

At the western end of the concourse, where we started, seagulls were being fed. You know the place: where the path takes a turn towards the overseas passenger terminal.

Guess who was in the ruck of birds shoving for free food? The art critic! I watched her pushing and pecking and bumping her body against all those round her. I hadn't realized art critics could be so fit. The humans with the scraps threw their largesse with no facial expression that I could see, but then many humans are inscrutable.

A seagull artist, spurning the crumbs, was high up on the scaffolding, filling in one of the areas of the mural that concern seagulls. A remarkable example of community effort. The seagull sections of mural are interspersed right along its length, which is a commentary on how thoroughly they have invaded the life of Sydney.

Our party walked round the Circular Quay West and Hickson Street, under the bridge, and stopped for a picnic at the little jetty just this side of Pier One. They opened their packets of sandwiches, uncorked a bottle of red wine, got out drinks for Julie and Donna, and a container of prepared food for me. I don't think my human people noticed the glum, ruminative seagull down on the bottom step of the jetty, fishing for tiddlers. But as the food and wine disappeared they made plenty of noise about the larrikins on the water, larrikin seagulls, true Australians, racing from wave to wave in their runabouts, sending spray everywhere, making an awful nuisance of themselves. The family made unfavourable observations about these things, and also about the bottles, cans and paper plates that other humans pitched into the Harbour.

Not even seagulls or debris could spoil the spot as a picnic place. There was so much to look at, so much to see. Occasionally trains rumbled across the bridge high overhead, yachts with white, red, blue, striped or rainbow sails dipped and glided by, fishing boats with their catch came back up the Harbour attended by clouds of gulls diving for scraps of fish.

We walked slowly back. At the site of the mural activity, the art-critic seagull was shaking her head and talking to any gull that would listen. I managed to get near and found that she was not only criticising matters of art, but had branched out into criticism of anything and everything that came into her head. I suppose I think that a thing of

93

art is part of the world looked at through one person's mind; and a piece of criticism is part of the world of art looked at with a similarly single vision. But what sort of vision is needed to view the whole world?

Universal critic, indeed!

When we were passing the giant statue of the seagull, near the gatekeeper's hut on the Opera House forecourt, I heard a human child in holiday clothes asking her mother, 'Did the seagulls build the statue of the seagull, Mummy?' Mother didn't know, but she didn't think so. At the same moment I tuned in to seagull talk and near me a child seagull was being told by its mother that a very long time ago the seagull statue *was* built by seagulls. It took many generations and the work was laborious and many thousands of heroic gulls gave their lives for it, but they did it in the knowledge that the fame of seagulls would be spread over the globe – gulls always knew the earth was a globe – and their place on the planet secure for ever. The child gull was suitably impressed and solemnly took off into the air, following mother gull.

I think there must be many levels of history, and many kinds of truth, and I looked up to the faces of my human companions to see if I could detect in them any signs of their reflecting on similar thoughts, but their faces showed nothing.

I guess it makes for a calm life, not to think much.

I saw Jeff one morning a year or two ago after he'd come home very late, looking pretty tired and thinned-out; his face occupied by thoughts. The part of his face where they were, was a part where I'd seen no thoughts before. He was sixteen. I think he'd discovered girls.

The statue of the ferry deckhand in Macquarie Street, who is frozen in the act of throwing her loop of rope over an imaginary bollard, shone in the midday sun. A pigeon, pear-shaped and pin-headed, sat on her outstretched arm. Just for a moment I had the irresponsible thought that perhaps the best way to make such a statue was to encase a real-life deckhand in metal which followed all the folds of her clothes and body, even the strands of her hair – and the effect would be startlingly real, as this statue is startlingly unreal.

By that I mean this statue's face had been distorted into a caricature of such faces; the brow ridge was too strong, the nose too thick, the forearms too heavy. I've seen the female deckhands often at the Quay; like woman bus drivers they're ordinary people no larger than life.

65 / I'm a Speculative Dog

I'm a speculative dog by nature, and today I've given myself a problem that occurred to me from my reading of the Book. I'm working out how much energy we'd require (I mean humans, of course) to accelerate a 1000-tonne payload to three-quarters the speed of light. At our present rocket efficiency and speeds it would take between 40,000 and 60,000 years to reach Alpha Centauri, only four and a bit light years distant. My opinion of humans is that the poor space travellers would be forgotten in a hundred years or less; and if a nuclear war destroyed the monitoring equipment, they'd be on their own for ever, generations and generations of them, living and dying, fighting and killing; animals in a space-ship; then at last all dead, a tomb going, going for ever: going nowhere.

The Guests. Why aren't they answering my questions? Why aren't they educating themselves? Why are they passengers? Why can't they answer my questions? Why haven't they already? There are so many things they should know, but don't; so many things to do and to be: but they don't, they can't, they won't! What's the matter with them?

Am I the one that's wrong? Has the Book poisoned me, somehow? Is information a poison?

I gritted my teeth and got down to my problem. If we consumed energy at our present rate for 10,000 years – that's how much energy we'd need to accelerate a 1000-tonne payload to three-quarters the speed of light, and that speed would make Alpha Centauri well over five years distant.

66 / Thoughts of a Meditative Dog

Clothes

I think it must be because they've worn clothes for so many years that humans look incomplete and awkward without them; almost pathetic.

Shoes

I wonder what it would be like to wear shoes and not to feel the ground.

Mortgage

I looked in vain for the mortgage that was said to be over the house, until I looked it up in the Book. I'd imagined a threatening cloud or something about to fall on the house and crush it.

Work

From the way work is spoken of round here, it's not much different from leisure.

Doctors

The Guests don't like doctors much. Yet they seem to get better of whatever ails them.

Conversation

Indecencies like politics and religion are frowned on. Sport is king, the weather is its consort, and complaining is the background.

Neighbours

Mrs Guest spends some time each week talking to her neighbours. Mr Guest avoids them. Mrs Guest thinks good neighbours essential: Mr Guest thinks of everyone who doesn't live at this house as a stranger, and sometimes he even seems surprised to see a woman and three children living at home with him.

My Kennel

Why are they surprised at my clean kennel? Demoralized animals – humans and all – are the only ones to foul their own nests.

The Old Lav

The small shed in the Guest's backyard, now used for a few largely unused tools, was once an outside lavatory. Some of the scents of the past are still locked in the concrete slab it stands on.

Fast Food

'Something's eating this dog,' Mr Guest remarked, 'Look at him wolf that food.'

He watched me some more. 'Do you think he's anxious about something?'

'Yes,' said Mrs Guest. 'Anxious to get it down and be off somewhere. He's a busy dog. Probably the busiest I've seen,' she added.

Human Music

Sometimes, when I hear their more serious music, I feel I hold in my mind every moment of my life; every one, all at once. But mostly, when that sort of music comes on, they turn it off, and put on music they understand. I wish I could hear it more often: I don't understand it either, but that's why I want it. Sometimes, while it's on, thoughts come into my mind that I've never had before.

Ordinary People

The Guests are ordinary Australians, and have no style. More, they're suspicious of it. To them, flair, style, class, are indistinguishable from the cheeky gloss of the car salesman and the benign dignity of the insurance man, and belong, in their eyes, to people trying to climb above their origins and leave old friends and neighbours behind. No one loved them so much, no mother poured so much sheer affection over them that they love themselves as naturally as they breathe. They are always slightly suspicious of themselves, as if suddenly they might do something embarrassing, and they wouldn't know till later, when someone told them.

Ambition

The sweetest desire of most humans at the end of a lifetime of effort, is to do nothing. They train for sport so hard and so often, that they can at last win, and with the winning comes relaxation and rest and the end of effort. They run to stop. I wish never to cease exerting myself, but not all the time, just on/off, on/off, in a way natural to me. Never to finish until at last my eyes shut of their own accord – because there's nothing stopping them.

Peace

Continual and unabated peace is unnatural in the family, in the sporting team, in the council chamber, as well as between nations.

Mrs Guest

'They'll only appreciate me when I'm horizontal,' she moans. It is a refrain she uses often.

She looks like someone who'll die from a dreadful disease, only she hasn't found the disease. The expectation of death, though, is stamped in her face.

She looks healthier when she's happy, and when she's not happy she feels quite sad. When she's sad, she seems to be thinking a great deal. Perhaps sadness is good for her, too.

She often complains she's so poor she can't even afford a bargain. It's not as true as she makes it sound. Sometimes she's so poor-spirited that even pessimism would be a lift. Yet every now and then she's capable of joy.

I think she's neurotic. There are one or two things she could be, but she doesn't know how to choose; besides, she doesn't really want to *be* anything, she just barely *is*. Mrs Guest is: patient, hardworking, has no aims, is living in a narrow channel, has few thoughts except for the beauty of the world around her in Woolloomooloo. She loves to find good points in other people; she thinks often of the pleasures of her youth; she thinks with regret of how exciting life was going to be, and how it never was.

Dear Mrs Guest,

Your talent is for watching, reflecting, then adjusting to ever-changing, ever-new circumstances. Try to accomplish one thing at a time; see how it goes, and if it's OK, do the next thing; if that's OK, do the next.

Don't get desperate and overthrow your life, or you'll throw away what is valuable along with the junk. The future must be worked for, every day; the current is against us: if we rest on our oars, we go backwards. Harmony and beauty are possible intermittently, but not as permanent states or features.

Mr Guest

He's subservient, but defiant;
An opportunist, yet lazy;
Self-forgiving and malicious.
He's against the government, but what is he *for?*
Nothing.
He's a big fish in a small family.

Mr Guest, you must not accept direction, you must question authority – it's your duty. No matter how loud you raise your voice, do it! Peace isn't the absence of noise: death is.

Mr Guest, think of next year; make provision for your children, your future, your drains, guttering, roof, waterpipes. Your family's waiting for a lead from you – you're supposed to know more about the world. These things go to make up what it means to husband – to be a husband.

Mr Guest, think less of the wages you get and more of the job you do. Every day you pass in routine is a day from your life. The future doesn't exist: this is your life, now!

Mr Guest sleeps strenuously. But though he snores he doesn't sleep alone: his house has three bedrooms and already Donna has to double up with Julie. Jeff's lucky, he has a room to be alone in.

Mr Guest's childhood was poor. His family lived in South Australia, his boyhood was rich in water, animals, fish, birds and trees. Once he went to work at Gove, then in Dampier. He didn't like either.

A lot of his friends are in cemeteries. He missed being killed in the war – his mate was killed beside him in the shell burst that knocked Mr Guest silly – and ever after he kept his head down: he wanted no trouble. A member of his platoon had helped him out of danger, and he'd been grateful. And uneasy. Something bothered him about it that he didn't want to think of. He never kept in touch after the war was over. When he came back from the war, he turned his back on the future, determined to put tomorrow behind him.

Mr Guest is what he appears to be, that's my conclusion. There's no mystery, no great sorrow, no broken heart, to explain what he is, what he does and what he doesn't do: nothing but what you see. That's what he is, and that's all he is.

I feel that once, one fine morning, he had gone unwary to his shaving mirror, and seen himself; seen himself clearly; seen, not his beard to be shaved, but his own usually hidden self looking out from frightened eyes. He had never recovered his confidence.

Around the house he's rather like a statue; he moves so rarely. He's of the sort that has feet of bronze – it's his head that's made of clay. He could never topple and fall flat: he'll stand still and firm and crumble from the top.

He would like to have said No to a number of things in his life, but he wasn't game.

When he thinks of final things, like death or retrenchment, fear and resignation shine calmly and equally in his eyes.

He watches the strivings of his fellow men with equanimity. Indifference is a better word.

This afternoon, when I walked up to him and got his smell, he was looking over the top of his newspaper at the earth of the backyard, thinking how, when he was working in the bush in his twenties, he enjoyed the company of sheep. Who said little, and never bullied him.

I stayed near him for some time. His next thoughts were of wandering the Coorong, as a boy in South Australia. Minutes later, he was on foot in Marble Bar, thinking – in Marble Bar – of how at school he'd been told Marble Bar was the hottest town in Australia, and here he was, in the place, and it wasn't.

He's not a finished man; not in his body, nor his mind; not in his speech, nor his idea of himself. He could be a work in progress, except I think he's been abandoned.

He is in his middle age, casually dying day by day of little things, things too small to notice: a pain in the knee, a feeling in the left hip that his leg won't support him; in fear of the next cold, the next influenza; in dread of cancer creeping up on him and gnawing his life away in terrible pain.

There is a motto in his room, framed. It was given him by his mother. 'THE SUN NEVER SETS ON FOOLS.' How he can bear to look at it I don't know.

Jeff

He's a self-indulgent youth, with a head full of bits and pieces. He likes to cuddle girls and drink what others drink.

> He tries to be tough, but isn't very tough;
> He tries to be quick, but isn't very;
> He tries to be smart, but isn't smart;
> He tries to be charming, but isn't often;
> He tries to be brave, but isn't brave at all;
> He tries to be cunning, but isn't very;
> He tries to be comical, but isn't intentionally.

I say this to him:

Drink more slowly. Do the things you're good at and forget the rest. You can't be born a man, you have to become one: most males never make it.

Try to remember that each person, each generation, has to learn over again all that history has passed along to us, and must make a fresh judgement on it.

Obey nature, your nature – if you love your neighbour and yourself equally.

If we look upon nature and our fellow humans and animals only as a field in which we find satisfaction of our needs, we're nothing but predators.

67 / Time Is So Broad

Time is so broad: it includes everything, dead and living. It's a sea, yet it's shaped like a river, and seems to move and flow, and we're all in it, moving and flowing. We face in its directions and think we're going forward.

But I think we're here, and stationary, and *it* moves.

68 / I Love to Run Alone

I love to run alone, but the new dog laws make it hard. It's a very artificial life, having to persuade human people to validate my existence by picking up my lead and trying to keep up with me on a long walk.

I say 'keep up with me', since it's well known by now that men descended from us, that is, from animals who go on four limbs, but at the cost of a great loss of speed over the ground.

I don't mean to imply that I look down on human people, because I don't. At least not much. In many ways I look up to them. For instance, when they stand near me. On the other hand, although I look down on seagulls in many ways, there are some ways in which I look up to them, greatly. In the air they're so graceful. Must there be something correspondingly graceful in their minds? You'd never know it. Their faces show an unparalleled stupidity and blankness in all circumstances.

Owls can swoop on creatures in the grass. Wagtails can skim the grass and suddenly climb high, land on a railing and swivel this way and that, with pride. Well justified, let me add. Seagulls can face into a wind, flutter and shake, and drop down vertically, wings beating, to a spot directly beneath them; and I mean facing into a high wind. I envy all these things.

Imagine a dog like me, graceful, with wings, swooping, skimming, banking, descending vertically: that's how I'd like to be. The trouble is that wings are in place of arms, and I have no wish to be without arms. How could I run, with only two legs? When I get these ambitious thoughts, the way I bring myself back to earth is to remember my four-footed relatives, the sheep, pigs, cows, rabbits, hanging from hooks in the butcher's shop. They've made the supreme sacrifice: I'm glad to be an onlooker at that drama.

I think I'd like to be willy wagtail most of all. Swooping, skimming, climbing, then to stand and prance, and wave my tail this way and that. Wagtails remind me of Darling. I know I can never do things like the willy does but I never cease wanting to. I think when I was born I was behind the door when lots of other things were handed out, but I got there in time to get two arms full of innocence.

69 / If They Stop Loving Us

I wonder will humans ever stop loving dogs? And cats. Cats, too. And birds.

If they stop being fond of us and caring whether we eat, what will happen to us?

I don't happen to believe that the work we do, whether minding, companionship, or security at night is worth anything; nothing, that is, except affection: affection for the worker, the work and the one worked-for. I like the Guests well enough – Julie most, then Jeff and Donna, then the adults – and what I do for them I'd do anyway. I believe they'd feed me just because they like me.

If they *did* stop liking animals, would it mean they'd soon stop liking each other, or would it be a sign they'd already stopped liking other humans?

70 / They Might Sell Me

I wonder if, when I've done this book, I could do lots more . . . Make my living at it?

Ah, there's a danger signal. I *have* a living. My employers trust me, and, mostly, I trust them – as long as I can keep an eye on them.

If people like my book, and get to hear that a dog wrote it, some get-rich-quick merchant might make me into a sideshow freak, and no one would pay attention to what my book is saying.

Worse, the Guests might sell me! After all, humans are in charge of most things, and as employers, they have the power to make a profit out of their employees. What a horrible thought . . . I wonder how I can guard against this happening?

I'll have to make sure Julie keeps my secret, and takes the manuscript to the publisher. She and I will make up a pseudonym, so no one will ever guess the author was a dog.

71 / A Visionary Dog

Hey! I'm a writer now! (Sometimes the thought hits me afresh and I get excited – as if it's the first time I thought of it.)

I'll be the first dog to have written a book and till the day I die I'll be proud a red setter did it.

No, that's mean. I'll be proud a *dog* did it. It could just as easily have been a basenji, an Australian native dog, a doberman, a terrier.

Trouble is, only humans can read it, so far. When will my own people learn? How can I get them to read?

Since we left off hunting in packs, like wolves or the African bands of big-eared dogs on the plains, and came over to the employ of humans, our culture has become shoddy and worn. We live in comfortable conditions, we've got lazy – our way of life is cheap.

Our disadvantage is, we're so alone. Each one in a little box in a million backyards. We're like . . .

What are we like?

We're like Mr Guest, in *his* little box. He's constantly trying to face the world alone. He goes out every day to face the world alone. Maybe that's OK – facing it – but he tries to understand it alone and unaided. And all the time the treasures, the savings, the bank of other minds are here, in the Book, in a million books, waiting for him to look. Other lands, other centuries, millions of forgotten geniuses, have left in libraries the records of their thoughts, their discoveries, their questions: the footprints of their minds. And he won't look. He leaves it to others, like the other dogs leave it to me.

At least this book is a start. But I'm forgetting. My Dictionary! My little Dictionary . . .

When will I get time for my Dictionary? I must hurry. Perhaps if I do without naps altogether . . .

At least through this book other dogs will hear of me.

Will news of my achievement inspire some young dog in the out-back, some restless individual in a city back street, some ambitious hound confined by the sprawling placidity of the wide suburbs?

Maybe one young lonely individual – in Leonora, in Dampier, maybe Mt Isa, doing minding work for a human family will hear and straightaway recognize a life's work calling her, calling him, to lift up all dog people and enlarge their horizons; a first step on the long road towards the gleaming goal I see at this moment of writing. When all living things will be able to make a conscious contribution to the world's culture.

72 / Questions for Mr Guest

What contribution to his planet has Mr Guest made? He helped create three children.

Does that mean he needn't do anything more, must keep his head down and stumble along as best he can until grave-time? Leaving the three children to do – maybe – what he didn't?

Is this why he doesn't seem to care that he omits to teach his children about stealing; about lying and hypocrisy; about crawling to authority; about fear of office-holders; about meanness, whining, complaining; about courage and cleanliness, honesty and frankness, decency and good humour, selflessness and good will?

They've had to struggle towards these things by themselves with more success than Mr Guest's efforts deserve. But, later, will their success in these things seem to them to come naturally, so they won't be able to voice them, as lessons learned, to *their* children, who may need the words and formulations?

He seems not to know that the 'old-fashioned' values were formed over thousands of years, the combined hammering out and smoothing down of human actions by thousands of unknown and unsung moral geniuses. He prefers to leave his children's education to what some money spinner said last Thursday in a popular song, a mass-selling book, or today's television.

73 / In This Country They Don't Eat Us

Just a short thought.

From what I see and hear, there are lots of human people who think of other humans as things – objects, stumps, rocks; animate obstacles to be knocked aside, run over or casually destroyed, but mostly ignored as if they don't exist.

If I'm right, and they really regard other humans as mere things, then it's no wonder they feel we are so different, we who go on four legs, or have wings, or fins. They plunder us! We are what they eat. Killing us is sport.

In this country they don't eat us dogs, or cats or lots of birds as humans do in other countries – monkeys, too, in some places, though you'd think the resemblances would stop them – but they made the rules, and if they were to change the rules we'd be bred for their jaws as other four-footed, finned and feathered creatures are.

I don't like feeling that my existence rests on a whim or a fashion among the master race. I resist it.

74 / But They Cut Up Animals Alive

I didn't know until I read it in the Book, that humans – for experiments – cut up animals while the animals are alive. Did you know that? I won't go on about the kittens who have their eyes sewn up at birth; the animals' brains pulsating in jars when the rest of the animal has been stripped away; the baby monkeys who have their heads removed and sewn on to their mothers' bodies. I'll merely tell you what I heard today.

I heard a young man talking to a girl outside the supermarket. He's a medical student. She used to go to the same school, but now has a job in a bank.

You know how young males – humans and dogs alike, and cats too, for all I know; and certainly seagulls – like to talk of fighting, and blood, and things horrible generally, to impress? That's how this medical student was.

He told how students and lecturers get around the provisions of the cruelty laws to get at and study brain material without causing pain.

The animal's head is held in clamps, a small area on the skull deadened by a local anaesthetic, and a hole bored painlessly, giving access to the brain. They need to study the brain matter unaffected by the chemical changes of either death or general anaesthetic. They retrieve the brain – which feels nothing since it has no nerves – by inserting a nozzle into the hole bored, then sucking the brain out, depositing it as a small heap of matter; rather like a squodge of toothpaste, but with a repellant colour.

I shivered when I heard this story, and just for a moment imagined I could smell blood. You know how, sometimes, you get the taste of blood in your mouth, and the smell of your own breath is the smell of blood? It was like that.

(I wonder if they'll get around to breeding human babies – in glass dishes or test tubes – for experiments on *their* brain matter.)

75 / The Smell of Blood

The smell of blood catapults me right back in time to six months of age, and across country to the place where I grew up. On the Plowright property there was an old horse the children used to ride; his name was Rover. He had the run of the timbered area across the creek. Our whole family went on a long search with two of the Plowright children when Rover hadn't turned up first thing Monday morning at the bottom fence of the ploughed land.

We found him dead. Some passing shooters had fired seven bullets into Rover's body behind his shoulder and forward of his flanks. From what my father said to me I learned that the shooters were using hollow-point bullets; the holes on the far side of Rover's body were big. Blood had run out and lay in pools beside him. The sun had been up about three hours and the blood smelled. That smell got into my nose and my memory and I will never be free of it.

I don't know if it's more cruel to shoot a horse just for fun, or to kill animals to run tests on their brain-matter.

76 / Glad and Light-hearted Things I Delight In

I got the idea for this chapter this morning. When you read about the things that delight me perhaps you'll understand me better than I can express myself. There are so many things I don't know how to say.

Nights of rain, when the wind lashes the pouring rain against my kennel and I'm warm and dry inside; checking every now and then that the Book isn't getting wet.

Afternoons when the sun comes out during a shower and the rain is silver spears.

A thin gum tree up the street that responds to the least wind, moving sinuously, this way, side-ways, back and forth, as if it's dancing. It has a strange effect on me. I think of the way Darling moves, even though dogs don't dance.

A bunch of small children with a teacher, going towards the Gardens; hand in hand, all of them.

After rain, when the drops get slower, falling off the bottom of the roof guttering on to leaves, and splashing on concrete.

A threatening storm turns north to avoid Sydney at the last moment: a few warm drops, a lightning flash or two, and it's all over.

A sudden storm, with pouring rain. It stops as soon as it starts, and everyone is cheerful. You can feel cheerfulness in the air.

Small white clouds riding high in the blue sky; in no hurry; not caring where they go.

Sheets of white paper that Julie gets for me. As I put them away, I wonder what I'll be writing on them.

When the whole family bursts out laughing and it takes me by surprise, and I can't help smiling, too.

A butterfly suddenly coming over the fence, swooping, climbing, going into the next backyard, just missing the fence, just missing the trees, the creepers – just missing everything.

Mrs Guest when she comes home from shopping with several things she's been dying to have to herself for an hour or two before the others come home.

Grass, in all shapes and sizes. Long grass with weeds, as well as short new-mown grass that's so good for showing off one's speed. When the men on their machines are cutting the grass in the Domain I can smell it, nearly a kilometre away.

A family of wrens at 9 in the morning and again at 5 o'clock, covering the same territory; first for breakfast, then for dinner.

When Donna was younger and made urgent movements to show she wanted her mother's breast. And some minutes later, when she rested from drinking, with her mother's nipple brushing the corner of her mouth, her cheeks were flushed delicately with an indescribable pink.

The uncurling leaves on the monstera that Mrs Guest planted; the latest to open out are light green and confused and wrinkled up, like children's bedclothes before they've been straightened out and the bed made tidy again.

Julie's hair when it's just washed and she's drying it, sitting in the sun. It shines with many different lights.

Donna doing her crude and wonderful drawings, and colouring-in the books her father buys for her.

Julie and her mother singing carols together at Christmas in the kitchen, standing side by side following the words and music, then linking arms as the music draws them closer together.

The sound of tea-cups first thing in the morning.

Many-coloured washing hung out on backyard lines to dry. Then a wind comes, and patches of colour flap about as if they're happy.

Small flower gardens in bloom in the tiny front yards in Wool-loomooloo.

Dogs and children playing on the grass, when the grass hasn't been cut and the clover is soft.

Grape vines in January, growing on the side fences of poor houses in Bourke Street.

Five ducklings, following their mother, swimming in the duckpond in the Gardens.

Water falling softly over low barricades, making musical noises.

Mr and Mrs Guest on the occasion in December – it was a hot day – when he bought a punnet of strawberries and gave them to her after he had secretly chilled them. She feels the heat; and just for a moment, feeling the cool fruit in her hand, she was young again, and, more important than that, courted.

Eucalypts covered with blossoms in summer; red blossoms, white, lemon: so many blossoms that you can hardly see the leaves.

Two babies playing on a blanket.

Racing home to read the Book, and finding that the next chapter is absorbing and full of interest. It makes me pleased and happy, and I can't help smiling. Sometimes the Guests see me, when I emerge from my kennel, smiling.

77 | The Artists' Model

Jeff decided to walk with me today. I find it very hard to manipulate Jeff. He's in the education machine, in the upper years at high school, and I think he's wide awake to people manipulating him. He's had years of experience. Saturday night he was out till about five on Sunday morning; he and his friends have learned to like parties and not all of them have to study for school. He doesn't talk to me much when we go for a walk, but I'm not complaining. I'm luckier than most, I have two adults, one youth and a girl, and sometimes the whole lot together, to walk with me.

You should have felt the ground tremble when that big truck passed. It roared up Bourke Street, which siphons off north-harbour traffic to the southern suburbs near the coast.

A pigeon passed me, waddling towards some spillage from a sandwich bag on the footpath. 'Have you eaten today?' I asked her. At least you can tell the women from the men among the pigeons. No one can mistake the heavy-set men pigeons, with their fatty necks that waddle out of phase with their body-waddle.

She blinked at me briefly as if she'd heard but was too busy to answer. I wondered if I'd soon be able to talk to pigeons. Yes, I thought as we went along at a fair pace (Jeff likes to step it out and I appreciate the difference) and if I can talk to pigeons what will I tell them? Can I pass on to them some of the things dog people have discovered and treasured and known for so long? I know birds are only birds, not people. I'd thought all my life, that because of the way their jaws are shaped, the size of their throats, the uses to which their tongues are put, that it would always be impossible for birds to talk, until I heard the Hobart gull. And they are capable of ambition – the art-critic wanting to branch out into being a Universal Critic!

At the Quay Jeff got himself one of the new seagull ice-creams. It's the most unusual ice-cream I've ever seen. A white seagull sat in the cone, and Jeff nonchalantly bit off its head in one bite. Inside the gull, the ice-cream was red. Several gulls watched this from a distance, as we passed their favourite feeding corner.

Jeff went up my favourite narrow lane in the Rocks area where he's an art student in his time off from school. We went up two steep flights of wooden stairs in what was once a warehouse, on to the floor where the students sat under the eye of their teacher, a man by turns fiery and benevolent, explanatory and dismissive, long-suffering and intolerant. Jeff talked to him.

I went to where a human person lay on a raised floor. She wore as few clothes as any dog person but was naked without clothes, whereas we aren't. I went right up to her and sat down. She smiled at me, and extended her arm. The hand on the end of the arm came down lightly on my head with the delicacy of tenderness and welcome. It was the most elegant pat I've ever willingly endured.

I sniffed at her, long and carefully, and took her smell in my nose, and down deep into me. I know I will stay with the Guests, because they are my employers and pay to have me registered, but if I'd been free and she'd said: Come with me, I'd have gone. She smelled of love and goodwill; her smell said she was level-headed and physically fit; it said she was female – whether she'd been a horse, a lion, an elephant or a dog, she was female in any form, in all ages, in every cell of her body. She was slim and fair; small-breasted and white-skinned; her hands were graceful, with two rings on her long fingers; one on her left hand, one on her right.

Jeff delivered his message and left. I was reluctant to follow right away, and he had to come back for me. The smell of that female person! It haunts me still: I've smelled it on no other person except Darling. If that model had been a dog person I don't know what I'd have done, but I couldn't have left that spot.

We were in no hurry to get back, Jeff and I. Particularly the latter. Seagull Park, between George Street and Circular Quay West, was infested, as usual, with gulls. I looked for the Universal Critic, but couldn't find her. There were plenty of dramas to see, though, and I managed to detain Jeff for a few minutes, in order to look at what went on. The same bullying and harassment; there was no change, only the faces were different.

In one of the waiting tourist buses there were seagull passengers. Quite at home they looked, sitting at the tinted windows, looking out. When the bus moved off, they looked just as tired and bored as any humans.

We waited and watched at the iron railings round the Quay while one of the new seagull ferries left number 6 wharf. I glimpsed the ferry captain – a fine young gull – and the staff – a middle-aged seagull with stained shirt – and the deckhand who throws the ropes round the iron bollards on the wharves. He was very young, not fully grown. Seagull passengers sat on the seats outside the closed compartment. I don't blame them for not wanting to go inside the glassed-in section: I hate it in there myself. I like to feel the breeze in my coat and see the water and waves just underneath me, riding by, not through salt-obscured glass.

As the little ferry made its way into Sydney Cove we stood at the seahorse railing and followed it with our eyes, Jeff and I. Could Jeff see the several human people riding the waves out near the Opera House edge, for all the world like large birds riding the waves? And when a line of seagulls threw some crumbs of food into the water, I wonder did Jeff see the flying humans balancing on the smooth bronze rail, swoop down on them and fly up again with crumbs in their mouths? I looked up at his face to see if I could tell, but I couldn't.

We walked round to the Farm Cove side of the Opera House, where another thing that caught my eye from across the harbour was the sight of human people sitting close together on the dolphins off Kirri-billi Point, as if settling down for the night.

I had no time this day to have a conversation with a gull, and I returned home with Jeff. He enjoyed jogging the last stretch across the Domain and down to the flat grass that forms the roof of the car park, and I enjoyed giving him the exercise. It's not always easy to resist the temptation to run ahead; I've noticed, though, when I've done this before, that it's often quite some time before he'll come with me again. I must keep to my resolve not to show how efficient four limbs are for running, or these new dog laws will finish me. I must have human company, or there'll be fines for the Guests.

78 / I Feel a Peculiar Loathing

I feel a peculiar loathing when I remember an embarrassment of my youth, as a country dog. I'd been told not to leave any messages inside the house, but I forgot. They'd fed me on some of their human food – which comes out messy – plus a small portion of fresh chopped meat, and played a game with me directly after I'd eaten. So right when I felt it, I did it. I was standing on a white fluffy rug.

They frightened me with sudden noises when they saw it, and I ran out of the house. They followed me, waving their arms. They shouted out loud what I'd done for everyone in the world to hear. I was so ashamed. They mentioned all the details at the tops of their voices. I stayed out till after dark and came back quietly.

The loathing I feel when I remember, is loathing of myself and of that memory. I think that even when I'm old and wobbly, I'll still remember, and still hear their shouts ringing in my skull.

Old Sorrowful Eyes round the corner has his memories still sharp and clear, even though he doesn't get around much, and has another dog under him, learning his job.

I think life, every day's life, must be precious and important when you're old. I can imagine you probably wake up and say, 'That's a surprise! I'm still here!' And treasure every moment of the day, looking at the street and the people and things around you with more concentration than usual, in case it's the last time you see them.

I suppose my father would have had these thoughts before he died. I was too young then even to feel much sorrow. But even if I had, not all the love in the world could have saved him when he came to die.

When I make mistakes now I don't reproach myself nearly as much.

79 / Gripes about Humans

Most humans have little money: yet they're all trying to buy the world on time payment.

They kill each other, singly and in wars, yet they're all going to die anyway. It's as if the survivor has somehow won something by not being next to die.

They allow lunatics in public office, people who crave power over others, who crave to see others obey them.

They kill killers, or hide them away out of sight, instead of putting them on permanent show in cities so their crimes can be read by those gazing at such creatures.

They freeze the worn-out bodies of those able to afford it, to be thawed in the future, when medical science can revive the dead. As if death is just a word.

They accept money as compensation for the loss of health or limbs, and for the death of their loved ones.

They need to communicate constantly, yet they speak in hundreds of different tongues.

Much of their populations are unaware of their countries' range of culture, or have no desire to know it. They are, effectively, citizens of nowhere.

Humans agree that money is essentially worthless, but all agree to value everything by it, including themselves.

Those who do the dirtiest and most dangerous work often receive the least reward for it.

Mankind considers that individuals may own pieces of the surface of the planet, and don't think this is ludicrous.

Humans paint parts of their bodies!

Don't humans understand that they need to work, need to be occupied? More and more people are now born on to the planet every year, so more jobs are needed for all sorts of people. But those who can affect the position are busy building machines to replace people. It can't come to any good.

They seem to organize their actions so there's inflation and recession, boom and bust: perhaps these happenings are accurate portraits of the human race. They're like kids who just won't be good. They could, if they tried, be restrained, prudent, careful, content with little, avoiding luxuries, turning a deaf ear to greed. Instead, they take all they can get, in any circumstances, and before long, there's nothing left but debts.

Humans are pack animals, like dogs are. They pine for a leader, someone to look at, to emulate, to please, to love. But it's not in their interests, if ever they want to grow up, to have this leader. Fortunately there is an apathy, a guilt, an uncertainty that usually pulls them up short of this authoritarian leader.

What I don't understand is the human attitude to the things I read in the Book every day. The Guests, for instance, the people round about, the ones I pass in the street – they don't seem to want to learn about what humans can know, and what humans can do. They haven't yet joined their civilization. All the information is filed away in libraries and so on, but very few ever look at it. It's left to a chance person, a student maybe, a dissatisfied and restless mind; but otherwise only those in the knowledge industry have close contact with it.

Humans in this country don't really know what they're doing! They get floods one year, but they never make lots of holes ready to store the rain when it comes; they never fill up the artesian basins. A few years later there's a drought, so they stand around and scratch their heads, wondering and cursing.

Every few decades humans have an armaments race and a war just to keep their economy going. Their economy is founded on death – on the unfortunate who starve when times are bad, or on the unfortunate who die in war.

Their whole way of living is a mess. They slide into boom times without knowing boom times were round the corner; they slide into recession helplessly, full of guesses but empty of knowledge as to how it's happening; they tumble into war with surprise, even though war has been hanging round for years, and all the time they're arming they've been protesting that they hate war and don't want it. Their human society seems permanent and stable, but that's only because things happen slowly; actually, it's a mess.

In the human world peace seems to run untidily all over the place, and looks like confusion. It's puzzling. It's ugly. War is organized, single-minded, definite, clear as day, and therefore beautiful. Some humans think of peace and war in these terms.

Are humans on the wrong track about their own history? Maybe they were here on earth as long as dogs have been; but were kept down to small groups, few in number, by large predators.

They're crazy. Humans were here in Australia more than 40,000 years ago. Yet they didn't know till recently. Don't they talk to each other? Don't they pass on what they know?

Humans have problems with poverty, disease, unemployment; they ought to organize themselves in ways that will help solve their problems, but they don't.

They can produce goods, but not everyone can have them. They ought to have everyone working on their problems, throwing up ideas, criticizing, making sure things change that are shown to be wrong. Why isn't it like that? But Mr Guest isn't like that. He's content with lots of things that don't work. There must be a lot like him who just go on day to day, not caring.

Much of their scientific searching is directed towards explaining themselves; wondering who they are, where they came from, where they're going, trying to find out what the world is made of, and where it came from.

They know almost nothing, yet. And we worshipped them. (I did, too. Once: not now.)

I'm sorry for them. They're wandering helplessly, like directionless robots gone astray, not programmed for what they're trying to do; programmed, instead, for a small range of reactions that constantly land them in trouble.

Here I am, living in their world, among them; I smell them, watch their movements, think some of their thoughts, care about their problems, but they have no means of knowing my thoughts, no way of listening to my suggestions.

No research they do is in any way directed towards giving them access to my brain, to the detailed knowledge I have, to the perspective I have on *their* affairs, to the thoughts I have, my dreams, my hopes and fears, my ambitions, my life.

No research they do is aimed at helping me to master speech, at assisting me to use my hands for the things *they* do with hands.

Sometimes I think they're selfish, and want to keep what they have from us, and never give us the chance to show what we're made of.

On planet earth, mankind is the root of all evil.

It may well be undesirable in the long run, for the planet to be dominated by these creatures, these humans.

Now that I'm older I find I often want to know what's really in me; I mean, what the thing is that's inside me. Is it a soul? Is it just a box of works sufficient to get me through life and a few emergencies or is it more than that? And if so, how does it compare with the similar internal mechanism of humans?

Humans have only so much love; they can't love strangers any more than they love themselves, and often, I've noticed, they don't love themselves all that much. Some detest themselves: how will *they* treat strangers, or neighbours? Who can tell?

One conclusion I've come to is that although humanity isn't OK as it is, it can't be improved. But the world can. I think Pangloss was right: this is the best world possible. All we have to do is improve it.

The animal that may evolve from humans in the future will not be their friend, nor they its friend. They will try to destroy it, since it will be different. Nor will it be human. They are human and will not extend that word to the newcomers; newcomers, looking at humans, will scorn to use it about themselves.

Them and their alternation of cold war and hot peace ... War settles nothing, just leaves its causes resting, festering. War stops only because one side can't go on – for the moment.

Such a lot of fuss, and war, and excitement; anarchy, waste, murder, anxiety, hatred, envy! How the world – now we hear more about what goes on in it – seems to resemble the individual's own heart and mind!

Is the whole of history, with its empires, wars, catastrophes, revolutions, rising powers, declining civilizations, some sort of mirror of the single human soul?

War is generally thought of as a bad thing, as is slavery. However, not all slavery is a curse; not all war is bad. The use of force is right against tyranny and for the restoration of free institutions. Freely undertaken slavery for a cause that benefits others hurts no one.

Please, humans, don't avoid *everything* unpleasant – if you do, far more unpleasant things may swallow you. Throughout history the disciplined and highly organized barbarian has driven out the civilized and gentle, the comfortable, the humane: those who live to enjoy life. The most civilized is in the greatest danger.

Humans, by and large, seem to think they're either savage and murderous animals or potentially nice people. It seems more accurate to me to say they can choose which to be. Though sometimes they change from one to the other on a whim.

I think they should consider what abilities they need to have to face emergencies, and what proclivities might incapacitate them in war-like conditions. They ought to keep all their abilities, but learn to drop temporarily those that don't apply to whatever fix they're in – whether peace or war – but always keep the full range of their abilities handy.

'Gripes about Humans' has turned out to be a long chapter in my book.

80 / Victor and the Seagle

He's a bulldog, but an uncommon one – he has intellectual leanings. He wants to be taken seriously when he speaks at meetings of other dogs, but his appearance is against him.

'Humans!' he complains. 'Look what they did to me.' Saying this, his mouth opens to show the small regular front teeth, together with large canines at the sides of his jaws. The muscles of his face bunch even when they seem to be stretching. It's true, he doesn't strike you as being an intellectual; his heavy brow-line creases itself up into a concertina of wrinkles.

'How can anyone believe *I* could think a thought – when I look so puzzled all the time?'

'How would you like to look?'

'Calm, serene, with a clear brow. Thinkers don't use all this effort of muscles to think. Their faces are relaxed; the thinking goes on in their heads. I wouldn't mind a blank expression, even. But humans gave me this jaw, this flat face, these forehead-wrinkles that make me look like an ape. Some sense of humour!'

'It's your thoughts that count,' I say.

'I never get them out. After two words someone always interrupts.'

'You don't look like an ape, to me,' I say.

'I want to look confident. I wish they'd made me taller. Look at you. People listen to you.'

I could do nothing for *him*. He was as he was.

But Victor did something for *me*. He told me of a seagull he'd seen, a seagull unlike any other. This bird spent no time scrounging for scraps, had no time for quarrelling with other gulls, simply flew over the harbour, flew out to sea, fishing the waters, riding waves, disdaining the grubby city ground, only coming to rest on earth on a mooring dolphin in the Harbour or on the Isle of Gulls, to sleep.

I questioned Victor, trying for every scrap of information about such an unusual seagull, but he was too taken up with the misfortune that had shaped his life, the humans responsible for breeding his ancestors to a certain shape and appearance, that he had little thought to spare for me.

'Just keep your eyes peeled; you'll see him,' he said. 'He's the gull that flies higher than all other gulls – as high as eagles. He's more like an eagle than a seagull.'

81 / The Dinosaur Dog

Today I got the wonderful, light-headed, full-chested smell of early summer flowers, that blows south to me in the warm northerly breeze from the suburbs across the harbour. I woke with the scent in my nose and sprang up immediately, ready to persuade Julie to come out with me.

I had to wait a bit, because they weren't awake. I read and re-read a particularly difficult chapter of the Book. Then it was a slow breakfast. When Julie came out to talk to me, I looked up at her for the required time, which she rightly translates as: where are we going?

She got my lead and said, 'We'll just follow our noses.' Which means she has no real aim, and that means I set the direction.

Kids were playing in the section of street outside – it's a part that's permanently blocked off to traffic so people can play there – and I was feeling so playful that I had to stop myself – and it was hard – from joining in and probably mucking up their game.

I have a lot of power, really. Did you know that I can stop their games immediately? All I have to do is threaten them with a loud voice and they stop instantly. They freeze. My teeth scare them. I didn't do it. Julie would have been put out. I like the fact that she's popular with all the kids round about. Everyone that sees her likes her, except some of the derelicts, who like no one.

Julie must have had the wind in her tail, so to speak, because she gave me a run across the green September grass of the Domain. She ran well, for a human. Crossing Art Gallery Road in the deep shade of the fig trees (Each time I pass them I think: these trees don't know their names.) we passed a derelict seagull sprawled on a bench at the base of a tree; I think this one had bad feet, the red-brown webs seemed to be painful, swollen and dark from exposure to all weathers. I half expected to see the odd plastic bag with a few possessions in it, like the human derelicts that wander round their limited territory.

Down the gentle slope towards the football area a seagull was haranguing half a dozen gulls that may or may not have been listen-ing, for all the world like the human Domain speakers on a Sunday afternoon, and just as loud and harsh. Julie decided she wanted to walk over to Hyde Park, so we turned and went out of the Domain along Art Gallery Road and by the cathedral, under the road and up again, making towards the spraying Archibald Fountain. We stood and watched humans from other countries and from country parts of Australia – the country begins just outside Sydney – take photographs of the things that were to hand, then we turned away and walked down to the saucer fountain, where a few gulls were having a splash, gulls that couldn't be bothered having a proper bath in the salt water of the Harbour.

121

Over on Elizabeth Street a gull stood on point duty, its beady eye trying to intimidate traffic in the instant before it surged forward and over the place where the gull had been. Julie wanted something to eat, and crossed the street to go down into Centrepoint for a snack.

When that was done we emerged and went back into the park. There's nothing like walking on grass to put you in a good temper. We ambled and stopped, looked and listened in that rectangle of Hyde Park, between College and Elizabeth and before Park Street, for quite a while. No one chased me out. I didn't catch sight of the Universal Critic, but I discovered, by listening intently to one of a group near the fountain, that seagulls, too, can be consumed with ambition. I heard one saying, of a heavy-set gull, who walked round with his head pulled down into his chest, thickening his neck and giving him a more obdurate look, 'He's chairman of everything already, what does he want to be? Premier of the State?' The obdurate one heard this and I saw his head rise up to gain attention, then sink down again into that hunched position as he answered: 'Not Premier! Prime Minister!' And turned away, planting his feet firmly one after the other. Wherever he walked, others got out of his way.

Over towards the Park Street edge of the park, we came on a group of gulls – near a wide shallow fountain, littered with gumleaves, that spits only thin quiet jets of water towards the centre of the pool; a group that was excitedly talking over news they'd received from overseas – presumably via the Overseas News Service for gulls – of the first seagull to conquer Everest. They were up in the air about it, particularly about the fact that this heroic gull had not been assisted by oxygen on the ascent. I wish Julie had been able to understand their talk.

We sat on the grass for a while, Julie looking about her and thinking human thoughts while I meditated on the life of dogs in general. I had my head forward on my arms, and seeing a labrador in harness as a seeing-eye dog I thought particularly of dogs that go about doing good.

From there it was a simple matter, for a dog with my imagination, to proceed directly to a consideration of the ancient legend of the Dinosaur Dog. This legend, which has survived so many millions of years, let alone millions of moons, has come down to us canines of the present day from the days of the Last Dinosaurs. The Dinosaur Dog was active in that far-off time, killing off the last dinosaurs – the hardy ones that survived the mass deaths caused by dinosaurs' inability to adjust themselves to the changes coming about on earth.

I know humans have their legends, but I doubt if they have one as terrible or as ancient as our legend of the huge and terrible beasts of long ago. I doubt very much that they have a legend as heroic as our legend of the Dinosaur Dog that killed off the huge and terrible beasts that oppressed the earth and its people long before humans became known. Down the generations the fight went on, until, after the last dinosaur fell and was torn into pieces small enough to be eaten, there were only a handful of Dinosaur Dogs left. These dogs, though, were big. They were too big for the rest of us ordinary dogs. Since they were *so* big, they were dangerous to us. They became the enemy. We had to be rid of them before they had time to breed up again into numbers where they could resist our hordes. We had to kill off the Dinosaur Dog. Whether we were right or wrong, our dogs thought then that the two breeds, with one so large, could not continue to exist side by side without deadly danger to our ranks.

The last three Dinosaur Dogs went down under the combined onslaught of three hundred packs of our best hunting dogs: one hundred packs to each Dinosaur Dog. It's sad to think back on, but our ancestors did what they thought was necessary to our survival, their descendants.

The Dinosaur Dog was too dangerous; he was too big for the rest of us.

I must have fallen asleep then. I dreamed of something I often think of in those spaces in the day between sitting down and getting up, between walking one way and suddenly deciding to go another: I dreamed of the many times I've been, in the evening, along Mrs Macquarie's Road to the headland called Mrs Macquarie's Point.

At night the small waves are tipped with a brightness, a sudden flash, yet it's a flash more subdued than the reflections of the shore lights. The shore-light reflections seem to be glued to the same patch of water, they dance about and are there when the waves move on. No matter how they dance, they dance in the same spot. Until you move; then they move with you. The flash I'm thinking of is in the water itself.

I like it. I often look at it. But I can't pick where it's going to flash next. There it is! It's a slow flash, more a spatter than anything. A phosphorescent spatter.

Julie must have roused me. I woke: not near the water, but in Hyde Park, and still sleepy. Look at those clouds. They're higher than birds fly. If you were up that high you could see over all the hills at once.

I don't have a word for it. I would like a magnificent old word from the Bible to keep its meaning in. I would take it out now and then and look at it, taste it, turn it over, feel it, and enjoy it.

I wonder if there's a bird which flies that high.

Of course there is. The one Victor told me of: the seagull that flies high as an eagle.

82 / The Willy Wagtail

As we came near the chess tables and the Cook Statue I saw a single wagtail persecuting a large glossy crow. The willy would come round to the back of the crow, take off and make passes behind the crow's neck and do clever aerobatics, fanning its tail feathers, spreading its wings, slashing figures of eight in the air, then back to ground, absurdly tiny as it followed the walking crow. It seemed to me that the crow knew perfectly well not only that it wasn't welcome, but also that it was useless trying to retaliate, for if it turned and lashed out with its great black savage beak, the willy simply wouldn't be there. The crow plodded forwards into the Australian shrubs at the foot of Cook, the wagtail flew to the top of one of the upturned lamps that illuminated Cook greenly all night, and harried the crow again. When it had the shelter of the bushes all round it, the crow stayed there, considering its position.

The wagtail didn't leave off. It waited till the crow emerged, pranced irritatingly in the air round the crow's head – well clear of its beak – and resumed its pursuit and brilliant antics behind the crow. The crow could see it, first this side and then that, behind its head. The crow gave up. It ran a step or two and took off heavily. The willy stood watching it, knowing that while he retained his mobility and mastery of the air at ground level, the crow could never touch him. The crow's wings beat powerfully – you could hear them – but his flight looked flat after the willy wagtail's.

83 / Teasdale McCann; Who Thinks, but Never Does

Sometimes when the human children play with me I know they want me to yell out. They like hearing distress. Trouble is, I'm usually happy and don't feel like yelling. What I'd rather do is yell at *them* unexpectedly, and make *them* jump. Some of Jeff's so-called friends used to squeeze orange peel in my face, so they could have a big laugh when I yelled and turned away trying to stop the burning in my eyes, rubbing at it with my hands – which weren't made for that work.

They were all playing this morning out on the shut-off section of the street where no cars can come, and all got it into their heads that they'd like to see me bolt. They prepared a trap for me – they were going to make a terrible din and cause me to yelp and run off. They know the ears of dog people are far more sensitive than their own to sharp noises.

I saw them at it, not long before, when I got to the corner of the house down the narrow path from the backyard. I came no further. I stood and thought. I knew what I would do; it was only a matter of waiting till they tried to frighten me. I wasn't nervous, but in general I'd rather have things done quickly, so I can react and get it over on the spot. I waited. My mother used to tell me, when I was facing similar circumstances: Pull yourself together. I was small, then.

They took their time getting ready for me, while I was there watching them, my face hidden at the base of the frangipani tree where the abelia grows from the soil near the side fence. I ruminated.

Minding people is an important job. As I've said, the pay is sometimes poor. But if you're independent, have a grasp of what your powers are, and a solid sense of self-respect, you can make it into a job with great scope.

125

We dogs are a special race of people. It's partly due to our sharing of a special spirit, which arises from our constitution and abilities and physical form. I call it the Spirit of Dog. That Spirit is what we move in. It's all around us; we share in it, move in it, taste it, we're made of it – yet it's like a bird, a quick bird that darts. Something like a willy wagtail.

I looked up at the children. Their faces were set, they were ready to trick me. Their faces reminded me of the faces of their parents, who seem so set when they go off to work in the mornings, and no less tight when they come back. Human people are born to worry, I think, as sure as flames go upwards. (Why *do* flames travel upwards?) That situation – human worry – probably comes about from insufficient thought about their problems in the first place, thought such as dog people give to past events and future possibilities.

I saw the kids were ready, so I rose, walked to the fence, sprang up and balanced briefly on top, then jumped down and trotted towards them. Exactly what they wanted. At the signal a great din of rubbish-tin lids broke out and I was supposed to yelp and look startled and make off up the street. I did only the third, and was soon slowing down to a trot, going towards the corner of Bourke Street where, nine or ten moons ago, a great friend of mine was killed. Run over by an early morning driver in a hurry to get a place to park before work. He didn't stop, and Joe died in a few minutes, with a broken back and ribs crushed.

The spot I knew from many times of seeing it. No stain remained, but I knew the pattern of the pieces of blue metal that surface in the bitumen just where his head lay. I got there within a few seconds of the accident, since I heard his cry of pain, and his three last words, 'They've finished me!' I ran up just as his eyes were closing and the life ran out of him and his piece of spirit left him and joined the aggregate of the surrounding Spirit of Dog, which floats free in the atmosphere.

I stood looking at the spot. 'Things are much the same, Joe,' I said. 'One new thing, I've begun to take an interest in seagulls. They're the most quarrelsome, vicious, selfish, inconsiderate birds I know. They're also very pretty when they fly and wheel and soar and stand head-on to the wind in the one spot. You'd like them, and there's one I've heard of that flies higher and comes down less than all the rest.'

I know the spirit of Joe heard me, but according to spirit rules he wasn't allowed to answer. I bet he's over in that part of the Sydney Domain where the grass runs past the swings downhill to the east and suddenly flattens out into turf over the roof of the car park. That was his favourite thing: running downhill and bounding on to the flat. Then turning, running up the slope a little way and racing back down, out over the flat again, back up the slope. The exhilaration of running possessed him, his eyes sparkled, his mouth hung wide in enjoyment, he was as relaxed as a child. He'd stop and look at you, then off again, up the slope, along a way, then back down at full pelt. I think he wished he was a pup again, to have an excuse to lose his footing, and roll down, over and over.

I mooched away along the part of the street where cars were, stopped and looked at myself in a hub cap. 'Stop being miserable,' I commanded. 'I'm not miserable,' I defended. 'Well, look out you don't *get* miserable,' I countered.

The world in hub caps is a world we dog people are familar with. It's a vision of a world strange and different. One's own self looms large in the foreground: everything recedes fast and is soon gone over a horizon you can't find when you turn round to look at it. (Each time my registration is renewed, I check my number in the nearest hub cap. The Guests don't think to tell me what it is.)

Further along Cathedral Street, past Bourke, I passed the house that Teasdale McCann looks after. I looked everywhere for him, and at last found him down in a warm nest of grass into which he snuggles like a cat. Teasdale McCann is thinking.

He wants to be a better dog. He loses sleep, his thoughts turn inwards, he hates himself. He suffers for his sins; I suspect he considers suicide. (Dogs hardly ever suicide.) All he succeeds in being, is – nothing. A dog who thinks and never does is not a real dog.

'How are things Teasdale?' I ask him.

He rouses himself with difficulty. That's how he is.

'Bad dreams, Hap,' he says. 'Bad dreams.' He always says bad dreams.

'Not more bad dreams?'

'You said it. More bad dreams.' He won't discuss it, won't go into the subject at all.

'How's Gualp?' I ask. Gualp is a frog, he's Teasdale's best friend.

'That Gualp is going off her head,' he says. 'They're sending her to the country.'

I begin to wonder what fantasy Teasdale is pulling out of that lugubrious head of his. Gualp is a male frog, what we call a bullfrog. Anyone can see that. You've just got to listen to him give throat on a hot summer night. But Teasdale and Gualp have been close friends for a dozen moons now, and Teasdale is very, very fond of Gualp. And insists he's a female. He's so fond of Gualp that you'd have to see it to believe it, but since the important things that happen with dogs, and frogs, never happen at times human people are around, you humans will never see it.

I think Teasdale McCann has never been able to rid himself of his masculine habits; any creature that he feels very, very fond of, just *has* to be a female. He couldn't take the thought that he could be so soft about anything male.

'What do you mean: *they're* sending her?' I ask. That can't be right.

'Well, I guess I might as well own up,' he said. He leaves long pauses between sentences. Sometimes you think he's never going to make it to the next one.

'I'm taking her.'

'You? How? I had visions of him curled up in his little meditation centre in the grass, but of not very much in the way of physical effort. But no one expected it of Teasdale, he *looked* a deep thinker.

'On my back, of course. I'll light out one night, pick her up, she'll jump on my back and in the dark I'll shoot across the Domain, along Art Gallery Road, to the first length of fence. She'll hop off, we'll say goodbye, and she'll make for the fold in the land there, where the water runs down to the fish pond. There's water all the way there, in the creek, and good earth banks. It'll be paradise for her. I've told her about the owls that get down there and how to watch out for them. I'll go and see her every now and then. We'll still be friends.'

'Have you any idea what's sending him off his head?' I asked.

He doesn't answer, he's turned off. But I know. It's being called she when he's he.

I went away thinking Teasdale McCann was a sad case. He'd never have the energy to go back and talk to his friend. Whatever sex he was. This would be goodbye for ever. I reckon Gualp, once he got his lift across the dangerous roads and up the hill, would be better advised to keep to himself and find a frog friend. And, as a first priority, give his attention to the birds and beasts of prey that get around in the Botanic Gardens after dark.

I was thinking so much about this that without being aware of it, I stopped and left a contribution next to the timber light pole on the corner of McElhone Street, the one with the number.

It was the very thing I'm always urging others not to do. Be discreet, be patient, wait for a bit of grass and some dirt, I tell them. Here I'd been and gone and done it myself. Oh well, no sense worrying about it, it was done.

It's understandable to everyone except human people. After all, the message dog people leave is basic. It says: 'I was here. Me. I made a difference. Here it is.'

I turned and left my difference and ran off home.

Anyway, they should forgive more. One person's need is another's crime. They never let you forget crimes against them.

84 / A Discreet Walk

Just then an argument burst out in the house. It reminded me of one of Jeff's boils last summer, when he sat on the back step and tenderly squeezed the place on his neck while his eyes, in the mirror, super-vized his fingers. I was sitting up straight, watching his face, then the boil; waiting. It was ripe and yellow, and it shot out suddenly. The bit that flew went on the bottom step, and the flesh around the base of the boil collapsed back and down to roughly skin level.

The argument seemed as sudden as that boil bursting. It was about a bottle that Mr Guest had bought from the grog shop and was hoping to open on Saturday night after the family dinner, by way of a treat. It was a special wine, and he meant well. Mrs Guest had found it, opened it and used it in cooking a special dish for the family. She meant well. Mr Guest doesn't often do something out of the ordinary for his family. Mrs Guest does, so perhaps that's why he was more upset than she was.

Anyway, it ended with Mr Guest hurling the bottle out of the kitchen window.

He should have opened it first. Glass flew everywhere.

Mrs Guest then got into top gear. Words flew like bullets. I went for a discreet walk. You can't beat an intelligent dog in tact and discretion.

85 / Nature Is Studying Itself

Julie had a Nature Study book on her knees, sitting up in the tree above me. She was deep in the book, so I didn't interrupt, just looked up now and then to see her face. She studies nature at school, and she was studying nature here. She was part of nature, studying nature; and I was part of nature, studying her who was a part of nature. It made a picture for me that I liked: everywhere nature is studying itself, and other bits of nature, every day.

86 / What a Miserable Dog

What a miserable dog I am! Do you remember how, back in Chapter 37 I was complaining about never being given things to do; never being issued with orders to follow, and blaming it on the Guests? I rubbished them, saying they had no goals, no ideas beyond surviving today and tomorrow.

I take it all back. Why do I need them to order me? I don't need anyone to tell me what to do. I know what to do.

In fact, I'm doing it. I'm learning every day, I'm making something as a result of what I've learned, and I'm passing on to others things I think will be of value to them.

What a lucky dog I am!

87 / I Don't Want to be Remembered by That

Once upon a time, on this very spot where I'm stretched out thinking, other people sat or walked or had their rough shelters, other dogs ran or lay stretched out thinking of their place in the world. They were as real as I am, their thoughts were real, their bodies. The trees stood mostly still, the wind blew, the white clouds shadowed the sun for a few minutes, then moved on, just like today. But they're gone, all of them, and one day I'll be gone too, and the Guests, and their neighbours, some of the houses, the dogs round about, all of them. All gone. There'll be death notices for some of the people, but none of the dogs. And that means me. I won't even be a footnote somewhere. In ages to come, the same air will blow round the globe, and no one will know I was here. It doesn't matter how I live or what I do, whether I kill people or whether I'm kind, it will still be the same and I will vanish.

So what?

I'll tell you so what! I won't vanish at all. Well, I will and I won't. The me that's writing this will vanish, but the me that's written down won't. The first member of the canine species to write a book...............

....

.... as long as history lasts.

That was a bit boastful. I've rubbed it out. I don't want to be remembered by that.

88 / If Life

If life, or things that combined to form nucleic acids, came to earth from space, did those nucleic acids come here simply to save themselves a bit longer? Were they outcasts? Refugees? Or were they formed in space and just happened to fall here? The Book doesn't know, it just mentions this as a possibility, a speculation. It's one of the things Jeff picked up at school, and delighted in telling Julie one Sunday when she'd come home from church. Julie knew perfectly well why it was said; but she had no stronger answer than a calm belief in what she'd been told. She wisely said nothing.

If only I could find the answer, or guess it. But it's too large and vague a thought for me; it's like trying to catch the atmosphere we live in.

If there are so many of these enzymes and molecules that go to make amino acids and all that stuff, in space, then maybe there's a tendency throughout the universe for life to happen. Maybe that's the way the universe is slanted.

And if we, here on planet earth, blow ourselves to atoms, then perhaps, if the climate remains favourable, life will rise again. I suppose there's not much chance that dogs will happen, or humans for that matter. Life might be limited to cockroaches, ants and spiders.

89 / An Austere Fate

The Guest family have freedoms I don't have, but they are anchored to their house for shelter, and they are compelled to go to their schools and places of work five days a week. I have a freedom they don't have. For most of the week I can come and go as I please, though less and less now due to the new dog laws; while they are interned daily in their work sheds, or filed in boxes called office blocks.

But on the whole I'd say that if I believed in fate, I'd think mine was an austere one. For a start, it's on my conscience that I want to help other dogs fit in better to this world, and yet I'm the only one I know who can read and write. How will I reach them? They're all separated, confined usually one to a house.

Another thing. There can't possibly be enough time in one dog's life to show all the peculiar things I've seen and heard. And read. I'll do what I can, but it can never be enough.

And who am I, to think I have it in me to help others? Who elected me?

There's only one answer to that. I elected myself. Who judged my fitness? I did. Am I honest? Well ... once or twice I've taken something that belonged to others – it was when I was a pup – but I have never lied.

Honesty doesn't make me smart.

Have I learned enough to be able to help others? Do I know enough?

I'll never know enough.

90 / The World's Not Made to Suit Me

The Guests aren't the only humans in the world. I wish I could get around a lot more and pick and choose whom I work for.

There could easily be a person I could have respect for, one who refuses to join all the others grubbing for money or looking to have people bow down in the face of riches, or loading himself with influence and power, always living in the future for trivial plastic goals. I might find a human person, a bit like me in the enjoyment of every day, every cloud, every leaf on a tree, every breath of wind; someone who knows each day is priceless, whether it's good or bad, grey or sunny.

Trouble is, I can't get around, I can't pick and choose, the world isn't made that way. I'll just have to do my own enjoying and live each day as thoroughly as I can.

At least I know of a seagull I admire, even if I've never seen him.

91 / How Big is the Ocean?

I have a dream that haunts me. I've never been to sea, but five times in my life I've dreamed I was at sea in a small ship, with lots of dog people: some big, some small, some black, white, red, grey, blue, brown, brindle, spotted, underslung, overfed – every shape and condition of canine. There's no captain and no crew; no engine and no oars. Some are sick, some fearing, some singing, some in prayer, some weeping. And some too stupid to know danger's face.

How big is the ocean, how far is the shore? None of us knows. What is our speed? Which is north? Where did we come from? We're all ignorant – all we know is we're dogs together and outside the boat we'd drown.

I had the dream just before we went to Hobart, and when I was in the blackness on the plane I remembered it.

I remembered it today while I was doing the calculations for space travel to the region of the nearest star. At present rocket speeds we'd take (I mean humans would take) something like 40,000 to 60,000 years to get to the nearest star to look for a suitable planet. What would happen in a spaceship in 60,000 years? What cruelty? What revolutions?

After they'd been gone for two or three generations parents would know no more than their children, and children – restricted to the company of the spaceship population – would know no more than their parents. Faction-fighting, murders, discrimination, destruction : the whole history of the world would begin again.

Eventually there would be people on board saying: Who are we? Where did we come from? Where are we going? What are we doing? They'd be just like humans now, who have the earth as their spaceship – they don't know who or what they are! Pictures of earth wouldn't be enough. Written descriptions wouldn't help. How would they last 100 years, or 1000!

Perhaps we're trapped here on earth, dogs and humans alike.

We'd better work on getting that rocket speed higher, I think. Much higher.

92 / I Think It's Me

Getting back to a thought I had earlier today, I've got a question. Yes, another one. And here it is: If the things that made life possible came here from outer space, things like nucleic acids, where did the nucleic acids come from, with their built-in instructions? I understand broadly what it is to be self-replicating, but how did a few chemicals get together so cleverly? Is there a lot more out there than we know?

I keep forgetting I'm just a bundle of chemicals, myself. With a little spark added – of consciousness.

So I know it's me that's thinking this.
I think it's me.

93 / God's Latest Children

The Book tells of delicate engineering that humans can do on the genetic material of living cells, inducing, say, a cell of one sort to produce a chemical it wouldn't produce in its natural, unaltered state.

Why can't we 'lesser' animals be improved by these methods, instead of humans messing about with us for trivial reasons, getting short legs or funny faces as a result of breeding and experiments?

Why don't human genetic engineers make an effort to lift other animals up to man's standards of ability? We could then claim the rights they claim. It could, it might, give humans a new incentive: to become better humans.

Mankind could still be the elder child of God: we'd be God's younger children.

94 / The Twelve Aspirations

It's hard to tell, but I think I'm about half way through writing my book. When I'm finished, I'd be happy to think that, apart from the story, the reader – or readers, if there's more than one – will find in it a lot of things about me, Archimedes. If they don't find them, then I suppose I haven't got them, but these are the things I hope they'll find:

> A knowledge of the frailties of human and dogkind
> A love of human and animal kind
> An ability to feel what others feel
> A person who tries to understand everything
> A desire for humans, dogs and even seagulls to be the best they can be
> Courage in emergencies
> Cheerfulness in adversity
> A feeling for justice, and fairness
> A love of mercy and generosity
> A person without guile
> A passion for forgiveness and tolerance

There's one more, but I don't have confidence that I've got it. I'd like to attain it.

It is:

> A sort of moral grandeur.

(I think I'll look up 'hubris' in the Book.)

In addition I'd like this book of mine to open vistas to those who read it.

If only one other dog could read! Then another and another, until there's a chain of dogs round the planet – learning, reading, thinking: lifting dogkind up to another level.

More than that, I would like to continue to live in the minds of those who read my book; and to know that those in whom I live are better persons because of the presence of my mind in theirs.

Perhaps I should have numbered this aspiration with the others, and called it the thirteenth.

95 / The Seagull like an Eagle

The Guest children were sitting on the grass, enjoying the sun. I looked around me, at the sailing boats and ferries on the water, at the gulls wheeling and flying low over the harbour waves. It was then I saw the seagull Victor told me of, the seagull like an eagle.

Way up, a lone flier glided up the Harbour into the westerly breeze, descended over Pinchgut – Fort Denison – and flew effortlessly over to the first dolphin, near Kirribilli Point. He glided down, pushed his wings against the wind and there he stood, facing the wind, his beak and legs bright red, chest out, snowy white.

It could only be the seagull like an eagle. He was so far away I had to squint a bit, and blink often, to see him clearly. If only he would come over this way!

I watched, never taking my eyes off that proud gull, till the children, roused by Donna, got to their feet and headed home, taking the eastern path, low by the water's edge, past the Domain swimming pool.

I turned and looked at the seagull like an eagle until a bend in the path took him out of my sight, and all the time he hadn't moved. I swallowed a bit, at having to leave and lose sight of the Seagle. Already I felt a great loss – but surely I'd catch sight of him again.

I didn't notice much on the way home; I was busy thinking how I'd use every chance I got to see him again. Perhaps I'd be able to talk to him.

What sorts of things would he say?

I resolved to take every opportunity for a walk.

96 / If We're ever Late

If ever we're late, Jeff and I, coming back from a walk around the Rocks, Jeff goes to the little hotel in Macquarie Place, the Customs House, and I wait while he gets a drink from the big, good-natured publican and walks over on to the grass and sits down with me there. The dark comes quickly and if it's summer you hear the soft flap of the fruit bats in the fig trees overhead as they fly erratically from tree to tree, grab a branch and flop down feet upwards, head swinging. Their cries are harsh, they're not glamour creatures at all, but I like them. Jeff lies on his back and looks up, speaking every time he sees a bat. The lights are turned on to show the undersides of the leaves; the undersides of the bats look brown and blotched.

Now and then the bats drop a fig, and you can hear it fall to the grass or on the flagstones and roll along a bit before stopping.

97 / One of the Weirdest Things

One of the weirdest things, to my mind, is the way everything in Sydney seems to empty and shut after five – and all day Sunday – when the city ought to be the brightest and most interesting place people can visit. I guess I'm a city dog.

Thursday nights they keep things open a little longer, but mostly in the better-lit parts: there's a dark spot between King Street and the Quay. I don't like it: it feels dead.

I appreciate the Botanic Gardens being shut at sunset, though. I've noticed a few human people take a walk then, just when the birds come out to talk and play round and pick up a last snack before bedtime. The parrots that no one sees by day, the wrens, the sparrows that work a full day shift, the starlings and mynahs, the white cockatoos making a great racket, the pigeons busy with heads down in the grass, the topknots, the soldier birds; all have a great time when the humans go home.

98 / The Message on the *Sirius* Anchor

One day when we were in Macquarie Place just on dusk and Jeff went into the Customs House hotel for a drink, I decided, just for the fun of it, that I'd leave a message up there on the iron anchor propped on the monument. The sign said it was the anchor from the *Sirius*, one of the first ships to bring us Europeans to this land.

Jeff brought his beer out to a seat in the open air and sat down on the side support of the old cannon. It amused him when I walked round the monument looking at it as if I was reading the inscription. I was. 'This anchor belonged to HMS *Sirius*, which convoyed the First Fleet, sailed from the Isle of Wight 13th May 1781, arrived in Botany Bay 20th January 1788, anchored in Sydney Cove Saturday 26 January 1788, and was wrecked . . .' and so on.

Over on the water bubbler with the iron lace-work surrounding it, was a verse from the Bible about the Water of Life, and the injunction, picked out in gold paint: 'Keep the pavement dry'. (Jeff doesn't know I can read, he's not as smart as Julie.) I was also gauging the height of the ledge that I'd have to reach and walk on in order to be in a position to leave my message. There was only one way up, and that was to balance on the touch-hole end of the cannon and leap from there. My attempts to climb onto the slippery steel were taken as play by Jeff, who playfully pushed me down each time I tried to get up.

I waited with the monumental patience of dog people down through the ages, until he went inside for another drink. It's hard to keep one's balance on metal that has the smoothness of age.

I tried to spring up from a standing start, clawed at the top ledge, and fell back. ('Clawed' is the wrong word, since my nails aren't made for penetration, they're far too blunt and rounded.)

I had two more tries and on the third I had two arms on the top and kept a grip with my elbows until I took another breath and swung my legs up, getting my left leg on top too. I was up. Jeff had come out by this time and looked a bit embarrassed at my drawing the attention of the people standing around in the open. It had got dark, and the harsh cries of fruit-bats overhead in the fig trees and the odd bat flying across the open spaces between the crowns of the trees, drew drinkers' eyes upwards. They pointed to figs that had been dropped by the bats.

I went over to the heavy end of the anchor and left a short message. The gathered people didn't seem to mind half as much as Jeff. I jumped down on to the cannon's barrel, skidded and slipped off and landed on my side. I think my having fallen did a great deal to help Jeff forgive me. Other dogs, when they came around that monument, would be able to catch my scent, but they wouldn't be able to tell exactly where it was; they'd be left sniffing the air in a mystified way, walking round and round the monument. The idea amused me. Even if they woke up to where it was, few would be able to follow: they don't all have my long legs.

Jeff stayed for two more drinks. In my spare time I went over in the half-lit darkness and read the obelisk.

> This obelisk
> was erected in
> Macquarie Place
> AD 1818
> to record that all the
> public roads
> leading to the interior
> of the colony
> are measured from it.
> L. Macquarie Esq
> Governor.

99 / There Was No Smell Like That

When Jeff finished his drinks we walked round to the Rocks. I ducked up the narrow laneway to the art school and raced up the flights of stairs, hoping to come across the lady lying there with no clothes on and other people looking at her and painting. I wasn't sure of my reception so when I got to the doorway I went softly. I kept my head down, hoping that since I could see less I would be less seen. (Vain hope, I know, but I still do it.)

But where I expected to nose against white, opulent flesh, I found an oldish man with the smell of rubber sandshoes on him, and sand from the beach, and a smell I've met before in caves by the ocean. Several plastic bags were stacked over against the timber wall, with his possessions in them. His raggy clothes were propped over the back of a chair. He reclined naked on the raised timber boards. He opened his mouth to smile at me. He had no teeth.

'Change!' called the drawing master. The man changed to a different position, this time with his rear towards the artists.

I left. No one spoke to me, threatened me, or criticised me; but I was disappointed. If only I could have smelled the woman who had been there before. There was no smell like that at my employers' home or anywhere else I'd been; I'd never smelled it before.

100 / Darling Likes Her Bath

It awakened in me feelings like those I had when I passed by Darling's place of work one morning and she was having her bath. The entire family was present, all admiring her, which pleased me a lot, and she stepped in the big pink plastic baby-bath into the warm water and stood sensibly while her shampoo was worked through her coat and the white foam and the bubbles ran down her flanks and she was rinsed and I could feel every touch they gave to her back and her sides, as their hands ran down her legs to her little feet, round her pretty neck and into her shapely ears. I know she likes her bath, even though her first instinct is to run when the plastic bath appears.

But there are other considerations. She enjoys the attention. Often she has the hands of the entire family over her, caressing her wet sleek body, drying her fine hair, making sure she keeps her mouth shut so she won't swallow soapy water. And when the bath is finished and she stands shining and almost dry, she waits a second and then, sure there's no more of the routine to come, off she bounds.

The time I watched, she saw me and came straight towards me. I love watching her come towards me. It's the way her feet come forward and down, and quickly and briefly touch the ground.

When it's my turn for a bath I'm not so cheerful. I feel good afterwards, but not while it's happening. Unfortunately for me, they allow Donna a free hand in the business. I know the bath is a kind of test: if you eventually submit with a fairly good grace you have shown a degree of co-operation, and they feel you have accepted a certain level of what they call 'civilization'.

Donna is full of affection. She gets herself as wet as me. But all the time she's grabbing me, hugging me, pushing me around when she means to be soaking me with soapy water, I'm off balance, out of sorts, feeling more than slightly ridiculous.

101 / I've Never Seen Myself Naked

Once Jeff came home drunk and threatened to shave me. His parents don't much like him drinking, but he does it.

I thought it was a joke, and maybe it was, but he went for the electric shaver he'd been given last birthday and brought it out to scare me. I began to take it seriously until I realized there was no electric connection outside the house. I relaxed, but – false alarm! He grabbed me to carry me inside. I'm a fair weight, and seeing he might mean business I struggled free from his one arm – the other held the shaver – and went for my life. He stood there calling me for a while, but I wouldn't come back till he went inside the house.

I've forgiven him. Took a while, though. I was really scared.

It occurs to me now that I've never seen myself naked. Without my red coat, I mean.

I hope I never do. There are some things it's better not to see. Better still, not even to think about.

102 / I Tried To Force My Throat

Once, when Julie came home from Sunday School she sat me down and gave me a lesson on God's judgment.

'God will judge what you've done, Archimedes,' she said, nodding at me for emphasis. 'And how you've done it, when you did it, and who you did it to.'

There was nothing I could say, though I wanted to. Jeff heard what she'd said, and made a point of interrupting.

'How do you know God exists?' he said, turning Julie's attention to what he thought was the fundamental question.

'I know,' she said.

What does it matter? I wanted to say. Whatever exists, there's a judgment: both God and judgment are in you ... (If only I could speak.) And if God and a continual judgment are not in you, you're only meat. Flesh and blood and bone – mobile meat.

I wanted to burst through into their world of spoken words; I concentrated, trying to form words with my lips and tongue and jaws, but no words came – I tried to force my throat and chest to master one word 'Wait'; my jaws moved sideways, but my tongue had no idea where to put itself. I felt a great pressure in my head; I felt dizzy.

I had to go away, even though Jeff had said things that had Julie in tears. I felt like a deserter in the face of the enemy.

103 / Joseph and Mary Seagull

The light, heady smell was wonderful. Julie and I had come into the Sandringham Garden part of Hyde Park, where the round sunken garden and its fountain were – with beds of flowers round in tiers like an audience – facing down to the patterned tile floor of the fountain, which was flat, and covered by a thin skin of water. There was a richness of flowers. We both went for a little run on the grass opposite the bowling club, just to work off the joyful spirits it roused in us.

The broken ring of white tea-roses round the Archibald fountain was in bloom. We inspected them, walking round, sniffing the air they lived in.

Julie wanted a rest, but not till after she'd climbed on the barrel of the cannon that faces east across College Street, just as she'd done since she was a kid. The smooth round steel was cool on the insides of her legs, her face said. She smiled and squaddled forwards up near the mouth of the cannon and gradually satisfied her desire to go back in time to when she was tiny. She got off and lay on the grass. I sat and put my head down and watched everything.

We were very still. So still, in fact, that a seagull who'd been talking to a group of eight or nine gulls, detached himself and walked quite near us. He was preoccupied and kept pacing backwards and forwards near us. I heard him muttering.

'Hey gull,' I said quietly, trying to get my voice down to the pitch of the Universal Critic's. 'Why so deep in thought?'

He stopped and looked at me. They have very narrow heads, front on. Not much space between the ears. It doesn't inspire much confidence in their cerebral output, but I suppose I shouldn't be prejudiced, or too quick to judge.

'It may interest you to know,' said the gull, 'that I regard my life here as a search for the meaning of existence.'

'Get away with you,' I said charitably. His words took me by surprise. A gull?

His voice was as low as the Critic's, but he was far more dignified, self-possessed. I regretted my hasty surprise, and made an effort to put things right.

'Strike my comment,' I said. 'It was the purest knee-jerk.'

'Perfectly understandable,' said the gull. 'You earthbound creatures are greatly affected by the fact that you can never rise above your surroundings.'

Julie had her eyes shut. I hoped she'd keep them shut until matters had gone further with this interesting gull. 'You're right,' I said.

The seagull searching for the meaning of existence was just in the mood to talk. As he told me his story I blessed the luck of the day and the circumstances that led us to meet.

'I started out, a very earnest person, and became, in my youth, a spiritual adviser to the young,' he said. 'My name is Joseph. The others call me Josephus because I have a little learning, but Joseph is my name.'

'OK, Joseph,' I said. 'I like the name. Mine's Archimedes.'

'I hope you've got the right name,' he said, looking along his nose. 'Anyway, the advising business got to me after a while, since I could see there were other more important, more urgent needs among the young of my people. Hygiene, for instance. I came to see that a lot of the ills of the seagull world were due to poor standards of hygiene. Gulls would pick up anything. They were getting the habit of taking the most miserable leavings that human people, and dog people' – he added with some emphasis – 'left lying around. Gone were the days when food was caught on the wave. Do you know that there are some of our citizens that spend their whole time in a round of going to Phillip Park for crumbs, sitting on the parapet of the New Zealand hotel killing time watching human traffic down William Street, visiting the Sydney Domain, the Botanic Gardens, the Quay, and playing in joy flights up the rising currents high above this very spot.' He cocked his head and looked up briefly. Sure enough, half a dozen young birds were lying with wings outstretched on the rising air and being carried high above the traffic to a point roughly level with the top of the law building. Then when they came to the edge of the other currents, they'd get off, wheel round and do the same thing again. Like human people coming in on the surf, then going out to come in on the same feeling again.

'Trouble is, some of those young ones have never been in the water except for urgent hygiene, and cooling in hot weather.' He regarded me with a strong look in his eyes. 'Would you credit that?' he said scornfully.

'Seems rather limited to me,' I admitted. 'I'd be in the water all the time if I was a gull.'

'Limited, yes,' he said. 'And do you know that the ones who still stick to the old ways, the gulls who get their living off the waves –they have no sickness, no problems with lice, no digestive upsets. I became a hygiene consultant. To spread the message of healthy living among all who would receive it. I became a youth and community officer responsible to the co-ordinating committee of the seagull standards organization. We're gulls, let us be the best gulls we can be: but you have no idea how that message fails to get a response from lots of the young. They neglect the old standards, fall sick, eat scraps instead of foraging for healthy seafood; and now I've come to the point where I believe that only a rescue operation can be any use. So now you see me: Joseph, the gull's friend, organizer, secretary, chief operative and dogsbody – no offence – to our young. It's heartbreaking trying to get some of the older members of our population to see that we have no future if the young fall by the wayside. Trying to get them to shell out a little of their surplus food to help the next generation. More and more of the young are on the streets, on the grass, begging. The old retire to public parks. That's understandable, but the young! I go to sleep sad every night when I remember how many are sleeping rough, washing only when it rains, not getting their protein, not keeping themselves smart, losing their self-respect.'

I'll swear there was a tear in his eye.

'It's so hard getting help, that we've decided, my wife Mary and I, to start a family and train our chicks to help others, to think first of others, to teach others to live together with mutual respect and love. As a matter of fact, she's got an egg on the way, due on the twenty-fifth. I wasn't expecting one so soon, but we'll be young parents and should have quite a brood before we're finished.'

I thought a while before saying anything. Joseph impressed me with his desire to serve others. I'd never have expected it from watching the way most gulls go on.

'It does you great credit,' I said. 'To want to help all and sundry.'

'Every gull is my neighbour,' Joseph said firmly. 'That's what I'll teach my chicks. All one family under one sky.' He suddenly took three hops backwards: Julie was stirring, her huge leg swung over without warning. Joseph had sensed the movement coming.

'I'm glad I met you,' I said to him. He'd have to go when Julie woke.

'Me too,' said Joseph. 'Look me up when you're here next.'

'With pleasure,' I said. 'Give my regards to your wife.'

'I will. Mary will be pleased there are dog people a gull can talk to.'

Julie sat up. Joseph took off. His trajectory was low, he landed over near the Archibald fountain. Birds have the best short cuts. Immediately he started in to talk to a group scrabbling for the crumbs of a pie that had spilled from a paper bag. He didn't touch any himself. He knew what he was, and who he was. I wondered what he and his wife would call their firstborn.

104 / Dogenes, the Philosopher Dog

I'd gone for a walk down on the flat, round the wharves, and went back up the slope of Dowling Street. When I got to the foot of the McElhone Steps I decided I'd climb up to Victoria Street. On the top landing I looked at something I'd noticed many times. It was a concrete platform on the other side of the barred iron fence. The platform supported an iron mast, painted silver.

On the far side of the platform was a narrowing ledge of rock, with some dry grass and weeds growing, and something else. There was a track, and along where the ledge merged into the rockface over a drop of about fifteen metres, an old partly dismantled wooden barrel. It had two round ends still, but not all of the bowed timbers, that once were gripped by hoop-iron to keep the complete barrel together. The missing slats made a doorway and a window: I went along there out of curiosity and I met the occupant of the barrel, a middle-aged dalmation.

He hadn't seen me when I saw him sitting in there, thinking, just like Diogenes in his barrel. I decided to call him Dogenes, after great

Diogenes. He hates it.

'Hi there,' I said. He didn't look at me.

'Eh? ... Oh. Yes. Well, er ... What did you say?'

'I said hello. I'm Happy.'

'There's not enough like you.'

'My name is Happy.'

'Is it?' he said. 'How can you tell?'

'This is your home?' I asked, just to get off the subject. I'm glad I didn't say Archimedes.

'Yes. But any other place would do as well. To me, home is a place to think.'

'What are you thinking today?'

'Where are all the past years gone.'

That stopped me. But only for a second or two. Here was a dog I could talk to. Perhaps if I mentioned Shakespeare *he* wouldn't think I was talking about a fish, like the other dogs round my way.

'The past years haven't gone anywhere. They're not things that can go.'

'What is a thing?' he said, gazing out over Woolloomooloo Bay. He rested his chin on the topmost stave of the side of the barrel, and closed his eyes. There was some sleepy dust in the corner of his left eye. Did he want me to answer? Or did he assume I couldn't?

'A thing is an illusion,' I remarked sturdily.

He came awake, his eyes opened, he regarded me gravely.

'Aha,' he said in a significant tone. The way he did this made me feel I was about to blush in embarrassment. But that's silly. (Just the same, my cheeks felt warmer than usual.) He was silent, looking at me. I felt compelled to go on.

'I mean, in the sense that physics describes atomic structure.'

He said nothing.

'The sub-atomic particles – or whatever they are – that spin in orbits round their nucleus, are called – at this moment – in the present state of the theory, you understand' – he nodded – 'protons, electrons, neutrons, positrons, and so on. At the very basis of matter there is a complicated spinning, orbiting, dancing movement. Since these things can be taken apart – and when they are, the electrons and so on still exist and go to make other things – then their present form can be regarded as temporary, and therefore an illusion in the sense that they once weren't; then became; then will disappear and be no more.'

Dogenes said nothing for a long while.

Then he said slowly, 'Do your employers' – he glanced at my collar and the registration tag – 'talk a lot about these things?'

'No.'

'Some?'

'The son is in his last high-school year. He mentions a little about physics, but he doesn't know much about it, just odd details.'

'Are you, or have you ever been, employed by physicists?'

'No.'

'Have you attended lectures, listened to cassettes, radio lectures, on the subject?'

'No.'

He looked away, rested his chin again on the barrel stave and closed his eyes. He stayed like that for long minutes.

At last he jumped up, opened his eyes, and stood nose to nose with me, all in the one movement.

'You can read!' he shouted. 'Read! You can read!' And stood looking at my eyes, shaking with excitement.

'Tell me! You can, can't you? You can read! Tell me! Admit it!'

It was my turn to clam up for a second or two. Even that was too short a time for Dogenes. He poked me with a paw, agitatedly, trying to pry loose the admission he craved to hear. Generous soul.

'Yes. I taught myself to read. When I'd done that, I found the Book.' And I told him about the Book.

He stared at my eyes for another long time ....

....

(I can't honestly say I knew what he was thinking.)

He began to try to speak. I didn't interrupt his efforts, but waited modestly until he was able to form the words. At last he managed it.

'How? How did you do it?'

'I began with a direct experience of the educative power of advertising; from there I moved to the fourth estate and its daily battle to educate the various publics.' I was really showing off.

'But how did you learn the first bit? How did you match those marks on the paper with the sound they have in the mouth, and the meaning in the mind?'

'I don't know.'

'You don't know? Rubbish! How can you learn, then know, without knowing how you do it?'

'I don't know. But I do: I *do* learn, I *do* know (I think), but I haven't the faintest idea how I do it. There's a step somewhere in this that I can take in my stride, that others can't, but I don't know which step it is. I'd like to work it out, but it's in the past now, and I don't know where to start.'

'Oh . . .' He thought about it, than asked with a humility that made me feel awkward. 'How did you come to read about your – physics?'

'I found the Book. I took it home. I read it. The *Book of Knowledge*'.

'Could you teach me?' His voice had a different note in it. I looked at him, he had tears in his eyes. How could I find time for teaching? I was so busy learning.

'I could try. Perhaps,' I said.

'Now?'

'I'm expected to be home soon.'

'Tomorrow?'

'I'll see. In the meantime get hold of a page of newspaper and try to decipher it. Read the pictures, then try to decode the words. If possible look over a human's shoulder, specially if there's talk about what's in the paper.'

'I can't. I have no registration. I'm on the run. I have to lie low and only go out for food.'

'Listen, I have to go now.' I took a quick look to see where the sun was. 'Tell me, have you heard of Shakespeare?'

'The Hamlet and Lear Shakespeare?'

'That's all I wanted to know. Get some newspaper out of one of the bins in Victoria Street and start trying to decode it. I'll be back when I can.'

I left, and went home. On the way I thought I shouldn't have tried to be clever about *things* – all the temporary objects made from the particles known to physics. *Things* are all we have.

105 / The Seagle

Each time I'd been out I looked as high and as far as I could, to catch a sight of the seagull like an eagle, but not once had I been lucky.

We were taking the long way home.

Everyone stopped at the north-west corner of the Opera House forecourt, where there's a small flight of steps down into the water. I put my arms up on the bronze rail and looked across the water, searching the air and the waves for the seagull that's like an eagle.

A movement below caught my eye. I looked down, and there he was, on the bottom step. At last I was somewhere near him! What would I say? What questions would I ask?

I spoke to him, but he made no answer, merely looked at me. I said a few things, about flying, about being a gull, but he wouldn't say a single thing. He didn't open his mouth.

It was just as I expected. His differences from other seagulls were so marked; how different he must have felt from a dog. How far removed. He turned away from me.

What a fine individual he was! I liked him now, where before I'd just admired him. How strong he looked! As I left, dragged behind the Guest children, I looked back a number of times. He was no gull, if the rest were gulls. He *was* like an eagle, compared to them. A seagull turned eagle – a seagle.

I looked back again. My seagle had taken off into the wind, and as I watched, he held his wings outstretched and rode up and up, taking the wind head-on. What a great flyer he was. Up and up, till at last he banked and turned off down the Harbour towards the Heads.

I sighed a lot on the way home. Julie noticed, but how could I tell her about the seagle?

106 / The World as Food

Yesterday settling down after my dinner, I read a chapter of the Book, then I lay down to think about the future.

What about the next 4000 million years? Would humans make a leap up to a more efficient sort of human, a type that can do and understand more? Would dogs be able gradually to do some of the things naturally that humans do now?

In the chapter I'd just read I learned that some bacteria can live in boiling geysers, and some in frozen Antarctica; some even without oxygen. It would be hard for man's wars to kill such creatures.

But how could the beginnings of the whole thing be random? I didn't understand. I'd need to read that part several times.

Perhaps if you put the whole universe into a plastic bag you'd find that life, here and there, is the usual thing. I guess you'd need to look hard.

If only the Book could show how to change rocks and sand, trees and every sort of plant into food for us . . . I've hunted through it many times, but I can't find anything on it. Surely, if we're made from the earth's elements, we can convert the earth to food for us. Either by changing the structures of the rocks and trees to suit our digestive abilities, or by changing ourselves genetically to suit the trees, rocks and sand.

107 / Next Time I Saw Dogenes

He was silent and immobile as before. I was breathing deeply after bounding up the McElhone stairs. I started in straightaway.

'Would you, Dogenes, call yours a philosophical temperament?'

'Philosophical mind,' he amended. 'And don't call me that name – I'm not happy being named after an ancient Greek.'

'I didn't know you'd be touchy.'

'It's not up to *you* to name *me*!'

I didn't agree. But I could see his side of it.

'I have a lot of questions on my mind,' I said.

He settled down into an even more comfortable position. He rested his eyes for a few seconds, opened them, gave a huge yawn, and settled his head on his dogpaws. (Why do I think of his as paws and mine as arms?)

'Let's hear 'em,' he said.

They're in the next chapter.

108 / A Chapter of Questions

'How is it I can think words?

'What do I think with? A mind, but what's that?

'Do I think? Or do I just rehearse words and assemble words I've heard? How is it I remember words I've heard?

'Where do I keep them?'

'How is it I can think in pictures? How do I see the picture in my head? What's there? Is it empty? Does it have a wall for the pictures to go on?'

'How can I see? Wouldn't it be black inside my head?

'Does my head light up inside, when I see things on a sunny day? It certainly seems as if the inside of my head is as light as what I see out there, but it can't be, it's all locked in, it must be black in there, black as pitch. It's only my eyes that are out in the light.'

'What's inside me, that keeps me going? A motor? What's inside me that asks these questions?'

'When I dream, and wake, knowing I've dreamed, how do I know I'm awake?'

'What is actually here? Do we know? Or are we part of it, so *much* part of it that we can never step back to see ourselves in it, and therefore just as we are?'

'The Book says all things are made of matter, but are they? Is a thought made of matter? What is matter? Is it me? Is it different from me? Or am I just part of matter? Is matter the boss of everything? Is mind matter?'

'Is the universe all one thing? Living, breathing, expanding, contracting like a living person? Expanding like a piece of life; a child, say? The sperm, the egg, the foetus, the baby, child, youth, adult, aged and shrunken, corpse, bones, dust of bones, nothing – is this all one thing? Is it all life?'

'Why do we sometimes try to be good? What's good? Something we all agree is good? If it's better than being bad, why is it? If you had only a day to live, why be good? Yet I hope I would.'

'All the books, mathematics, science, laws, music, art; are these products of humans' love of order? Did humans acquire a taste for them once they invented language, and found there was order to be had with language as a tool? Do they think that by finding out things, setting down everything clearly in ranks and rows and files, that they'll tame the chaos of the world, and finally, somehow, understand it?'

'Then again, how can they bear to live, how can they, and we, continue to live, if there are questions with no answers? Perhaps that's the answer: life ignores questions. Just goes on and on, expanding and contracting, breathing in and out: food in, processed food out; water in, water out.'

'Perhaps the best we can do is to manage to live with uncertainty, though without hesitation. (I'd rather be uncertain all my life than rely on a fairy tale.) And never despair: despair is obscene.'

I stopped, and Dogenes said nothing. He said nothing for so long that I began to talk again. Somehow, having met a dog I could talk to, I was impatient with silence.

'If you ask me there are six senses, not the five they usually tell you. Even the Book lists only five: Taste, Touch, Smell, Sound, Sight. What about Thought? *I* feel what I think, don't you? As a matter of fact, most of the time I think, I seem to feel myself thinking with my whole body.

'Think about it, and see what you feel. Even if you don't agree, I think you'll feel there's some merit in it and the Book hasn't had the last word on thinking, or on the other five senses.'

Still he didn't say a word. I assumed he was listening, since he hadn't moved. He gazed out over Woolloomooloo Bay towards the city skyline, so dramatic yet so strangely domestic. I went on, speaking my thoughts.

'Things can exist in language alone, without having a further existence, a more touchable one. What does it mean not-to-be? Is there some *thing* that there isn't? Of course there is: a word. To-be is merely a thing made sometime, somewhere, as an afterthought, to show we're capable of making a word to explain a part of our consciousness. Turning the word upside down, or putting a negative sign to it, may be a good invention, like a new mathematics, but it's still an invented thing: it doesn't correspond necessarily to any reality, unless by chance we find one to fit. In which case the original bad habit is furthered, and we will continue to expect that every time we make a word to fit a 'reality' we perceive, there will be a corresponding anti-word to fit its 'opposite', or negation.'

I tailed off into a long silence.

109 / A Philosopher Without Answers

In the last chapter I came to the end of my questions for one day.

I settled into a listening position, and waited. Dogenes said nothing.

I waited some more. I put my head up, scratched my chin, looked down at him again. He was hardly breathing, and didn't move at all. Down near the wharves massive trucks rolled heavily on the bitumen. A cargo ship from Japan was being pulled backwards away from its berth by three tug boats, ready for sailing out of the Heads to another destination. The city skyline with its tall and graceful buildings gave no hint, from outside, of the activity inside them.

I suppose my being a dog and an employee, a city dog, a speculative dog, has done a lot to make me the way I am. But, just the same, the way I am has done a lot to make me enjoy being speculative and to love the city I live in.

I looked at my friend. I considered calling him Dogenes, but decided against it. Instead, I gingerly moved my right arm over towards him and touched his shoulder. He opened his eyes.

'Well,' I said. 'They're my questions. Where are the answers?'

'I don't have the answers.'

'How can you call yourself a philosopher if you have no answers?'

'I'm a philosopher-without-answers. All I have are questions. Just like you. My object is to increase the number of questions. If I do that I'll consider my time has been well spent.'

110 / I'm Having My Feet Done Today

The sun is coming up over the roofs and shines on the bark of my friend Jack Jacaranda, above me. I'm having my feet done today. I heard them arranging it last night when they brought out my dinner – my daily stipend for duty done and standard devotion.

Now I've had my breakfast, read two chapters of the Book, and Jeff, Julie, Donna and I are on our way to the man who does my nails. We have to cross Hyde Park, and I'm in luck. There's the Shakespearian duck – a Falstaff of a fellow who struts and swaggers fatly when he gets out of the water. He is brown and has a brilliant green collar. I like the way he struts. Over the other side of the Pool of Remembrance are two men plotting the downfall of the Shakespearian duck; if they have their way and lay a trap for him with that string they're holding, they'll get one end round his feet and pull him through the water to them. After that, one quick stretch and he's meat. Poor table birds. Pain and cruelty is their world.

In the sun on the eastern side of the pool is a great convocation of gulls. They carpet a special patch of green grass that's always greener than the rest. When they split up into groups and take off for other parts of the park, or for the gardens down by the sea wall, or the Quay, or Lady Macquarie's Point, the Domain or the smaller parks, they let their baser natures have free rein and are beasts to each other, taking their friends' food, scaring off all gulls willing to allow themselves to be scared off, working themselves into ecstasies of rage.

But always the thought is at the back of my mind: they can fly, swoop, soar, and descend vertically. (Into a stiff breeze they can keep their heads up, work their wings, and with a little movement side to side, come down on a spot directly beneath them.) I'll never outgrow my admiration for their cleverness in the air.

111 / Feelings That Make Me Think I Could Do Anything

I like having my feet done. The vet asks me to jump up on a table and I have to lie on my side while his shining steel clippers take my nails down to a comfortable length. I like them short: long is fine for grass, but most of the time I'm on the black carpet of bitumen humans like; and for that, short is best.

Humans are lucky. They can't fly in the way seagulls can; but they fly after a fashion in their clumsy air buses that ferry them from one city to another, travelling mostly straight. They're lucky in another way, too: they have music. I heard Jeff one day telling his parents of things he'd learned at school, things about music being a treasured part of life in ages gone by. I listened as intently as I could, for two reasons: one, that I listen to as much music as I can, to try to find out from it why it fascinates me; and two, because in dog culture the past ages are only sketchily drawn and remembered in the form of myth. As for instance, in the story of the Huge and Terrible Beasts, and the Dinosaur Dog.

So humans have music and they can fly, or nearly fly. I envy them. In general I look up to human people simply because they're higher off the ground, and in my cynical moments I tell myself that's the only reason; but when I'm more detached and taking a fairer view, there are quite a few ways in which I admire them. Admire's not too strong a word. But if only I had access to more of the things they've treasured up in books. Particularly things of the past. Humans ought to talk to me more. I wish I knew humans who'd talk to me over the whole range of subjects they think of. The Book has only so much in it: there are many more books I've never seen.

Julie could come out each night after tea and read to me from her books. I've heard her recite to her mother and father at the table but I've had to strain to hear the words. When the radio's left on in the day time I sometimes hear things about the rest of the world that hold my

160

interest in a way few other things do, except the Book, and talk of the past life of the earth. At such times I sit or lie motionless, drinking in every word; wanting the words never to stop.

But they do. And I have to be satisfied with what I get. Well, I'm not.

Then music comes from the house and I float away on dreams that are sometimes full of colours and warm smells and feelings that make me think I could do anything: that nothing is beyond me, no task too hard.

Then the ordinary routines of the day take over, and it seems to me then that the wonders of the past and the wonders of the future are separated by the sleep of the present, and I begin to doubt that I'll ever achieve anything. I say to myself: buck up! Let's join past and future with our very best efforts in the present.

The music is on continuously in the vet's surgery and he has finished my nails. I anticipate the word, get to my feet and jump to the floor. The man gives me a pat, more to congratulate himself on his way with dog people, than me on my manners, intelligence and self-restraint.

112 / The Manly Ferry

This is also our day for a ferry-ride. We go from the vet's place back to Hyde Park, and begin to walk north on the wide path right through the middle of it. High fig trees are on either side, and close over our heads, leaving only a few patches of sun. It's cool, under the trees. We stop at Park Street, cross with the lights and head for the Archibald fountain. It is spraying out its water in the shape of a fan as we approach, coming up behind Apollo, whose body is gleaming wet. People are taking photographs of each other with the wet figures as a background. Women sit with pink-cheeked babies on the clean grass. Men lie full stretch, asleep in their socks. Pretty women walk smartly

161

to the shops, or away towards the cathedral and the car park. Jeff looks everywhere for the little black-suited man with the white hard-hat who walks bent over his wheeled trolley that holds all his wordly possessions. He says that last time he saw the man was two years before; and then the trolley's rubber tyres had gone, leaving it to run on steel rims. But today he can't see the little old man anywhere. He *does* find the big man with the grey suit and Finnish face who walks the city and inhabits the park, winter and summer, fully-dressed except for bare feet. Huge toenails grow from his swollen brown feet, and bend over to the ground; some overlap, making walking painful. No one has ever heard him speak.

Donna listens to Jeff, Julie watches Donna's face. Jeff stands at his tallest, looking around for more things to interest his sisters. People from the country hold their heads back to look up at the tall buildings that stand clean and bright in the sun. The Sydney Tower gleams, standing proudly above Centrepoint, its gold splendid against the blue sky, contrasting with the coloured granite, the stone, the concrete of smaller buildings.

We cross to the beginning of Macquarie Street and Jeff points out the cleaned ancient bricks of the early barracks, the old Mint building, and the statues of the people of Sydney, the line of statues that goes down to the Opera House. At the old Hospital, site of the first tent hospital in the early days, Donna is lifted up to touch the pig on its snout, where the yellow brass shows through, and innocently on the other place people touch for luck in getting babies.

Jeff and Julie don't explain this to Donna.

We go down the hill, accompanied by the line of statues. Today my favourite is the old derelict, who stands taller above other citizens in unmoving effigy than ever he did in life. A seagull has landed on his head and added to his crown of white and grey. The sculptor made him with his trouser buttons coming open and the buttons of his long coat in the wrong button holes so the coat is out of line. He carries in his left hand a bag that's coming to pieces and getting ready to spill out the bottle it tries to hold, and in his right he clutches a sherry bottle's neck as if he thinks it might escape, but it's he that can't escape the clutches of the bottle, not the other way round. In his partly open mouth is a loosely rolled cigarette, with a few centimetres of ash and only a centimetre to go before it burns his lips. I've known that statue since I came here to Sydney, and the ash has never fallen yet. Little children have it pointed out to them, some of the countless children who come here in the holidays from other parts of Australia, just to see Sydney and feel the life of it around them.

Donna likes most the statue of the barrister with a bundle of legal papers under his arm, one hand steadying his wig as he hurries along to court, his gown flying behind him. She finds the 'dress' on the man funny, and wonders about his outstretched front leg, which has no support. She wants to wait and see if he'll fall.

On the ferry, we climb to the top deck. We sit in the open and up the back because there I can sit on a seat out of sight of the driver. We all love the open air, and the deep satisfying smell of the salt seawater.

At Manly Beach the children and Jeff went into the water. I minded their things up on the promenade. Just down a metre or two from where I was lying, seagulls in a patch of sand were holding a court. The seagull magistrate had a malefactor before him, a seagull starting-price bookmaker who had been caught in a police gull raid, betting on the surf races. Even at this stage, the criminal gull sneaked looks at the humans breasting the waves, estimating odds. On the outskirts of the court, which had no other premises than the patch of sand the magistrate chose, stood a hefty gull. I heard some guarded comments from gull onlookers about 'Mr Big', as they looked across at him. From the little they said I gathered he was something of a standover gull, who made life unpleasant for those who went against his wishes. The court broke up, police gulls took away the offender, and Mr Big departed with gravity. The gulls that remained got into a heated conversation about the criminal element. Some were for relentless prosecution of all offences against existing laws; others for changes in laws to bring them into line with what gulls wanted for their society; and still others were more interested in the compact between police gulls and the criminal element. They hold strongly to the opinion that the criminal gulls guaranteed not to bring their in-house quarrels and disciplinary measures out into the street, not to involve the general public of gulls in their activities, as long as police gulls turned a blind eye to some of their basic activities that they felt necessary to their economic survival.

113 / The Sermon on the Beach

A little further along the sand was a religious service for young seagulls. I heard the speaker say, 'This is about survival. To survive the message is: fit in! If humans push this way, go round the other way. If they take your special spot for sitting or foraging or just thinking: find another. Don't sweat about it, don't fume and get excited: be calm, ride with the punches, go with the push. Blessed are those that fit in.'

The young gulls faced the speaker, none made any comment. I found it hard to tell if they'd heard, or, if they'd heard, whether they'd taken any notice, but I suppose I was looking on their faces for signs that I'm used to on dog faces, signs of recognition and attention that are too subtle for human people to catch, even if they took the time to look. 'Blessed are those who stop fights and squabbles; blessed are those who don't get off their bikes easily but keep cool; blessed are those that are not all the time conniving and working the percentages just to get crumbs, for they shall hold their heads high.'

114 / The Eleven Commandments

Along the beach a short way a parsonical gull was looking benevolently at a small group of young gulls, and going through the Seagull Commandments with them.

'You shall not bow down to humankind or serve them.

'You shall not prefer any form of life above another and that goes for seagulls too.

'Remember that every day is holy, there is no difference between days.

'You shall not lay up any food for tomorrow: there will always be food tomorrow.

'Honour all gulls, but not above other forms of life.

'You are not to kill except for food.

'If you are uncomfortable, lash out and get comfortable. If you can't live without something, take it.

'But you are not to try things that are impossible. Never steal unless you are stronger than the one you steal from; better still, never steal at all.

'You are not to covet anything you aren't strong enough or quick enough to take, for this leads to frustration.

'You are not to tell lies about other gulls unless the lies are true.

'Protect your back at all times. If something doesn't fit your ideas and doesn't fit them for a long time – change the rules, the ideas, the lot. What is, is.

'I have said you shall not bow down to humankind. I say it again: honour all life but bow down to nothing.

'Observe these ways and you needn't fear when you come before the Big Beak.'

115 / I Love Ferry Rides

I'm not allowed to go swimming in the same water as humans. How-ever, they swim in water that's tainted by their own excreta. Sewer outfall pipes are a common sight on beaches.

We walked back along the Corso, towards the ferry wharf. A sturdy young gull strode along talking to himself. I was near enough to hear him say something about Algull, IBM and Cobol. He was in com-puters, obviously.

I love ferry rides. I sit and look down at the swirl of water away from the bow and watch it boil and fizz and all the eddies tumbling over one another. People enjoying the Opera House – just being near it and round it – watched us in the ferry, and we watched them. Some waved. Julie lifted my right arm and waved back at them with it. I didn't mind.

In a shop window at the Quay was the skeleton of a sea crab, its shell a spotted green, its underparts shading to bone-white. When my time comes I hope I go out better than that. I mean I'd hate to be a crab, caught for food, and have my insides eaten and my shell displayed in a window. They didn't even have a card with the crab's name written on it.

We climbed the steps up to the Gardens and walked by the Gover-nor's residence, then over the rise down into the hollow where the stream flows by the kiosk and restaurant. We stopped for ice-creams. I always refuse to have a lick of their ice-creamy paper when they finish. If they'd just buy me a whole one! They know I have no pockets for money. It's an awful temptation to have just one lick, but I won't.

We came down the steep grass behind the Art Gallery near the pubs in the quiet streets of Woolloomooloo and crossed Lincoln Cre-sent near Plunkett Street School. I love that name! I caught sight of

Rita there. Rita's part airedale, part cocker; she has the athletic flair of the one and the cheerfulness of the other. She's about twenty-four moons old, and has an appetite, that's never satisfied, for romance and making love. She hungers to be wildly popular, and she is. She has so many lovers, though, that no one loves her. And always at the tail of any visit she makes, after the wild caperings and the unstinted affection poured out on all and sundry, there's a little sadness. Something's incomplete, something's missing; and she doesn't know what it is.

116 / The Island Where Gulls Go To Sleep

Gulls appear to have no masters, but I think there's a network among them, if not of control, then of some sort of authority. They appear to do no work, but I don't know about that either. They appear pretty stupid and useless. Maybe they're not. If it's a matter of what 'seems', then they're selfish, bullying individuals. I wish I knew more about them. If I could talk to enough of them to give myself a fair chance of understanding them – if I could mentally tune in to them and know more of what they say to each other . . .

I suppose that you could say I'm haunted by gulls, how they look and what they do, the way gulls are haunted by humans: the human presence everywhere; their buildings; the fact they're likely suddenly to appear anywhere. Sometimes, in a place where there was a clear patch of earth for gulls to alight or walk on, suddenly there are chattering jackhammers and roaring holes in the ground; then buildings growing up out of rock, high into the air.

To gulls, man must seem a tyrant, since gulls have to adjust their actions to what man builds; and where he chooses to go, they must keep out of the way. Whereas to dogs, man is manageable. Not always and never completely, but within certain limits a good dog, a smart dog, can so arrange things, tidy up the appearance of situations, that man can be brought to heel, to good sense and a regular way of living.

I used to wonder if gulls take any shelter at all, during the night. I thought perhaps they went in under the roofs of caves, or down under wharves. But wharves would be dangerous, because large rats come out at night near the water-line, all round the harbour, in every bay and inlet.

Did they get into trees? I always wished there was someone I could ask.

Perhaps they sat out on waves, but no, that wouldn't do. There'd be far more Hoppys and Stumpies if they did that, and one-legged gulls.

Then last summer the whole family went on a ferry and we passed the offshore Isle of Gulls where the gulls go to sleep. It was early in the season and Mr Guest pointed out some birds still nesting. It was no wonder I'd never seen them sitting in trees around the Gardens or at night on rocks near Mrs Macquarie's Point. They had a whole island.

117 / Conversation with Dogenes

The day was hot. We'd attempted a reading lesson together, but Dogenes couldn't get even the simplest idea of matching the letters to sounds. Perhaps his isolation from human company has too severely limited his experience and powers.

'You say the Book says that right down to the smallest bits all this' – he gestured round at the silver-painted steel mast near his barrel, the dry clumps of grass, the rock ledge, the sand, the brick wall at our backs – 'is made of, that the bits are particles?'

'That's what it says, but they admit that the sub-atomic particles may not be the last word, and I think they'd have to admit it.'

'You mean the ultimate particle must itself be made of something?'

'Yes, I do.'

'These particles – I prefer bits – these bits; can they feel or think or want?' said Dogenes.

'I don't know.'

'Can they be dissatisfied?'

What an unusual question.

'What's in your mind?' I asked.

'How do they get close to each other and bind on? How do they push other things away?'

'It's to do with the electric charge they have.'

'And we're built up of these strange spinning things binding tightly together, and when we die the protons, electrons, neutrons, and so forth, they go to form other things, and they live for thirty million years, or for ever?

'Nothing can live forever, I think, except the space in which everything exists. But yes, we live a short time and the bits we're made of live for an enormous length of time ... I wonder if getting old and dying has anything to do with some of the bits being old, too, and decaying at the end of their life-span.'

He said nothing, and I had nothing to add. We sat silent. Then he spoke again.

'So all these spinning bits bound together in all sorts of combinations make up our bodies. OK. But where in all that cake-mixture is the thing that makes us move and talk and think?'

'Well, the Book doesn't say. Doesn't even guess. But my guess is that the life in us, is just the sum of all the natural functions of all the little bits. Attractions, repellings, hurtings, learnings, experiences, memories, dangers, chemical pushings and clingings, electrical yesses and nos; a whole intensely complicated world of friends and enemies, pleasant feelings and unpleasant, of hungers and fullness.

'I think that the cross-linkings and wonderful complexity of each person-world multiply greatly the effects and abilities of all the little functions – digestive and oxidation, energizing and building, chemical and electrical – so that the most complicated are the cleverest.

'But we're still transient beings. Not-here; then here; then not-here again. And the bits live on. Those bits were called in and used for a time, then go on to form other things.'

'Yes, that's the thing! Life happens, bits coalesce, consciousness arises. At the level of the smallest, bits draw together. Drawing together is the thing.'

169

'I love the world,' I said. 'But that's no wonder: I'm made of it, made with its parts that are available here: all the calcium, phosphorous, hydrogen, oxygen, nitrogen, iron, zinc, copper and the rest of the trace elements we need to keep the chemical balance of our blood, bones, brain, nerves.'

'And at the same time life is so close to death,' said Dogenes.

'Yes. So close.'

'And life loves us,' he added.

'Life loves life,' I said.

'Love and life are drawing together, aren't they?'

'Yes, and a pushing away of what we don't like, or what's danger-ous.'

'Or foreign.'

'Sometimes. Not always. Foreign things *can* be safe.'

'Do you think,' he asked, 'that life will go on forever?'

'Once it arose, you mean?'

'Yes.'

'I think so. I think life, or the things that push for life, are stronger than the things that make for death and the end of life. I don't know why I say that, it's a feeling in me. But I think questions will go on forever, my friend. In the beginning was the word.'

Dogenes kept silent for a while, then asked if we might get on with the reading lesson.

'Do you think I'll ever get the hang of it?' he asked anxiously.

'It'll come to you suddenly, one day,' I assured him. We settled down to a page of newspaper I'd brought.

He wasn't making much progress, though. When we'd done, he got back to talking. He loved to talk.

'If we weren't; then are; then will disappear; we're like bubbles of water, that form, then unform. Where's the bubble then?'

'Out of existence, with the water still there,' I answered.

'Yes. And our length of life makes us merely longer-living than bubbles.'

'Or ants, or flies, or seagulls,' I said.

'What's it all for?'

'That's easy! It's for *it*. The purpose is to be *it*. The purpose of anything is to be itself. Anything that has it in it to live, may live on, if it can.'

He was still chewing it over when I left. At the bottom of McElhone steps I looked up and there he sat, looking out over the bay to the

Botanic Gardens and the city buildings and towers floating above the green of grass and trees, like a sort of dream.

I went home through the streets, strangely grateful for the ordinariness of Woolloomooloo, yet not entirely a part of it, for into my head had come the idea to write a history of the world. *A Dog's History of the World*.

118 / He's Not So Smart

Next time I saw him, Dogenes was reluctant to do his reading lesson and I thought, after half an hour, that I'd give it a miss. He wanted to learn, but just couldn't get the idea that a T or an R remained T or R wherever they appeared; nor the idea that there's a sound linked to each letter. This last idea was the main obstacle.

The word DOG he seemed to show great interest in, but next time he saw it, in different word-surroundings and a different size, he didn't see why it should still mean the same. Perhaps his weakness was that he couldn't understand that something composed of several shapes on a flat piece of paper could *mean* anything, or that there was any obligation on anyone to make a sound in response to the sight of marks made on a surface.

I know he's a thinker, and has a philosophical cast of mind, in the old sense, but I think perhaps he's not all that smart.

I stayed to talk. Perhaps plenty of talking could help him.

119 / Not Entirely Anything

'What about *God?*' said Dogenes.

'What *about* God?'

'Would it be reasonable to say that people wouldn't seek God if there was no God there?'

'No. I don't think so.'

'I didn't suppose you would. Where do ideas of God come from?'

'From here,' I said, tapping my brain case. 'The brain, where the creative imagination lives; where heaven and hell, inventions, troubles and blessings start.'

'Why do they need God and religion to prop up their moral system?'

'I don't know. But if they need a God, they need a God. Some don't see the need. But moral obligations – they can't be escaped. We can't *not* help the starving, or the injured, whether we think we're answerable to God or society at large.'

'I suppose you're an agnostic dog?' he said.

'Not entirely. I think "not entirely" describes me – not entirely anything.'

120 / Living in the City

What I miss most, living in the city, is not having lots of company. Our family was so nice and big! There were always voices. Employment isolates you, locks you up in a function, and there you stay. I'm married to my job. The fun and frolics of childhood are far behind me, and I'll never again see the family I loved.

At least they like me here at the Guest's place. I hope I have a natural old age and a slow sinking to death.

I'm luckier than the unemployed, who get taken away to a transit camp for fourteen days and if unsold – well, I said it before. Even pigeons and human derelicts, both sorts in shabby clothes, both scavenging, both unemployed – even they aren't treated like dogs.

The light goes quickly, at sunset. It doesn't muck about. There's a sudden gentling of the light, then the shutters descend, quick as water gurgling down a pipe, leaving nothing. Yet it's so much a place of light that the dark always seems strange, uneasy, as if it doesn't belong and isn't convincing.

A storm was coming up this afternoon from the west, like a strange beast whose shape no one had seen before. Come to think of it, it's possible that every cloud-pattern is never exactly repeated. I might have seen a sky no one else has seen in all the history of clouds. Hey, there's an idea! *A History of Clouds*.

The storm didn't arrive. Like so many other things here, it seemed to be happening, but swung away to the north, and didn't happen at all, leaving a gap where it should have been.

Living in the city you have the feeling, night and day, that there are so many people out there beyond the city. Why, then, do the suburbs seem empty? Why does it take so long to get out there, and to get away, back to the safety of the city?

173

(Suburban Sydney is a vast carpet spread out over a stone foundation. I have the feeling, as night pushes the light callously out of the way to the west, that a sufficiently strong arm could lift the edge of that carpet, roll up the suburbs, and tip them all into the Pacific.)

Out there, past the suburbs, the trees are aloof, the hot distances indifferent. Anything may come or go; anything may be done: the land won't change. Peoples may arrive, survive, disappear: the land itself doesn't care. It's supremely indifferent to life, death, existence itself. Whoever comes here may live here, if they can. If they do and can; or can't; or don't come – it's all the same to Australia.

So often it seems the country has been asleep for 50,000 years and more; dozing off, waking a little, then off to sleep again. And the face of the land itself; the stillness of the air in desert and forest valley; the haze over distances; the land so often described as waiting: waiting to be used, to be seen, to be loved.

Will it wake, shake its head, get to its feet. . .? And if it does, then what?

Or is it not asleep at all? Is there something else? Is there a malady not yet detected, evading description? Has no one diagnosed its sickness, has no one cared enough – or is it a sickness never encountered before? Is it a sickness of eye, of voice, of brain, of muscles, of imagination?

If only I could provide answers, but it's all I can do to try to understand. With a short life like a dog's, I'll have to hurry, if I'm even going to understand a fraction of it.

The whites came from far countries and when they got here the spirit of the land – the Aborigines' land – entered them just as it entered the Aborigines, with its life of dreaming sleep, and they, as if to the feeling born, began seriously, determinedly, to dream and not to care. They don't care . . . for the things the old countries care for. They don't care . . . for anything. 'It's the same to us; It'll all be the same in a hundred years; She'll be apples; Don't worry about it; Get out in the sun; She'll be sweet.'

But maybe that's not the whole story. Maybe this bottom-of-the-soul not-caring, is the clearing of the way for a new spirit – a caring for something that the old nations don't know; something that Australia, in its very soil, its air, its dreaming stillness – means.

Could it be a reconciling of differences, a levelling of privileges; an allowing of freedom to be different, to be included or be alone, a harmony of disparities; a willingness to go with the tide of nature; a silence in the face of a silent universe?

Perhaps our poor soil, our inarticulate land, with its brutal alternation of fire, flood and drought, has a new word for the world, for the humankind of the future. I wonder what that word is? Maybe it is to love their neighbour as they love themselves: that is, not too much.

Perhaps the secret of Australia and its silence is the key to the world's future.

121 / I Saw the Seagle Again Today

I saw the Seagle again today, high up, riding on the air. The sun gets in my eyes when I look straight up, my hand isn't big enough to shade my eyes, so I close one eye and do the best I can.

I pointed him out to Dogenes, but he doesn't seem to get the same kick out of the Seagle that I do. He's a good chap, and I get on well with Dogenes, but he's very literal-minded, and to him a bird is a bird, and seagulls are squarking nuisances. Even their flying is an ordinary thing to him; he sees nothing more in it than that they have wings, so it's natural they can fly.

I don't try to persuade him to my opinion. That would be patronizing.

He doesn't recognize any of the letters I've shown him, singly, or the sounds that go with them; nor does he remember MAN or DOG or TREE from one day to the next. Perhaps I take it too quickly, or there's something wrong with the way I'm showing him.

I hope he gets the hang of it in the end. Then the two of us can teach two more. Sometimes I daydream about it all happening, and more and more dogs reading and the whole thing snowballing. Then the lords of the planet would *have* to take us seriously, all of us; not just one dog who happened to be unusual.

122 / He Never Got Off and Walked

Sometimes my feet hurt. Not often, but Jeff used to take me for a run the easy way. Easy for him, that is. He rode his bike; I was on a lead that he held looped round his wrist.

Do you see the pressure I was under? Obviously, if I ran slower, or to one side, Jeff would come a cropper, off the bike. There'd be grazes and blame. I had to keep up a dead-level steady pace, and that's something I don't like. It's not the way I work. I like a few spirited bounds, then a stop. Then maybe a sprint, but not for long. Another stop. Another direction. I love variety, turning, stopping, starting fresh.

The dead-level pace hurt my feelings; and my feet suffered, too. I used to think, looking up at him, happy and at ease on his bike, 'I wish you'd get off and walk.'

He never did. I was glad when he sold it.

123 / Today I Refuse Sadness

Mrs Guest was singing part of a song in the kitchen as she cut up some vegetables for the evening meal. Just a line 'Through all life's sadness. . .' then hummed the rest, not having the words.

Life's sadness? What sadness? Was I ever sad? Was it sadness when I hurt my foot? When rations were short?

What's sadness? A cloudy day? Never! Some of the most beautiful days are full of clouds. Thunderstorms? Certainly not. Thunder and heavy rain and brilliant lightning make a day heroic. A sick child? Yes, often sickness is sadness, but the life inside the child will pull it back up to health.

Sadness is sickness – when death crowns an empty life, when energy is lacking, when promise remains unfulfilled, when opportunities are missed by laziness, stupidity, dullness.

I remember a sadness once, but the memory's fading. My father was dying and I was sad because I hadn't seen or known of the long and good life he'd had. I was uninformed.

Perhaps I'll be sad again. Perhaps I'll hurt my foot again. But not today. Today I refuse sadness. I refuse to recognize it.

124 / Do You Think I Want Justice Done To Me?

Jeff said to his father, as they sat in the sun on the tiny front verandah of the house, 'Come the revolution, and the world won't have different social classes. All people will be one class: just people.'

His father said, 'I believed that once, son.' His voice was kinder than usual. 'I believed in justice for all, and thought that would be a good thing.'

'A good thing! It's a basic right, Dad.'

'Think of it son. Do you think I want justice done to me?'

'Why not, Dad?'

'Think about it. Take a little time. Justice? For what I've done and what I haven't done? Hardly. As for one class of people – I don't even think it's a good idea any more. If you get rid of formal class divisions there'll spring up as many divisions as there are people. Humans want to be different from others: content to be lower than some, higher than others. But above all: different. Do you want to be the same as me, or your sister, or your cousin Wayne? No you don't. People feel comfortable with themselves when they can see what marks them off from others, no matter how close the others are to them.'

In fairness to myself I must state that Mr Guest had given no sign that he had these thoughts in *him*, or that he could get them out so clearly.

I'd like to have piped up and told them that the class divisions Jeff was thinking of were verbal constructs put up by humans for ease of classification, and don't reflect the real world; but as you know, I can say nothing, only write.

Another thing: what happens in Jeff's revolution? Are the poor made rich, or the rich poor? Is there bloodshed? For the sake of justice for all, are the rich killed off? Are the poor liquidated so the world will look less untidy and miserable? Ah, Jeff. Politics is too serious a business to be left to the uprooted, the exiles, the disappointed, the unemployed, the failures: such people must be cared for, not followed as leaders.

125 / The Salt of the Earth

Those who are soft, who cannot bear to take every principle, however good, to its logical conclusion, who hesitate to be cruelly thorough-going, who would rather remain human; these are citizens worthy of a better world. However unconsciously they prefer the human to any other thing, these are the salt of the earth.

In the next chapter, I'll tell you why this applies to the Guests.

126 / The Avant-Garde of the Mind

It seems to me the Guests are just like millions of ordinary people – mostly apathetic, often lazy, usually hard to move, fairly ignorant, without much ambition; yet I set it down here that the Guests are the salt of the earth, for they and their unnumbered and unsung millions form an immense counterweight to the planned brilliance of new, ambitious, universal theories; to the impatient opportunists; to the persuaders; to the flexible, excited intellectuals with their passionate haste for change. And the fact that they'll stay together, even though in some dislike for each other, even though they may drift continents apart always feeling kinship with each other – one family against the world – will mean dismay and a thorn in the side for utopians, governments, church, welfare agencies, kings and presidents.

All great, encapsulating ideas are wrong in some respect, and should never be implemented in a lump. The intellectuals must never have power, they're too easily carried away in the direction of comprehensive – and quick – solutions. Just as intellectuals must never be our police, and government must be ordinary: government of the ordinary, by the ordinary, for the ordinary.

To intellectuals, the mundane real world is neither known nor loved; it is feared as chaotic, disorderly, messy, incoherent: it's a problem to be solved. When it's solved, of course, they can turn their attention to problems more worthy of their intellects; more profound, nearer the vanguard of human thought, and further from grubby, day-to-day banalities – which form, have formed and will always form the staple diet of the peoples of the world.

127 / What Is To Be Done?

If we're not to have intellectuals in power who ought we have? Businessmen? Farmers, engineers, sportsmen, heavy drinkers? Shoe menders, housewives, teachers, labourers (hoboes, derelicts?), the nobility, TV repairmen, asylum inmates, cab drivers?

Philosophers with doctrines and all-embracing systems? (Yes, but only one or two; never a clutch of philosophers.)

Politicians? Yes. But what's a politician? A mix of all men; a bit of each; a seat on which everyone has sat. Let's have politicians, who love to talk to people; who, without people, are nothing. Let's also mind constantly what we're about. Let's hang on to alternatives, and to the maximum amount of freedom: freedom from government, freedom from the rich, from the military, from money and greed, from friends; never allowing ourselves too much freedom, for too much freedom for citizens plays into the hands of and lets loose the baleful, the cruel, the merciless, the torturers, the empire-builders, the gangsters.

128 / The Impatient Radicals

I've been through the part of the Book that deals with the history of ideas and I find a strange thing. The clever ones, those who have the great new ideas, the startling changes, the breathtaking developments, are very few. On the other hand, the not-so-clever ones, those who are clever enough to understand once they've heard the new ideas, make a special thing of the new knowledge, of familiarity with all the radical ideas, and this familiarity does them no good. They begin to want to hurry the ideas, they begin to have special hurry-up ideas.

I've come across lots of these hurry-up ideas, these short-cuts, and they're a disaster every time. In each case it seems to me it would have been better to let the ideas develop, the ideas that led to new institutions – and to let those ideas and institutions grow at their own pace, as the programmed fruit grows on vine and tree, bush and plant.

There is, simply, no hurry. Only a hurry in the excited minds of the intellectually labile, the hurry-up radicals, for whom a change in the fashion of ideas is the supreme good, not the health of any one of the ideas.

There's no hurry. We're not going anywhere. The motion of history is an illusion.

These hurry-up radicals, lacking leadership ability in practical and daily affairs, want to be leaders in ideas. They detect the idea-fashion and move to the front of the advancing pack. But the idea is stationary. There is no movement. There's no need for leaders. We're not going anywhere: time and history pass *us* by. They can never stop until we do. We, and we through our descendants, are there at the end as we – and our ancestors – were there at the beginning. Time has wasted, history is gone; but we, and our ancestors, and our descendants, are here. We are the important elements: history and time are nothing; they are words we use for flows we do not understand.

129 / Twenty Institutions To Be Guarded

Before I go any further, here is a list of things which I think are precious, and which ought to be preserved, whatever changes are planned for 'society'. (That Jeff has certainly set me going with his 'revolution'.)

>Honesty, and reverence for truth
>Love of peace, hatred of tyranny
>Humanity, diversity
>Freedom of speech
>Freedom of opinions
>Freedom of religion
>Freedom of press
>Freedom to travel without hindrance
>Love of tradition and rejection of tradition: optional
>Representative democracy
>Agreed rule of law
>Equality before the law
>Equality of opportunity
>Good government
>Justice and fairness
>A sense of proportion
>A sense of humour
>Restraint and compassion
>Tolerance, gentleness, brotherliness
>Courage to fight those who would destroy these things or who would destroy the individual's ability to practise them; and by 'courage to fight' I mean courage to fight and perhaps die; and by 'courage to fight those who would destroy these things', I mean courage to fight those anywhere – in one's own country or elsewhere – who would destroy these things.

130 / Wedding of the Gulls

It was the third Saturday of the holidays.

Julie and I walked left at the Robert Burns statue and into the small curved slice of garden behind Burns. It was an impulse, since I was leading. Julie allows herself to wander when she's dreaming or thinking.

Down the slope near the garden beds was a wedding party of gulls. We made sure they had plenty of room for a take-off and therefore needn't fly away just because we were there. The proceedings hadn't started. Julie sat on the bottom step of Robbie Burns, and I settled on all fours, with my arms in front of me and my head up. I pretended to be looking at the little stone cottage behind the opposite fence, but I can see very well sideways without turning my head.

From their chatter I found the groom was a member of the gull firewatch service, the bride a food researcher specializing in infants' food in these times of decreasing stocks of fish under the wave. The couple's parents were both members of the gull conservationist movement. Gull conservationists work to save the customs and attitudes of the past, since they can't do much about habitat and food stocks, which are at the tender of mercy of the human elite.

Their marriage ceremony is different from ours. Each person, in turn, went out in front of the assembled crowd and made a statement of his and her desire to live with the other, and a reasonable certainty that they felt like having the arrangement last for some time. There were expressions used here that I didn't understand. They may have indicated some freedom in the relationship, so that either could go at any time, but I'm only guessing. It's what I'd want.

I guess when I talk about Darling, what I mean is that I find her so interesting, – everything she does, everything she says, the way she does things, the way she looks, – so perhaps that means I would find her interesting for a longer time than I would any other female dog person. She's so beautiful.

I'd much rather say I love her – that's far more satisfying.

Suddenly they all flew off. I must have been daydreaming through part of the ceremony. Their energetic fluttering and the creaky sound of wingbeats roused Julie and she stood up.

131 / Come Away, Happiness!

My red coat is shiny as the sun today. Most days I feel good, and have no complaints, but today I feel wonderful! I don't think my feeling good depends on what food I get. When I have better food I feel no better than when the family has a scratch tea and I get scraps. It's not considered the thing among the people I respect most to be happy and satisfied and comfortable with things as they are. There are lots of injustices, and they should be got rid of; but I suspect others will take their place. There's poverty and starvation, and they should be remedied, but those things break out somewhere else. I'm often ashamed of thinking how well I feel when others are dying of this and that, and my early education from my father made me want to do something about the bad things around me, and if I couldn't do anything, at least to feel bad about them. But my trouble is, I can't feel bad for long, I'm not made that way. But what if the person with the discontent, the urge to reform and abolish, as soon as he gets what he wants, finds more things to abolish and to reform? What has he gained? Why can't it be that the person who looks around, sees what's up, and fits in immediately, is the smarter type of dog? Surely he's more adaptable. If the reforms and abolishments happen, I bet I know who'll fit in best with them, and right away: the adaptable one. It may be that the one with the divine discontent will be just as discontented when he gets the revolution he wants. Perhaps he'd be a danger in the new-born world, wanting a revolution *after* the revolution, and have to be put down.

'Come away, come away, Happiness!' called Julie. Happiness she

184

calls me when she means Your Happiness. It's something between Julie and me. I'm not sure I should have mentioned it. I ran joyfully to her and pretended to jump up on her. She likes it, but not so much when I really do it, since often my feet are dirty and I haven't noticed. Her mother always notices.

I swished my tail round to see how it looked. The part on top was shiny and had the sun in it; if you put your eyes close to it, you can see the tiny spots of red, green, purple, yellow and white that the light of the sun shows up. The feathery part underneath, which makes up by far the most of the colour of my tail, is a deep chestnut, shining and silky.

I felt so good! I ran on ahead and tried to run up the first Moreton Bay fig tree, and Julie laughed. She laughed *with* me, while I laughed inside. There's nothing like running on grass to put you in a good temper.

132 / Mr Big

Down in the hollow of the Domain where the men play lunchtime football through the winter, and touch football in summer, I saw Mr Big the seagull. Don't you think it's something to be amused at, that even seagulls have their Mr Bigs? Dog people do, and cats, horses, cows and pigs as well. Ants must, and cockroaches. We have lots of cockroaches in this part of Sydney.

Mr Big looks all ways at once. Seagull people give way before him, without his having to run threateningly at them, and they look after him when he's passed by. He knows everything. He's honoured among thieves. His wings make no sound. He steals everything, gives nothing in return. Everything flows to him, nothing from him, apart from orders. What he doesn't steal is stolen for him and given to him as a present. Seagull researchers have worked for years to find the reason for his hold over the minds and hearts of other gulls, but they're still back where they started. They can't account for it.

Mr Big holds court at the bottom of the depression there, where grass stretches in all directions. I suppose he wants always to have advance notice of any move against him. Gulls can swoop, but Mr Big's understrappers keep watch at all times. No one knows where he sleeps at night.

What a contrast he is with Mr Hadaby, a dog person of my acquaintance. Hadaby is a stateless refugee who arrived in our district from unknown parts; his only possessions were a black patch over the left half of his face, and a limp. He arrived round the corner of Bland Street one Monday morning around ten moons ago; the day was brilliant after a weekend of rain, and the human heart expansive. At least in the case of the woman in the white-painted house, who'd lost her canine security person three moons before in an industrial accident. She saw Mr Hadaby at just the right instant, spoke to him and invited him round the back of the house, where she prepared a dish for him of cold leftovers from her meal of the previous night, and a dish of water, and introduced him to the luxurious accommodations of his predecessor. It was more a lounge than a kennel; the lady's late husband had constructed it on weekends as a project to keep him out of the house, and lavished lots of time, money and ingenuity on it. There were two beds, one for winter and one for the hot months; a door that swung shut and could be opened by a push, but could be held back in an open position in summer; a mirror; playthings such as rubber toys to push round, and to chew in anxious moments; scenes of country life round the walls in a panorama without beginning or end; eyeholes on all four sides in case the occupant wanted to see out but not be seen and there was more.

Mr Hadaby arrived stateless and furtive. He is still furtive and stateless. He's surrounded by love and comfort, but every waking hour he's unsafe and afraid. He tells his friends of his dreams, which are many and just as fearsome as the legends of the huge and terrible beasts, except to Mr Hadaby they are real and here, and the time is now. His life is terror. He says nothing of his past life, but terror possesses him at the mention of it.

After they've talked to him, friends of mine walk away saying to each other, 'He had to be joking. He hadda be exaggerating.' That's how Mr Hadaby got his name. Mr Big wouldn't have understood one tremor of Mr Hadaby's. Mr Big's digestion flows smoothly, he inclines to fat, he watches all sides calmly, impassively. He is a success, and that success flows from within him and sets the mould for his actions, his confidence, his achievements, and allows his imagination full play.

If you think Mr Hadaby the dog person and Mr Big the seagull are a sharp contrast, consider my old friend Eugenia. She's dead now, and it's the manner of her death that will show you what I mean. We weren't close, but we went back a long way. She was a good person.

133 / The Beautiful Death of Eugenia

When Eugenia came to die, she took to her kennel, which she'd named 'Wyebark', and called to her nearest friends to come and take her final message to all who knew her round the district. Eight loyal friends gathered and sat to hear her last words.

'Never mind a funeral,' she said. 'Send my love to all our street and all the streets over that way and that way and that way and that way.' She pointed with a weakly raised paw in the four directions. 'I've had a fortunate life. Plenty of good friends, a fine boss to work for, I've set my own hours and given loyal service, and even though I've refused to bark I've guarded these premises every day of my life here. Hard times and soft, good and bad, I've never found anything to grumble at, but everything to feel grateful for, that my parents had me for a child.

'So take my message to all the dog people you know and tell them: Every moon remember Eugenia, who lived for friends and good times and the knowledge of duty done; who loved each day as it came, and now has to die, like all things; who lived and died without a moan.'

She paused for breath, looked round at us all, sighed a long sigh, letting all her breath out. Her head dropped a little, she took a deep breath of air, let out one glorious bark of the sort she'd repudiated all these years of her life. It was short and sharp. She clashed her teeth once, and smiled at us all. Then she died like that, with the smile still on her face as her head fell to a spot between her arms, after which she moved no more.

We made rather a loud farewell of it once she couldn't hear us, and her employers came out to see what was up. They took no notice of Eugenia's wishes and gave her a grand funeral in a place of honour in their backyard, under the lemon tree. There was a cross, and a border, and her name on the headstone. The children of the family cried and the street mourned one week. For two days I had dreams of the animals in the trees of the Botanic Gardens, and of the birds who gather there after sundown, when the gardens are shut to humans and it's a free go.

The dreams I had, though, were mysterious to me, for they were silent, as if I was seeing behind my closed eyes the place where Eugenia's soul had gone when her head dropped and life left her. And what a beautiful place for her to inhabit. Humans don't know what a paradise the Botanic Gardens are in the dark hours, and it wouldn't help to tell them.

For the two days after that I dreamed I was alone and in a place I didn't know. No one knew me, I had no friends, there was no one for me to mind, no one to mind if I was there. I could see the place in my dreams, the houses and streets, but I had never been there, and knew where no streets led.

Those mornings I was glad to wake up.

Whenever I wonder about my own death I come back to the question I asked when death first came into my mind, when my father died: will there be such life, such enjoyment then? It's hard to imagine, remembering my parents, and my friends that have died, and now Eugenia, that those dead faces and helpless bodies without feeling could be enjoying anything at all, let alone something as glorious and satisfying as this life.

I think I would like to die in the sea; float down and rest on sand where everything's muffled and nothing's grand. A watery grave for me.

188

134 / Problems of Dog People

If the Guests would come out walking with me every time I wanted them to, their lives would be a lot richer. They'd be physically fit for a start, since at the moment they spend a lot of time sitting, either at tables or at the wheel of a car.

I dream of a day when all dog people will have attained their proper dignity, when their language will be known far and wide, when communication back and forth between human and dog people, between cats and seagulls, between all classes and divisions of animal and bird and insect – yes, and even fish – will be an accomplished fact. I know I've said it before, but I'm full of it: I can't help saying it again. I don't mean to say this will be a panacea for the ills of the human world, the dog world, or any other world, but it could make for something approaching justice between the varieties of living things on the earth.

We'd started on our Sunday walk, the whole family of Guests, and me. It had taken me nearly an hour of energy and agitation to get some action on this vital question. We started off, and round the corner from Cathedral Street into Dowling we came across Basher. He's not exactly one of my friends, because I'm not one who likes fighting, but since I can meet him if he forces things, we have a mutual respect. I knew him a long time ago, when I first came to the city. We were never close, but I saw him regularly and I watched him change from an anxious youth into a critical adult, then through a stage of intolerance which still persists, into an aggressive and terrifying middle age, which probably will remain with him until the feebleness of advanced years modifies his rage somewhat. Anxious, critical, intolerant, aggressive, terrifying, feeble: an interesting progression.

Basher has a dog face, but a violent soul, the soul of an assassin. As he stands over small dog people, coercing them for this or that purpose, or just even for the exercise of it, or from habit, or because he feels like it – he's got a million reasons to be standing over others and making them either fight or obey – his face is empty and wretched. Not like most dogs I know, who have interesting faces.

My father taught me that the dog who thinks is superior to the dog who fights. Except in defence, my mother always put in. No, even in defence, said my father; the dog who thinks is the better dog. Have it your way, said my mother, who was just as good a fighter as my father, and in some moods, better.

Basher was having one of his aggressive days, not allowing any dog traffic past his place of work, in any direction. If dogs didn't want to fight, they withdrew and had to go round the block. If he could, he'd stand over everyone he came across. He's just as bad as humans. With humans, the strong stand over the weak, the rich over the poor, big nations over small; and they wonder, hypocritically, at the wreck of peace. Yes, he reminds me of humans. He, too, likes to have little wars, just to test his weapons.

Basher wanted to stop me, but he knew I'd fight. On the other hand there was that thing inside him, stirring him to take no notice of consequence or logic, or anything; gripping him inside and twisting him in the way it wanted him to go. Yet the thing doing this inside him was still part of him; it was his *own* self. In a sense he was powerless. But not quite. He moved forward. He looked away, as if forgetting he'd moved. He moved forward again. He put his mouth back in the beginnings of a snarl, his teeth appeared but no sound. He looked away again and the snarl relaxed. The force inside gripped him again and he'd like to have dashed out showing his armaments, but by this time we were past. Only in exceptional circumstances is it permitted or understandable to let people past, then go after them. That's for heelers: cattle dogs. At least he moved forward as he fought the urge: he hadn't moved backwards.

Courage is a problem for dog people. Such a lot is expected of us. And the primitive habits of the hunt, when they start to well up from inside, are hard to hold off.

Servility is another problem. I'm ashamed of some of my friends, they seem so suited to servility. They sit up and beg on the least excuse. They look touching, they make human people laugh. They think they have to be entertaining whenever human people are looking.

190

Triviality is another hurdle. Many dogs never seem to think of constructive things; many merely criticise, and at the top of their voices. And when they get together to chew over the events of the week, all they can talk about is conditions of work – guard duty, injustice, meals served up at the wrong times: petty complaints.

I dream of a time when all dog people will open their hearts to the world and enjoy everything around them; when they will open their minds to the things that matter, never criticise just to be saying something, but use their time thinking.

135 / These Thoughts Occupied Me

These thoughts occupied me till we were passing number 11 wharf at Woolloomooloo. We crossed the wide curving street and began to climb the flights of steps up to Art Gallery Road.

I'd never seen a dwarf gull before.

There is a flat place leading off the steps, a place of grass where you can have a little run before resuming your way to the top of the rise. A tiny seagull with a big head and short body waddled in a hurry over to an assembly of two dozen gulls, gathered round a dead body. The others climbed the steps; I took Julie over near the gulls so I could hear what was said. In gull talk, a funeral service was being held over the body of '. . . our dear relative and friend, Mr Biscuit. Not all of us approved of his neglect of the traditional ways, or his predilection for the human biscuit, but we're all full of sorrow at his passing. We must resist the temptation to link his dietary habits with his demise, dear friends. It was his time to die and he died: that's all we can say about it. To his immediate family I extend the sympathetic feelings of us all.'

Julie hurried me off to catch up with the others before I had time to see what they did with the corpse. Did they bury it? Did they take it out over the water and drop it in? I'll never know.

I kept up an anchoring pressure on my lead, but Julie didn't notice. I suppose she was thinking too. She didn't slow down. It was a day full of sun. On such days it's natural to walk along with eyes down, which is halfway to thinking, already.

We didn't stop until we were at the rise at Mrs Macquarie's Point, which is a great place to sit. The human people sat at first, then all gradually slipped into a lying position. I put my head down on my arms, then I too tipped over sideways, head on the grass, arms and legs stretched to their furthest extent. I usually lie first on my left side, then later on my right.

Once when I got lost, as a child, I was a long way from home and I waited and waited for someone to turn up that knew who I was, but no one came. It got so dark I couldn't see, couldn't see anything at all. I'd been keeping out of people's way, because even a small dog could be rounded up and put away in a death camp. I got near a lighted bus shelter, and spent the time trying not to be afraid, and trying to remember which way it was to go home. I couldn't remember at all. At last they came for me, my father had followed the general line of the way he thought I might be headed when I'd gone for my run. It was just that I was growing and I could go much further without getting tired and I didn't realize it. I remember how happy I felt when we got home and the whole family was there!

I suppose it was the thought of my lost day that reminded me of Deirdre of long ago. I knew her many many moons ago, we were close friends. I hadn't seen her for a long time till she came to work for a family in Forbes Street. Her friends from the other place are all gone now, but she still looks for them. Yes, looks for them. Of course they're not round here at all. She gets loose and wanders far away, and often has to be brought back to her human family and they have to pay the expenses for bringing her back.

I saw her a few weeks ago, just after the last moon.

'They're vanished,' she said. 'Where can they be?'

'People move away,' I said. 'You can't expect your old friends to be always around, not in this world,' I added wisely. It was no help, and I knew it.

'I have no peace without the familiar faces,' she said.

'Make new friends,' I suggested.

'They were beautiful,' she lamented. 'I'll never get friends like they were. I dream they went west to the open country, where they say there are mountains, but I don't really know. They're all scattered and I'll never see any of them ever again.'

She began to cry. I made a sympathetic noise, but I felt helpless. You always say the wrong thing when you try to help people.

I was brought up not only not to cry at disappointments, but not even to feel disappointment. I don't think it's helped all that much. I don't mean to deny I was sad or disappointed: I mean not even to recognize sadness; to take no notice; to let it happen but not feel it.

That's the way I've always been. I just hope that if ever anything's the matter with Darling I won't treat it as if it was happening to me: I hope I give her every bit of attention and sympathy and love that she needs. It's all very well me turning my face away as if nothing has happened, when bad things happen to me, but I'll need to be on the alert for what happens to Darling. She shouldn't have to go without one single drop of feeling just because I was trained to be numb.

Maybe it wasn't so much that I was trained that way. Perhaps it's me, just as I am, just as I would have been anyway.

'Don't you remember,' Deirdre said, 'When we used to be so happy together, you and I, and sometimes love each other?'

'Yes Deidre, I remember. Of course I remember.' I'm afraid I said 'of course' purely because while she'd been talking it seemed to me that I didn't remember all that well, at all. And it worried me. Deirdre deserved someone who remembered every little thing that happened. I remembered most, and it was lovely, but what embarrassed me was the powerful thought that though I remembered the main things, my time with Darling – and the sort of wave of joy that carries me up every time I think of her – seems to have become such a column of light in my vision and my thoughts and everything I do, that other things and times seem to be a little on the pale side. As if they're ghosts, and you can almost see through them. Not insubstantial exactly: just not as substantial as they were.

For some reason there came into my head the sight I had of the fish in the dentist's tank when I went with Julie the last time she had a filling. Some of the fish there, you can see their insides: their outer flesh is fine or papery, almost insubstantial. It was a shock to me. Julie laughed and told the dentist how I stared and stared at the fish with their inner workings, their guts, their digestive system, their hearts, their private parts all on show to everyone who cared to look. I looked at the heads of those pale fish to see if their minds were on show, but I could see nothing but that pale shining exterior.

The dentist didn't laugh. Julie doesn't realize that not everyone in the world loves Archimedes. To him, I was only there on sufferance, because the whole family goes to have their teeth done at his surgery.

I was in a delicious state. Lying there on my left side, ready to roll over to my right. The image of Darling, once in my head, began to dim everything else. What a pretty dog she is! How attractively she moves about! How deceptively she takes a corner! What a seductive voice! I was prepared to spend the rest of my time on the grass letting thoughts of her run and skip through my mind, but a harsh seagull voice near me informed me that I was listening to the Port of Sydney Gulls' Shipping Movements Officer. She was giving information to a team of five young harbour-going gulls about the arrival times of the first of the fishing boats, due in the Harbour shortly. The young messenger gulls took off and the Movements Officer strutted important-ly about and busied herself with a piece of meat pie that had spilled on the grass behind a white-painted park seat.

The gulls' noise awakened my family; they began to make the sounds they make when they think they ought to sit up, or even stand up, but haven't worked up the energy yet.

On the way down the path to where the Farm Cove pathway begins its half-circle, I passed a middle-aged gull scolding two very young seagulls; she was telling them, for the millionth time, she said, to keep away from gulls like that Hopalong and the Show Pony; that promis-cuous behaviour carried with it certain drawbacks, which they were now experiencing. She'd see them back at the clinic, and if they didn't have it in them to be good, then for heaven's sake be careful.

On the flat grass on our left a group of seagull joggers scampered up and down. Their legs aren't suited to proper running. They were watched by several overweight members of their family, who were engrossed in a lively conversation about weight-watchers, seagull style. The words – Seagull Swimming Club – caught my ear: it was part of a complaint by a child gull. He wanted to go swimming in the pool, and his parents insisted there was no chance of that now it was nearly summer; that sort of thing was for the winter.

I'd seen gulls in the Domain pool during the winter, though I had no idea they belonged to a club. July days I'd seen them in the late afternoon, some on the side doing a little flutter and landing in the water in the float position; others paddling about. Others still, unable to resist the seagull temptation to scare off others, would take off from the water, fly a metre or two and land on another gull, bombing and splashing and being a nuisance. Some stayed on the tiled edge, watching.

I wouldn't have been surprised to see some seagull-racing, or talk of betting on the horses, since I knew they often went to the races at Randwick, and even as far inland as Rosehill racecourse. Or talking about Lotto numbers, or scratching instant lottery numbers. Seagulls had taken over the culture that was all round them in Australia; I wouldn't have been surprised if they had music concerts just as humans do in the Opera House, with a Toscanini seagull and a pompous audience, elderly and well-off, making up the front rows.

What I did see was an old gull with arthritis. She called aloud in her pain and pecked at the place where the pain was. I could have told her not to, but the old ones can't change. She pecked fitfully, having a rest from it when the pain of the peck overcame the pain of the degeneration. Poor thing, I thought as we passed by, someday her pain will be scattered on the wind and we'll all breathe a little more of someone else's pain.

Somebody else's pain is tolerably easy to bear.

136 / Last Night I Saw a Shooting Star

Last night I saw a shooting star. I wish I could talk about it with the Guests. Jeff would know something about shooting stars. Not much – he doesn't know much about anything, although he knows lots of bits about lots of things – but it would be a start. It would be something to talk about every time we had a minute or two. And I could talk to Julie about the sorts of things she knows; her music and the things she's learning from her mother about making clothes and putting ingredients together for meals; and to Donna when she gets bigger and begins to understand some of the things around her. And when Mr Guest sits out in the sun, or on his little front verandah, he'd find time to talk and discuss things. He doesn't talk much to anyone here, perhaps he talks more with the men at work. And the mother, she doesn't talk much with the family either: she likes to let herself go with other women who understand the things she understands. She and I could find lots of things in common to think over together, since I'm here most of the time, like she is, and I see what goes on, and everything that happens around the place concerns me as much as the Guests.

It would be a fascinating life. I could fill the whole day with interesting things. As I got older and my walks shorter, the days would still be full of interest, with talk or just sitting enjoying things we all knew well and had talked about often.

I could go to their schools, and learn more about things that are only mentioned in the Book; things there's no space for in it.

I wish it wasn't just a dream.

I could go to university! And ask professors about things in the Book that I think aren't right . . . or where the Book seems to say too much, or not enough.

Hey! Wait a second! What about all my work – my *Dog's Dictionary*, and *A Dog's History of the World?* How can I be thinking of all that talking, about professors and university, when I've got so much to do?

What a pity there's not time for everything. I guess all I can do is make a choice – and I've *made* the choice.

137 / We All Got up Suddenly

We all got up suddenly from around the duckpond in the Gardens and resumed our walk on the flat ground near the harbour wall. The grass there is deliciously fresh, I love walking on it. I'd run except my family would get into trouble. Three dogs I know slightly were up the slope near the rose-beds. There's an all-black, a brown, and a black-and-white with prick ears and a curl-over tail. They're great mates and go everywhere together. One hasn't got a registration tag, so the others need to be on the look-out in case he gets caught. You'll see them around nightfall, next time you go there, if you're lucky: two fossicking near a rubbish tin, and the third keeping watch. They take the watch duties in turn; they also take them seriously. I've spoken to them once or twice, but in general they don't need much conversation, they know each other's minds so well, and they don't need other company. I like best to be by myself, so that's fine, but now and again I have that old feeling of what it's like to be in company with reliable dogs, and I long for it. Only briefly: the hunting days are past. Learning is next in the history of dogs.

Ladies with busy legs jogged round the bitumen pathway next to the harbour wall, scattering us. Over on the grass near food that had spilled behind a park seat, some gulls searched. One was half a leg short, he hopped along, from his left leg on to the same one; his stump ended well short of the ground. It looked as if it had been bitten off cleanly while he sat on a wave. Seagulls' feet don't look particularly edible to me, but I guess one small trainee shark had been taught to bite first and chew later. It must have been an interesting lesson, to find there was no meat to speak of on that little red souvenir.

I like that about sharks. They go straight in to the attack. I'm not like that myself. I like to look and check first. I'd like to be brave, but always something tells me I haven't enough information, so I delay and look a bit longer and check the difficulties. Take that jump of mine.

There's a place around near the northern gate of the Gardens, above the bronze statue of the seated satyr with the satisfied *and* anticipatory grin.

The jump is one I hope to make some day. It's a standing jump from one large rock to another. If you fail, and fall, there's a nasty drop; I'd probably skin my nose on the rough surface of the vertical face of rock, and I hate anything happening to my nose. Every so often I have a go at the jump, standing on the take-off rock and estimating the distance over the chasm. I make a movement forward, then back. So far, for every forward movement I've made, there's been a backward one. Most times I don't think I can make it, or that I won't ever make it. Other times I'm almost ready to go; I *could* make it, if only I used every muscle to its full extent.

197

It bothers me that I'm not daring enough just to walk up and do it.

We left the bitumen path and went across the grass up a slope that meets the iron fence surrounding the Governor's castle. A few rough steps take you to a small plateau and from there it's gradually downhill to the north gates near the satyr and my jump place. My companions knew that over on the left was my favourite stand of bamboo, where if you wait, you hear the bamboo talking. We stood there near the thick trunks that people had carved initials on, and other messages, and high overhead the diminishing trunks rubbed against each other.

The Guests have their own thoughts. They said remarkably little during this walk. I can't help thinking as I go; I think continually.

Perhaps the stumpy seagull had been thinking as he sat the wave, or his mind wandered.

We left the bamboo clump. And just then out of the Governor's grounds came the beautiful singing of a bird I'd never heard before. I jumped about, trying to interest my family in this new sound, but all they would say was in the nature of reproof to me for excitability, and to themselves that I probably wanted to catch and eat the bird. Can you beat that? Do they really know so little about me after all this time? I've spent my whole adult life with them. How could they possibly imagine I would hurt a bird, a singing bird? It isn't as if they've ever seen me savaging one. They assume I'm a heartless primitive butcher, on no evidence at all.

I shouldn't think too badly of them. They're thoughtless, that's all. On the other hand, we're all animals to them, and they've seen me tearing into my meat as if I was starving, and that's on occasions when I've had merely a reasonable appetite. I know they like a show, and I like to please them, so perhaps I've only myself to blame if they think I'm a ravening monster, red in tooth and claw.

Perhaps I am selective in my fastidious feelings of benevolence for singing birds. I remember once when I was young, not living here in the city, I saw a cow. I could smell her; it was the same smell as when my then family gave me steak once a week. Even then, young as I was, I felt the juices run at the sight, the smell, and the thought of the cow and what its flesh meant in my dish.

I wanted to stay and look up to see what bird it was that was singing, but they pressed on and I had to go. As we went past the satyr I glanced up at my jump. Would I make the jump if I knew lots of people were watching? Would an audience supply the missing push that I needed? Dog's Death-Defying Leap! They could stage it in the Opera House, and the family could watch. Well, maybe not: the Guests can't afford to go there.

As we passed the satyr and down through the iron gate the sound came to us of Man-'o-War jetty as the waves lifted it and let it down within its guide posts. It's for all the world like a moaning, crying thing. Donna thought so, and Julie, for they both exclaimed at it, and were so curious that the whole party walked over to it and on to the iron-grey timber planks.

It's not very modest of me to want to do my jump in public, and I'm not game enough yet to do it in real life. But I'd like to be heard about. I'd love people to know my name.

(I wonder how I come to get such ideas. None of my friends says anything like that. Perhaps they keep it to themselves. I haven't said anything to them, either. Maybe *they'd* never guess *I'd* have such thoughts.)

The jetty moaned continually. You'd swear it was a living thing. I wonder do those little waves ever stop. You'd hardly think such tiny things would have such power, yet I suppose there's a lot of water underneath each one, and it weighs a lot. When you come to think of it the water weighs nearly as much as the same amount of rock would.

138 / Where Are the Days Gone?

It's a helpless feeling, knowing you know so little. In addition to things I know I don't know, there are all the mysterious things no one knows. For instance, in my quiet moments back home when the family is in the house and in bed, and I'm outside guarding them, I think of the days that are gone by, and where they are, and I feel the idea makes no sense. How can they be anywhere? But if they existed, why not? Didn't they really exist? And the feeling I have that those days have taken some of me with them, yet I still feel the same. It *is* mysterious, isn't it?

It's a bit like looking up at small white clouds on a hot day, fluffy intangible things that begin to disappear as you're looking, or begin to form, seemingly from nothing!

The thought I most often get as I look at them, is that what I'm feeling, the pattern size and spacing of the clouds, has very likely never been exactly the same before. Ever. And those always-different shapes have looked down on the earth before dogs were dogs and humans humans. They were there, innocently doing their cloud-business, while all the wars went on that have ever been fought; all the good things, all the bad.

139 / The Seagle Was out at Sea

We were walking on the forecourt of the Opera House, along with lots of other people, human and dog people, and the moans of the jetty behind us – the old Man-o'-War steps – getting fainter. Making for the Quay we passed the fig tree growing from a fissure in the high vertical rockface beneath the rise on which the Governor's castle sits. Julie stopped to point it out to Donna, but very small children are not much interested in natural objects like that. I was more interested, because at that moment it seemed to me that the situation of that fig was like my situation. It was flattened against the rock, arms clinging, frightened of falling, yet not letting go its grip; insecure yet with its own niche to cling to. I wish I could have told them what I thought.

On the footpath nearby were pigeons gathered round some spillage. Man-pigeons strutted and harried the women-pigeons, who were really only concerned to get on with picking up crumbs. The man-pigeons tried to persuade them away from food, but the females weren't having any, and turned their backs. You should have seen me scatter them! I ran a few steps at them, and they took off. Man-pigeons try to get off with every lady-pigeon in sight, but not once have I ever seen one succeed. I think those lady-pigeons are respectable married mothers and get quite enough attention back home in the nest. And maybe they've had it up to here with laying eggs.

On the other side of the road, past the covered walkway and the kiosk, a Japanese fishing boat was in at the small visitors' wharf, rows of sharks' fins hanging out to dry.

Lots of people gathered on the wharf looking at the equipment, the fishing traps, the mooring gear, the sharks' fins, and the one or two fishermen that appeared on deck briefly and went below. I noticed some of my family, after they'd looked enough at the ship, looking at the people gathered to watch: plenty of tourists, the sort of people who are never in one place long enough to unpack. (In their faces you can almost see the question: where's the airport from here?)

On the way round to the busy part of the Quay where the shops are, I overheard some seagull talk about the gull weather-report service, but I couldn't see where the talk came from, there were too many human legs blocking my vision.

They all stopped for ice-creams. I waited, and as I kept an eye on things I noticed from the top part of my vision a speck in the sky. I looked up. Against the sun a high bird floated, so far up you couldn't see its wings move. It was a dark bird, not a seagull. I wonder how many types of birds there are, perhaps there are birds that fly way up there all the time and hardly ever come down. The Book says not all birds have been classified. If so, I probably won't ever be able to know much about them, not like I can about seagulls. I looked for quite a while but didn't see the seagle. He was probably out at sea.

I felt a slight twinge of affection for gulls in that moment. It passed, however, when I heard near me a seagull loudly boasting to other gulls that he was just down from the country to see the sights and that he'd already got a crick in his neck, and why wasn't there more space and more green places because he'd got used to lots of grass where he lived, and when was it going to rain. Another broke in with the latest on the weather, and I recognized the voice I'd heard on the way round. I felt pleased that I was beginning to detect differences in seagull voices without seeing the individuals.

The farmer went on, though, about how hard the work was out in the country and the rewards bitter, with uncertainty and failure *dogging* every footstep – I don't know where he got *that* word – when one of his listeners, reeling under the flow of complaints, broke in on his monologue and advised him to contact Life Line if he wanted help. The farmer, an obtuse gull with a head capable of holding only his own concerns, was confused at this sudden change in the conversation. He thought they'd been listening, because no one else was talking. They began a dance round him, mocking his slowness of wit. He retreated, looking back, then flew off, angry.

'Good riddance to bad rubbish!' the remaining gulls cried, and resumed watching a young boy trying to catch fish through the iron bars of the Quay railing.

Donna was tired by this time; so was I. I don't know why, it had been a leisurely walk. Perhaps the weather was changing. I'm very sensitive to change in the weather. A sudden hot day or dry winds from the west, and I get tired and want nothing so much as my kennel at home by the back door, and the Book.

We crossed Alfred Street near the Paragon Hotel and an excited bark drew all our eyes. There, coming down Loftus Street was a lucky dog on a motorbike. From sheer joy, excitement, and the love of speed, he barked attention to himself and his friend, who handled the bike while the dog sat just ahead of him in a wire basket attached to the handle-bars. He tried to watch everything he passed, but things were going too fast. He blinked a lot, from the wind getting in his eyes.

Julie and Donna laughed, the older people smiled.

We went home. I lay gratefully on the mat outside my little house, and went to sleep.

140 / A Carpet of Gulls

I had a dream. It was night, I was in a forest of big trees close together. Apes swung in the branches, and humans with no clothes on swung about too. I wasn't scared, there was nothing to be scared about in the dream; I just woke up puzzled. Did it mean something? It was day, the sun still high, I fell asleep again.

This time I dreamed I was out in the harbour, swimming for the shore. It was night and a flight of gulls with nowhere to land tried to land on me. There was only my head showing above water, so they landed on that, pushing me under. Each time I went under, they took off, and when I surfaced, they stood on my head again. Clusters of them. When I went under, they settled on the water. When I surfaced my head came up underneath a thick mat of birds packed tightly together. I couldn't surface. I went down and tried to swim underwater, looking up for a hole in the carpet of gulls. My breath was running out, so I let myself sink down further, then shot to the surface, parting the fat bodies violently. After that they let me alone, but kept pace with me as I swam for the shore, sitting on the water and paddling with their feet. It was an eerie feeling, having them round me, keeping pace.

I woke sweating, and began to pant. It wasn't time for my meal, but I'd have dearly loved a dish of water. A dish of water? What sort of dog am I? There's a leaky tap in the backyard, and a pool of fresh water under it. I must have been half-asleep not to remember that.

141 / Everything Flows

I've been thinking . . . It's all very well for me to start off confidently asserting that dogs are people, then gradually finding reasons to begin thinking all sorts of other beings are people, too; it seems to me now that the question becomes not what makes people, but what is life? Because I think that's where the original question will lead.

And the answer I've come up with is that life is everything that is.

Let me explain, if I can. (The fact of whether or not I can explain this satisfactorily has no bearing on whether it's so.)

I've looked at myself, and at other living organisms, in the light of what I've found in the Book. I've learned about involuntary systems of the body – human, animal, bird, fish and insect, about automatic systems of those same bodies: the reflexes, the processes of mending, and balancing fluid levels and the outputs of glands; about the action in digestion of the flora of the gut – bacteria that did not originate within us – which produce proteins from what passes within their reach; systems of repair (oh, I've said that before!). Of preparing for bodily emergencies, preparing for ripening and ageing processes; systems of resting, wearing out, growing new things to make up for the loss of others: and all these things go on without our conscious direction and control.

If all these things happen in us, – heartbeat, breathing, blood-pressure regulation, arterial dilation and constriction, automatic muscle spasms to enable us to swallow, automatic gastric secretion to break down 'food' into assimilable chemicals, balance systems to keep us upright, nerves that can form habits so that we don't need to think how to run, descend stairs, or scratch an itch, but simply do it – then how much of us is ourselves? Isn't what's left over from this list trivial? Aren't we at the controls of a ship that's on automatic pilot? So that whatever we elect to do, it's within the bounds of the system inside, which governs our existence?

Is the heat and cold balance of the earth alive? Are rocks alive, that change, but so much more slowly than we can detect? Are butterflies intelligent, that fly erratically to foil birds? Are bubbles alive, that move away when touched? Are viruses so stupid, when we have no man-made defences against them, but leave it to our bodies' automatic chemical factory to identify them then synthesize a chemical that will invade and destroy the stranger? Is gravity alive, that seems so automatic, yet so subtle that it penetrates every part of us? Is the atmosphere alive, that seems part automatic, part wilful, yet somehow has the nous to stay in balance? Is the atmosphere alive? The earth; that seems to receive a constant supply of minerals from inside the planet, and spread them out, ready for use? The ocean; that maintains its heat balance, mineral balance, and never rears up and overflows the earth?

If we speeded up the processes of living things – the growth of a tree, the building of a mountain chain, the erosion of a myriad hills – to the speeds that are familiar to us, we would see that everything flows. What is around us is fluid.

Just the same, to get back to what is alive, let me take you to see a tree, one of the gum trees, bleeding thick red gum. Someone has chopped carelessly through its bark, and the tree sends gum to stop the wound, and protect its circulation. The tree is alive. But isn't it also smart? It has done, whether automatically or voluntarily, what is necessary to protect itself.

I think the tree knows exactly what it's doing.

Let me show you a thistle. I've knocked off the top of this stem; the pores of the thistle are bleeding a milky sap. It's alive. But isn't it also smart? The sap will dry, and the circulation in the plant will adjust to its new boundaries.

We have a little problem. Others have had it, and solved it to their satisfaction; we will solve it to ours. After us, others will come who will solve it differently because they see it differently.

We can't draw a line between what's alive or dead; nor can we draw a line between what's intelligent and what isn't.

Where do people stop, and *things* begin?

I propose to solve it my way. A person is anyone who bleeds or flows. So, those things are all people, who make the world what it is – a system in balance. Therefore a plant is a person, birds are people; and my beloved rock, Grok, is a person – which I always knew.

Trees, rocks, plants, birds, grubs – they're all people. They must be respected, and allowed their rights. My tree has its rights; my Grok has, too.

Anyone who loves, gives the loved person rights of respect, affection, care. How can we not love all who share the planet with us and make it what it is – our home, flesh of our flesh? Not only the humans, but all the other people: non-human animals, trees, grasses, flowers, rocks, birds, all the rest.

142 / A Soft Day

I woke early today, because it was warm, perhaps. I lay in my little house before dawn, noticing how the trees at night move their leaves slightly in the windless air. Perhaps they talk to each other and hear the quietest whispers. It was going to be a soft day.

The weekdays will be empty soon, with Jeff and Julie going back to school in two weeks. I'll make a point of going to see Darling. I'll explain to her why I haven't been round and why we can't see each other more often. I'll tell her tonight if I get a walk round that way. Sometimes when we talk to each other we don't need words; I ask a question with my face, she answers with her eyes or her mouth with the milk-white teeth and pink tongue. She's beautiful to look at and to think of, but when I'm near her and her smell is in my nose, I'm different and the world is different too: better, brighter, stronger, more colourful, with interest and excitement in every slightest detail.

143 / I Made a Resolve Last Night

I made a resolve last night as I was going to sleep that I would never try again to interest my dog friends in a return to the old ways. I know all the reasons against a revolt of the dogs, but every so often I get the urge – I don't know where it comes from: it wells up inside me – to persuade them that the old ways were best. The hunting past, solidarity, all-for-one and one-for-all. But I know now I was wrong to think so. The pattern of human settlement is such that if we went back to pack ways, we'd be banished to the outskirts of the cities and the borders of settled land. Eventually they'd stamp us out, with poisoned baits, shooting parties, helicopter spotting. They cover the earth; it would take a universal disaster to clear them out so we'd have more space.

Mind you, if such a disaster came, I'd be all for a return to the wild. I know some humans are worried about the prospect of a war more devastating than anything so far imagined, but not enough are worried enough to be sure of stopping it. I daresay enough of us dog people will survive such a holocaust to build up a good population, but I doubt that I could join the pack again: I'm too different. I've changed too much to fit in. I'd be lost without the Book.

There's another reason why I'm not sure about going back to the wild. Humans have had a big hand in creating genetic differences in us dogs, with the result that some are huge, some tiny, some are good runners, others can hardly get themselves along and keep their stomachs off the ground. In the wild there's no question about who'd be the boss, and it's quite likely I myself would be only a minor dog in the hierarchy. When I think of that brash John Doberman and his great white teeth . . .

With humans, there's no question that to them I'm inferior. They call me 'Here, boy!' when I'm more than a boy. And so on. But within the confines of my place here, I have no one bossing me all day long, like I'd have if I were a subordinate to some cut-throat dog in the bush. And it's usually the cut-throats that get to be leader.

I'll think about it a bit more.

144 / Not a Gun Dog: A Gull Dog

I made a resolve, to do the best I could to make the last two weeks of the school holidays interesting and enjoyable for the Guest children. With this in mind I got Julie's attention as soon as I heard her wake up.

'Hey Julie!' I called.

'Good morning, Happy,' she said. 'We're off to the beach today.' And went to get my breakfast.

I saw two ducks in Hyde Park Pool of Remembrance that morning when we started out again to walk from the War Memorial through the middle of Hyde Park down to the Quay, to catch a ferry to the beach. I'd seen the same ducks at the duckpond in the Gardens. If I'd been living rough – no work and no registration disc, like Dogenes – I could get through the iron railings there at night and get a duck, when I was hungry. But no, I think I'd have to be really returned to the wild to do that. As it is now, I can't bear to do more than chase them. And I usually over-run the little beasts. What happens is, I work up a thirst and get hungry and still can't catch them. They dodge and twist at the last moment and I over-run them.

It's just practice. If I gave it more time I'd be OK.

On the beach Julie was in her swimming costume and I in my usual attire, guarding her things. She's just at the stage where she's turning into a woman, and putting things on her skin that say, 'Smell me!'

I stood guard, and enjoyed myself, thanks to having learned some seagull talk. The seagull interpreter service for immigrant gulls was going well. I had no idea those birds had so many languages – if you'd asked me before I'd have guessed that all seagulls speak one seagull language. That's absurd. Human people don't; even dog people don't.

There were gull police and a gull drug squad; not even among gulls were you allowed to do what you liked.

In one gathering near the wall of the promenade, where gulls gather, I heard some excitement over a gull sportsman who'd won the Seagull Hundred Metres race.

When Julie came back from her swim and we went up the deserted part of the beach, I passed gulls putting bits of raw meat over holes in the sand, near the water, to get worms to poke their heads up. One worm caught in this way was more than twice the length of the gull. Once out of the hole, the rest of the gulls fell on it with cries of enthusiasm. They love fresh meat.

There were gulls drinking at the Pink Dolphin, and coming back in the ferry I saw gulls on the firefloat.

When Julie went to the Ladies at the Quay, I slipped round and in at the place marked Gentlemen. But when I approached the urinals – I'm perfectly capable of putting up a leg and aiming as well as humans – they hunted me out. Yet the dog laws grumble about us doing it on the footpaths! Humans really try to have it each way, don't they?

When we got home I wasn't tired. Nevertheless I sat down on my mat with an air of patience. I began to think about seagulls generally, and all I had learned about them in the past weeks.

They're only birds, but I'd begun to have a queer affection for the seagull race. I call them stupid but I remember they can fly and I can't.

Here I am, one of a family that used to be in the gun-dog business. Now, for at least these few months, I've been a gull dog.

145 / The Seagle Only Looked at Me!

When the Guests stopped and rested on the grass I went off a little way alone. They think I'm 'exploring' on such occasions. I was standing alone in a wide grassy place, when my eyes caught a movement high up that was unlike the movements of other birds: it was slower, more powerful, less hurried. I raised my head and recognized the seagle. He was flying a great circle in the sky, and coming gradually earthwards.

I stood admiring him and following the widening circle he was drawing in my picture of the blue sky. Soon he was flying round me in one long curve that had me turning my head to keep up with him. Then he was level with me and swept round in a long graceful sweep, elevated the leading edge of his wings, pushed against the air, and stopped with his feet on the ground, perfectly balanced. He was only a few metres from me.

I waited for him to say something. I don't know why, I guess it was respect.

He stood and looked at me. I waited some more, until curiosity compelled me to talk.

'Why are you different from other seagulls?' I said. He looked straight at me, his eyes unmoving. In his eyes I saw the sea – the marvellous sea that encircles all land – in all its storm-swept strength, eternal battlefield of bitter fights for food and survival; the loneliness of the flier that looked down alone, swooped alone, and, alone, flew back to a rock with salty prey, the antithesis of all the co-operative methods that dogs have used since we became dogs. He said nothing. Slowly, in the space between us, I caught a ghostly sight of my precious Book. It was a shape in the air, transparent, before it disappeared.

'I call you the seagle, because you're an eagle compared with other seagulls,' I went on, but my thoughts clung half to the image of the

210

Book, and half to him.

Without answering, he took off. I imagined then that he looked down on me for crawling to him, as he flew straight and low and rose gradually. Then, surprisingly, he turned and did a circle round me, and this time he *was* looking down on me. I waved my tail, but he looked away and up and flew towards the harbour. I guess even if he was going out to sea, he liked to have water under him rather than just dry land with streets and buildings.

I wonder what he meant by just looking at me and saying nothing? Did he mean that being a seagull, and fishing the waves was enough – he needed neither speech nor an organized society, such as other gulls had? Did he mean that, being himself, he didn't need me, either, as he didn't need other gulls? Or even to talk to me? And that I shouldn't cross boundaries and try to speak to him, but be only and always what I am – a dog?

And the ghostly shape of the Book, rising between us. What did it mean?

Perhaps the seagle's silence was his message to me; that he relied on his wings, on his own strength; that he would live as himself, an individual cut off from the flock of gulls, without the benefits of co-operation; and when his eye was dim and his strength failed, he would die alone, without support from his kind: alone and without sorrow.

That afternoon, when I got home, I went straight to my kennel and uncovered the Book. The seagle was trying to send me a message perhaps. I felt a little ashamed of what I was about to do, but I did it just the same. I lifted the front and back covers, brought them together, then I let the corners fall back to the case they were in. The Book fell open, at a random place. I leaned forward to read what was there in front of me.

'In any society tolerance and freedom must be restricted if they are to live. Too much or too little intervention by government or anyone will kill them.

'Complete freedom would end in freedom's death, and boundless tolerance would stamp tolerance out, for then the violent and tyrannical would be unrestrained.

'The heart has reason on its side when it says: give everyone as much freedom as possible.

211

'Give me a country where the people have room to breathe, and there is as much diversity of people, opinions and action as possible; where conflicting aims and contrary views are followed and expressed; where everyone's free to look at any of society's problems; where everyone can criticise; where policies can be changed if they're shown to be bad; where those in power can be moved out – without violence and bloodshed.

'Nothing can guarantee freedom. Those to whom it is precious must be on the alert all the time.'

It was a defence of freedom, written by someone to whom democracy was precious. It had nothing to do with heroism of the lone individual, but with societies, crowds, great numbers of people, all doing the things they'd chosen to do, all trying to rub along together with the least amount of friction and the least amount of interference.

Perhaps it was for dogs, too. And seagulls. It was certainly for Jeff. But one thing was clear, it wasn't a message from the seagle.

I knew then that although I admired the seagle, his life wasn't for me. For better or worse, my life was amongst others. All my abilities, even though some recent ones seemed to mark me out as different from other dogs, were suited to life among others, lots of others, whether dogs or humans, or both. I'm a pack-dog, whether it's a dog-pack or man-pack. I'm made to rub along with others, to be part of crowds and to love it, even though I have a life of my own, apart from others, when I'm alone with the Book. Both sides of my nature must be given a run, regularly and often, and then I'm truly a dog for the world I live in.

The seagle was a hero, but he lived like a hermit, even though an adventurous one: he didn't muck in with the others, he kept away from seagull crowds and the complications that came with them. It wasn't enough. It was a bit like running away.

146 / Perhaps I Was a Hero

When I was a child we had such pleasure at home. We lived in a large wild place, my brothers and sisters and I played all day long and went tired to bed every night. Now I'm lucky if I'm so tired that I drop off to sleep right away. Ten to one my mind will be gnawing at something in the Book.

One of our games when we were small was played with a sock belonging to the youngest boy of the family we lived with; it had his smell. We raced round with it and tried to take it off each other. I think they only gave it to us to play with when the boy finished with it. When we got hold of a big boot Mr Plowright wore, we exercised our teeth on it, enjoying the game for the restless feeling in our growing teeth, and for the smell of the big man. Sometimes he would hold it out for us, then wrench it away, to see how fast we could snap back and grip the leather. I still feel the leather between my teeth when I think of it, and the side of my mouth remembers its touch.

One day a machine with a frightful noise came, and we hid. Under the house we ran and didn't come out till it was gone. Then all the wildness was gone: the long grass, the thistles with the milk where the house cat used to wait for birds, the long pleasant bushes the humans called 'weeds'.

The wildness came again, gradually, and once again it was destroyed. Our playground, the great backyard that we knew since we'd been pups, was never the same, and when we were adolescent, the family split up. I think I remember hearing the human people saying they were going to go somewhere north, on the coast, but I can't be sure. It seems so long ago.

It's sad thinking that if I went back to that happy place there's nobody I'd know, any more. All grown and gone away.

I have a happy nature, though. It's a great asset. I enjoy the place I live and the people I work for. I know some sad people – dog people –

but I think they haven't seen the good things I've seen.

There's my acquaintance McDog, who goes round saying 'Hell and destruction', and I have no idea why. He's got a good place to work after being close to destruction himself. He was caught on the streets, and put in a concentration camp where all the dogs knew they were done for, but luckily a family went there looking for a dog, and took him. With luck like that, he should be leaping in the air and laughing.

It's the second last week of the holidays. I'd wanted to make yesterday a super day, but somehow everything seemed to go by so fast, I had no time to enjoy it. I'll try to get the whole family out today; it'll be a quieter, slower day.

I succeeded in getting the entire Guest family to come walking with me. It was a cloudless blue day, the smells of the flowering trees all round, the summer flowers out, even the new leaf growth seemed as green as it was in Spring.

Bees are a hazard for dogs, especially when the clover is in bloom, as it is now. I nearly got a sting. We came up Cathedral Street and crossed by the entrance to the parking station. There's a patch of clover up the rise in the Domain just by the thin carpet of bitumen that leads to the twin paperbarks at the junction of the paths. That clover, if it's lucky, doesn't get cut savagely in early Spring; the park men leave it to bloom and it's good to walk on. It was a wounded bee that nearly got me, as I incautiously put my nose down as I do every dozen steps.

I reared back and Jeff laughed. I didn't mind. They'd all come out with me, I could stand a laugh or two.

The first seagull I saw was stout and middle-aged, and wanted to be a duck. That's what he was saying to his friends. He kept saying it as we were passing, and his friends were agitated. They began to scream at him to shut up.

Why are they so fond of harassing each other? The gull who wanted to be a duck was very likely only trying to stir the others to some sort of frenzy. But why were they so ready to fly off the handle? They love to oppress others of their own kind. I daresay they'd do it to everyone else, if they were big enough. And if they were as big as dinosaurs, nothing would be safe.

'That one looks like the original Mongolian Trotting Duck,' said Mr Guest unexpectedly. He was talking of the same gull! He and I never have much to do with each other, but I warmed to him then.

'Moonflowers to her breast she caught,' sang Julie suddenly. Everyone looked at her.

'She's been reading poetry again,' explained Jeff. Her mother and father didn't need the explanation, but continued to look at her for a while. Dogs notice every look.

In silence we enjoyed the walk as it unfolded on the pleasant grass of the Gardens and came past the bamboo and again to the satyr and, above him, to my jump.

I don't know what possessed me. Many times I've stood on that rock and moved forward as if to spring, then back as if to settle and sit. Not game. I never really thought I could make it to the other rock over the gap.

I just walked up to it, didn't stop, just steadied myself, and simply sprang with all my strength. Just like that.

Julie didn't even have time to gasp. I made it. One second I was steadying myself for the leap, the next I was standing on the other side of the chasm. As if it was nothing out of the ordinary.

They all cried out, as if they knew it was a hurdle to me and I'd come through a test. The noise continued for a while and drew the attention of people passing by on the grass outside the iron railings. Without properly considering what I was about I turned casually and gathered myself in a split second and sprang back. The welcome noise and sounds of praise rang in my ears as I modestly stepped down to where they all stood.

I was grinning broadly, mouth wide, tongue nearly touching the ground. Julie and Jeff patted me, and brought Donna to give me a pat on the head. (The others stroke me with their pats: Donna gives a sort of bang on my skull. I don't mind.) I wonder how they knew that jump was a fearsome thing to me all that time? Perhaps I should revise my opinion of them: they seem to notice things I don't notice them noticing. How strange it is to have your ideas of other people's capabilities turned round.

And how strange that I just walked up to it and did it, where for so long I'd stopped and thought and estimated and considered what would happen if I fell, and let my mind play around every possibility of failure, and never once attempted it.

Perhaps I was a hero.
Perhaps it was a new growing-up.

147 / Conquering the Picnic

As we walked through the iron gate, all of us one nice big family, I felt my step lighter and carried my head high. I looked up, and way up there in the breeze over the harbour swung the seagle, enjoying his power over the air, exulting in the strength of his wings, turning on a rising current, banking, riding the oncoming air that swept under him holding him up, sending him higher. For many minutes he banked, dived shallowly, turned into the wind and rose; back again, loving it. The seagle was enjoying himself, just as much as I did when I stood on the far side of my completed high jump.

I thought about it. The sky is too high for me. It belongs to birds like the seagle up there. The earth will do, for me. Feet and strong springy legs are better than wings for me, anyway. I'm satisfied with what I've got.

When we walked through the Rocks I pointed out the seagulls riding the carousel; I'm not sure my family saw what I was pointing at. A pity.

I felt for a moment I was seeing a new sort of gull, but I knew my feeling was wrong: I was simply seeing things about gulls that I hadn't noticed before my Hobart trip. Some gulls are happy and given to enjoyment; some ride high and fish the sea for food and never eat human scraps; and above all, they have a life among themselves, a civilization, that I'd never suspected.

The family ate, and walked, and came back through the Domain past the Art Gallery. We stopped at the swings. Gulls were in and out of the jungle bars, the iron contraption the human children climb in and out of. Gulls were on the seesaw, dozens of them on each end, making it go down at one end, then flying to the high end to weigh that down. They were having a whale of a time pecking at each other, it's true, but enjoying themselves in their primitive fashion.

Over the road gulls walked in at both doors of the brown-painted public toilets; some into the gents, some the ladies.

Gulls flew to the top of the slippery dip and skidded down on their bottoms. Even when they put their feet out, they skidded, since their hard skin is very slippery on metal.

On the top bar of the swings, gulls flew to one end and lined up in a row to drop one at a time from the other end. They kept their wings folded until they were a metre from the ground and saved themselves at the last moment. You should have heard the harsh hoarse cries, the excited bullying!

People gathered to watch.

Then an awful thing happened. Hundreds of seagulls marched together down the eastern slope towards a spot where human people had a large white cloth spread. The many items of a picnic stood shoulder to shoulder on it. Suddenly the gulls took to the air and descended in a cloud of wings and harsh cries on the picnic. The picnickers ran, leaving the cloth, the meats, drinks, plates full of food. The gulls hoed in; ate, fought, screamed. The whole Guest family laughed, and so did I. The civilization of the gulls had temporarily routed the civilization of the human picnic.

148 / I'm Not a Religious Dog

I went to church on Sunday. It was the small, graceful church in Brougham Street, St Columbkille's. No one seemed to see me go in the door and I made my way up the outer aisle to the altar. I'm not familiar with church services, but I could detect a feeling, an atmosphere in the place among the people there, that the altar was not to be messed around with. I kept away from it.

The man standing there talking to the seated people looked at me, but I could tell he was not going to make any aggressive movement towards me. I stayed a bit, then went slowly up the back of the church to listen. I liked that atmosphere. I'd never felt it before. I guess I liked the idea that humans are capable of some sort of awe, a reverence, before things they don't understand.

I stayed inside until the people came out. I heard some person say, 'That dog's waiting for us to go so he can go in and make his confession.'

It wasn't true. I was listening to the man talk about the good Samaritan, and was sorry he was finished.

I'm not a religious dog, but I agreed with the man's message. If a person was injured, I would always help. If someone was dying of hunger, I must feed him. There are no circumstances I can think of in which feeding him and saving his life is not my duty.

As I watched the people coming out of the church, standing around talking quietly among themselves, I wished I had all the human faculties, so I could join civilization and teach other dogs to join, too. I could also have asked questions.

On the walk home I thought about the church and the people I'd seen; and about God.

The sort of people milling around outside the church looked like ordinary people, who aroused little interest in others. Perhaps they hoped God would express an interest. But why, as the Book said, did He want to be loved by them, when He made them? What would He gain by being loved by those people? They were just ordinary people.

What would their love amount to?

I thought of the punishments I'd heard Julie mentioning, that were to be given out to sinners, and heaven and hell as ultimate destinations. But I'm a mature four-year-old dog, and to my mind heaven is hell and hell heaven. They're identical, and there's only one door. The difference is in the nature of the person who enters the door. Nor is that door death; it's a conscious choice, an individual decision.

My heavens are numerous. Sometimes I'm in heaven when there are lots of people around, as in Pitt Street, at the Quay, or in the Gardens on Sunday; other times I'm in heaven, alone in my kennel with the Book. My heaven is portable, I carry it with me.

I wandered down near the wharves in Woolloomooloo Bay,

remembering parts of the holy writings of the Hebrews that I'd read when I was new to the Book (their Bible is contained in the Book).

The God of the earlier part of it seems to me blood-thirsty, selfish and ego-ridden. All the righteous killings, the slaughter of babies, the command to worship *only* God, the commands to sing God's praises continually: all this doesn't sit too well with a modern sort of dog, especially a setter; tolerant and good-natured. Why would God want to be feared?

The God of the second part of it is too spiritual and not practical enough. The teachings of Jesus can't be followed by an ordinary person – they're too heaven-oriented, too detached from the everyday world, and in parts seem to carry mild contradictions within them. Perhaps he was misquoted.

On these writings several religions have been founded. One tells its followers they are God's chosen people; another tells its followers they won't die, but will live for ever; that there will be a second coming of Jesus Christ; fostering beliefs that human society will become perfect some day, maybe soon. Some people think we are – or they are – perpetually in the Last Days.

I suppose I'll never understand human religions, beyond guessing that humans invented the Hereafter because they can't face dying; their self-love is so big they can't stand not being here: feeling, since they are so different from all other life around them (so they think) that they shouldn't share the same fate, but have some extra privilege after death to match the privilege of being superior in life.

I know there's more to their religions than this; lonely old women gain a sense of purpose in life and religious people generally are given purpose and a spiritual life to explore, within the bosom of their God, and in practice their new purpose in life is to prepare for death.

My idea of purpose in life is different, and quite humble. It has to do with everyday things, one in particular, and has a peculiar poignancy for me. If, as my meaning to life has it, the purpose of being here is not to prepare for the Hereafter, for oneself, but to make sure of a here-after for one's progeny then what am I? If I've produced progeny, I don't know them. Even if I'm mated with another setter, I'm taken away once my job is done, and never see either her or my off-spring.

Under-privileged dogs don't have the best of it in a privileged world dominated by a human elite.

149 / My Religion

If I were inventing a religion, it would be one suited to the life on earth of a healthy, self-respecting dog, a dog who owes nothing and who is owed nothing. This frame of mind – which is my private description of a religion – would be based on my own frame of mind: innocent, guileless, patient, cheerful – joyful, even, intelligent, energetic, generous, forgiving, disengaged and thoughtful, unwilling to take orders and too detached to give them.

(I'm trying to be as objective as I can be. Don't think I'm blowing my own trumpet. All my family was all those things. We setters are lucky – the way humans bred us just happened to turn out right.)

I would start out by saying that God began the family of life; from dinosaurs to dogs, from man to monkeys, fish in the sea, birds in the air, animals on land.

People are part of each other, not brothers and sisters so much as other selves; other selves are extensions of our own selves.

In a family that *is* a family, all is forgiven even though some family members persist in doing bad things. So in my religion:

all must be forgiven, including ourselves;
nothing is to be ignored;
and some are to be forgiven *and* restrained;
including ourselves, for the sake of the rest.

Morality would be part of my religion.

Why should I do the right thing, as most people see it? Why? That's easy. Because if I do the thing that's in the interests of others, and they do the things that are in the interest of others, which includes me, then we'll all be better off. It's a matter of loving my neighbour as much as – no more, no less than – I love myself; whether I'm a dog or a human, whether my neighbour is human or a dog, cat or seagull, fish or fruit, tree or mountain lake.

My religion would say: touch everything as you would be touched, for every living thing is a person. We are responsible for what we do to them all: responsible to all other people; responsible to the running total that's kept inside us – the running total of our actions.

I would extend citizenship to all, and everything.

Then my religion would say in the words of Australian fairness: OK, all living things are citizens, so let's help them all up, let's give them the benefit of everything the world knows and has, for life on this earth is an end in itself; our only life, our only earth, our only end. I'd say to humans, the upper class of the world: move over a bit and make room for the rest of us people, the world's proletariat. Give us a fair go.

Kindness is the foundation of my religion. Love is too strong, too wild, too liable to excess and cruelty: kindness is more temperate, more even, more fair.

If I were given the chance to talk about my religion to the young and growing, I'd start by telling them of The Ten Things – you'll find them in chapter 55. Next, I'd tell them of the sort of person I'd like to be for all the suns and moons of my life, and this can be found in chapter 94. It's called the Twelve Aspirations.

150 / Under the Veneer of Nature Lie the Floor Boards of the Universe

Next time I went with Jeff to the art class, there were paintings on the students' easels that caught my eye. One was a painting of a household petrol-mower cutting grass and flowers in the Garden of Eden, and gradually isolating Eve and her leopard, while under the grass that was mown could be seen the parallel pattern of floor boards.

The other students were ringing the changes on the same subject:

'Under the floor boards of nature lies the chaos of civilization.'

'Under the veneer of history lies the chaos of the past.'

'Beneath the poultice of crowds lies the timeless individual.'

'Below the veneer of nature lies the scaffolding of the universe.'

I left the place with a peculiar feeling in my head, as if a bell was ringing somewhere, but I had no idea where it was, or what had caused it to ring. Suddenly I turned round as if something pulled at me; I bounded up the two flights of stairs again, and walked over to the far corner of the studio where a student, whose work I hadn't looked at, sat painting. On her easel was a fantastic outpouring of colours and shapes. The title underneath read: 'Under everything, at the heart of all things, there is life and strength and joy.'

I left the place for the second time, one happy dog, my tongue extended luxuriously, my eyes moist.

151 / A Dog like Me

I wonder what a dog like me is a step on the way to?

When Dogenes can read, I'll teach him how to put down his thoughts in words, then we'll both teach young dogs, and they can teach others . . .

It will grow and grow. If each dog can teach four dogs in a year, how soon will we reach a thousand-strong? I must work it out later.

Perhaps, after me, others will come with a mightier message, but my mission is to do the foundation work – to teach. To show them what there is to know, and how to go about it. Those who come after me can build on this, they can have great thoughts, and see the world in new ways that will lift the lives of all dogs, so they can be included in the civilization of the world.

The task I see after that is to lift other animals up to our level.

I see a world where humans, animals, birds – all take part in the running of the world, so that one section is not a victim of the others, and all others on earth are not victims of humankind.

152 / I Tried to Sing Once

When Jeff was younger he used to take me for much longer walks in another direction. He knew a girl south of the city and we'd walk along Elizabeth Street, way past the old brewery. He'd talk to his girl in one of a row of houses in Goodlet Street and I was allowed to go into the vacant block and look round. Since he used to go Saturdays and that was a day for matinees at the Nimrod Theatre, I often thought I'd like to have a look inside.

I tried for months. One afternoon it was very hot. I lingered at the door. When the coast was clear I bolted for the steps and flew up. There are a number of flights; I didn't stop to count. The top doors were open a bit and as I squeezed in I saw down between dark heads a marvellous riot of colours, with lights playing over the flashing reds and yellows of the set. Actors came out of some doors in the set, and went in at others; talking, shouting, being excited, laughing, grabbing other actors in their arms – it was wonderful! I'd never seen anything like it before – not in the street, nor at home, not in the Gardens, not anywhere else, only there, in the theatre.

I couldn't help it. I gave a yell. Humans call it a 'bark'. I wanted to encourage the actors to go on being dashing and exciting, and the audience to listen and enjoy it all. Besides, the play made me excited. 'Yell!' I said.

All heads turned, as if I was on stage. From the near darkness two figures got up, whispering menacingly. I fled. Down the flights of stairs I raced, barely registering the spotlit rows of photographs, posters, paintings on the walls.

Whoosh! Out the front door and into the sunlight, jumped the steps, down the sloping path, into Goodlet Street. Jeff hadn't noticed I'd been gone. There he was, hanging on the front gate of the girl's house – one of a row of neat terraces, brightly painted and well looked after. I sat down, panting a bit, and listened.

It was theatre of a sort, listening to Jeff and Maria. A much quieter theatre. Maybe more intense.

We never go there now. His girl friend's name now is Sandra. She calls herself Sandy, but he doesn't. He hardly ever uses her name, at least when talking to her.

If I were a human person I don't think I'd be an actor. I tried to sing once. I'll never do it again, no matter how they try to get me to. They begged and kidded me until I gave in and tried a few bars of a song that was popular when I was a boy. They all fell about, helpless with laughter. I didn't think my singing was all that much worse than Mrs Foops, the cat next door, when she sings. They think she's charming.

If you ask me, that cat's voice is plaintive, at best.

153 / Stages of a Dog's Life

Guess what? There's a grey hair in my coat! Am I falling to pieces? I wish I knew exactly how old I am so that I could work out if I was young to be going grey, or old; or just average. I wonder how old Nipper really is – he looks older than me, he's got lots of grey. And Old Sorrowful has a grey moustache round his face.

I wonder if I've slowed down a lot. Running, I mean. Perhaps I ought to sharpen up by running at a seagull or two. I could hide behind a fig tree and rush out and grab a seagull sandwich.

I hope I'm not going downhill already.

I don't think I'll run at seagulls. If I do, I won't grab them, I don't like the idea of having a mouthful of feathers. I'm not a cat, after all. Cats don't care what they eat.

In my lifetime I've passed through the classic stages of a dog's life; the curiosity of the small child, the interest of the adolescent, the energy and knowledge of the adult, and now I hope I'm headed for the wisdom of age. I missed out on the disillusion that afflicts many canines in their middle years.

I notice lots of human people don't get to the wisdom stage, no matter how long they live. They seem to lose confidence in themselves in middle life, they seem to be in fear of younger generations treading on their heels. They get older and older, sillier and sillier, and their young do well to pay them no attention.

154 / At Dogenes' Place

I wondered how he got on for food, since he was an unregistered outlaw with every man's hand against him. There were several rubbish tins along Victoria Street; I asked him if he searched them with his paws for scraps.

'If I was ever looking for something to eat, they're the first places I wouldn't look,' he said. 'Humans have gone through them long before I get there. Every scruffy derelict that comes along looks down into them, puts a hand in. And there are so many derelicts among humans. No, I get fed. Three different stops I have, and I accept food from their tables. *They* call it scraps,' he said, with a look at me. 'But it's food to me. I give them, in return, the glow of generosity without even a whisker of responsibility. Humans take readily to that.'

Dogenes isn't getting the hang of reading at all. I'm very disappointed in him.

A great loneliness seems to roll up like a cloud and hang suspended over me, when I think that perhaps I'll be the only dog who has made the jump from the traditional canine role of quiet and cynical onlooker, to a reader of humans' words. (I wonder if there are dogs in China, Germany, India, who can read the languages of those countries?)

But where did this loneliness come from? It came from me, not

225

Dogenes. It's in *me*, I carry it in me, ready to get under it when I feel down. Well, that's a start; perhaps if I know where it comes from, I can control it. Maybe that doesn't follow, but I can try.

The fact remains that as far as I know, I'm the only dog ever to read. And when I die, there'll be no one.

I'd better try harder with Dogenes, and look for some other bright dogs to teach. Maybe I'd have a better chance of succeeding if I taught younger dogs. And there's Darling. She's bright and quick, and full of energy; I'll mention it to her.

But I hardly ever get to see her.

Oh well, I'll do what I can. First thing in the morning I'll go to see Dogenes and give him a reading lesson. I hope he doesn't let impatience and frustration get the better of him.

I'm going to go right back to the beginning, and take him through everything, as if it's fresh to me, even. I hope he responds.

Of course he'll respond. I see him looking at me, as I'm talking about words, and nothing could be gentler than the expression on his weathered face. (He has fine silver hairs on his muzzle, near both sides of his nose; two on one side; three on the right.) His eyes are grave and quiet; his manner is soaked in the most hospitable habit of mind, the most brotherly tolerance, the most direct honesty and frankness. I like him a lot; I just wish he would get the hang of reading.

I'll give it my best effort. Above all, I must be patient, and practise what I preach. Nothing's ever late, in all the world – it's always early days.

If I *do* fail with Dogenes, then somehow I must get out and do something serious about breeding. Some child of mine may have my ability too.

Oh, if only there was a way I could be sure of passing on what I know before I get old, and die.

155 / Most of Me Will Die

Some day these hands, these faithful legs, these two brown eyes and
their mysterious brain, this tail, and featherings, too – will crumble.
I'll be long dead. I hope they say of me:

> In a soft age I sang of hard work,
> Hard thought, of thinking for the future;
> Of the living jewel of patience, eyes that see
> Wide horizons and the long view;
> Of strength and independence; the steadfast
> Virtue of constant attention to life's problems
> As they arise. In a makeshift age
> I reminded my friends of freedom, justice,
> Kindness, mercy; the tyranny of things;
> The poison of envy; the vice of discontent;
> The chains that are possessions; of love for living things
> And for the gentle planet; of love for love.
> In a selfish age I sang of generosity
> Extending a hand to everything that breathes;
> In a cruel age I sang of brotherly love
> And the raising of the proletariat of this world.

> Most of me shall die, but not these.

156 / The End

Now it's time to get all my papers and notes together, write them up and put them in order. Julie will take the whole bundle of manuscript around to the publishers to see if someone likes it.

Next I must get on with my *Dog's Dictionary*, and make notes for *A Dog's History of the World*, and after that, *The History of Clouds*.

The Guest children will be back at school shortly, so I'll have long stretches of time each day to myself.

PS: The printer allowed me to put this extra bit in.

I thought you'd like to know that after Julie read the manuscript for me, she persuaded her father to rig up a light in my kennel. It's a bed lamp; all I have to do is press down on the plastic thing to turn it on. When I've read enough of the Book and it's time to go to bed and my eyes can't stay open, I press it down again and the light goes off. Like this.

Goodnight to you, and pleasant dreams.

MORE ABOUT PENGUINS AND PELICANS

For further information about books available from Penguin,
please write to Dept EP, Penguin Books Ltd, Harmondsworth,
Middlesex UB7 ODA.

In the U.S.A.: For a complete list of books available from Penguin
Books, 229 Murray Hill Parkway, East Rutherford, New Jersey 07073.

In Canada: For a complete list of books available from Penguin in
Canada write to Penguin Books Canada Ltd, 2801 John Street,
Markham, Ontario L3R 1B4.

In Australia: For a complete list of books available from Penguin in
Australia write to the Marketing Department, Penguin Books Australia
Ltd, P.O. Box 257, Ringwood, Victoria 3134.

In New Zealand: For a complete list of books available from Penguin
in New Zealand write to the Marketing Department, Penguin Books
(N.Z.) Ltd, Takapuna, Auckland 9.

ALSO BY DAVID IRELAND

THE GLASS CANOE

The Southern Cross is a pub, an old, battered and experienced place, somewhere in the centre of Sydney. Meat Man is a regular, a very regular regular, who views his world — the world of the pub and its clientele — through his beer glass, his glass canoe which transports them all to other worlds, worlds of fighting and loving and, above all, drinking.

The grand saga of the Southern Cross or the tragic futility of humanity at a watering hole? Perhaps, it's all to be taken on a bent elbow with another swallow.

CITY OF WOMEN

The city of women is love, Billie Shockley says. But in the city of women that is her world, love takes strange forms.

The city is Sydney, from its familiar streets and gardens men have been banished. Their existence still threatens its precincts and Old Man Death moves rapaciously and relentlessly among its citizens. Billie observes them — their hedonism, rivalry, passions, cruelty, power, fragility. Reflecting her own anguish at the loss of love and youth, they suffer brutality and decay.

But she tells her gentle leopard, she will never admit it's all over.

DOUBLE AGENT

DAVID IRELAND AND HIS WORK

HELEN DANIEL

David Ireland's novels have won Australia's most prestigious literary prizes and have been damned as literary 'sewage'; they have been prescribed for some literature courses and banned from others. But they cannot be ignored. Ireland lurks under cover to ambush the reader. His novels — from the grim energy of *The Unknown Industrial Prisoner* to the optimism of *A Woman of the Future* — take apart contemporary society, enjoying a pungent delight in exposing its absurdities.

What is David Ireland: master of 'literary subterfuge' or writer of 'blasphemous hogwash'? Helen Daniel has pursued this evasive, reticent writer in search of the inspiration behind his work. And, paradoxically, she has discovered much of the private man in his very public writings.